T0314813

ASSETS

ASSETS

by Robert Cameron

FireStep
Press

FireStep Publishing
Gemini House
136-140 Old Shoreham Road
Brighton
BN3 7BD

www.firesteppublishing.com

First published by FireStep Press, an imprint
of FireStep Publishing in 2013

© Robert Cameron, 2013

All rights reserved. Without limiting the rights under copyright reserved, no part of this
publication may be reproduced, stored in or introduced into
a retreival system or transmitted in any form or by any means (electronic mechanical
photocopying, recording or otherwise) without the prior written permission of both the
copyright owner and the above publisher of this book.

A CIP catalogue reference for this book is available in the British Library.

ISBN 978-1-908487-50-6

Designed by FireStep Publishing
Cover by Ryan Gearing
Typeset by Graham Hales, Derby

Contents

For my amazing parents, who have supported me through everything I have done.

Acknowledgements

Thank you to everyone who has helped me with the
Sterling trilogy.
Aga, my first point of call when I'm stuck for ideas.
Christine Howe, who doesn't have to help but from whom
I learn so much during our editing process.
I improve because of you.
Firestep and Ryan Gearing for believing in the project.
For my family, friends and loved ones. Thank you.

www.rcameronbooks.com

The following story has been highly dramatised.

Prologue

Each night the dream grew worse, more vivid, more exaggerated every time it played back in his sleeping head. The dust, the lack of light, the rancid stench of the enemy soldier's breath. His gurgling slashed neck spurting blood and coagulating in his beard. The same blood soaking into Cam's clothes as he pushed the knife deeper and deeper into his victim's neck. Even whilst sleeping, Cam's spine shivered when the man's broken bones ground against one another.

The nightmare had evolved over the past few months from a faded memory to a movie quality vision. The ending however, was always the same. The desperate shouts of his colleagues screaming for help.

"CAM WHERE ARE YOU?"

Then the explosion.

Chapter 1

"Are we sure this is going to happen today?" Asked the official looking man.

"Yes, at least this afternoon anyway." Replied the intelligence officer looking at his watch. The time read 03:46. The intelligence officer sighed with sheer exhaustion, the past few days had seemed to last forever. "We have to act now, before he goes off the grid. If we're not careful we'll lose him."

"Look, I'm so far out of my comfort zone with this," said the government official. "I'm going to have to go with your advice on this one, give me some options and I'll approve the one that'll give us the best outcome."

"OK." The intelligence officer held up a mobile phone. "I have a man on the end of this phone who could arrange for this problem to go away," he said placing the phone down and activating the loud speaker.

"Hello Al."

"Good morning gentlemen, I believe you have something for me."

"Al, I have with me, Mr Mcguire. He has been authorised to give us the go ahead to deal with this little problem. Would you like to explain who you are and what it is that you do?"

"Certainly, good morning Mr Mcguire. My name is Al and I'm the handler of a group of individuals whom we call Assets."

"OK yes, I've heard of the Asset program. I had no idea it was active."

"Well it is and I'm sure you are aware that my guys don't officially exist, therefore we can be slightly more extreme with our methods in making things happen the way we want them to."

"Excellent," laughed Mr Mcguire. "What do you have in mind?"

"You have an individual who you want to disappear," said Al. "If I can make it look like an assassination by some other organisation, we can get rid of the problem and blame it on a foreign intelligence service. How does that sound?"

"That's perfect," said Mr Mcguire in disbelief. "And you can do this?"

"Child's play," replied Al.

"OK, do what needs to be done and I'll be in your debt."

"I'm glad to hear you say that because I need a little help getting one of my projects off the ground."

"Al! Now is neither the time or the place for this." Interrupted the intelligence officer.

"Neil, my guys are seasoned operators, each one has more experience overseas than on home soil. It makes no sense only using them here in the UK," said Al, still fighting the fight he had been for the past year and a half.

"What is it you need from me?" Asked Mcguire.

"I want to branch out internationally. I want to take the Assets to the enemy." Al paused and waited for the reply. The intelligence officer looked over at Mcguire who was deep in thought.

"These guys are nothing but misfits," said the intelligence officer. "Some are even criminals."

"Circumstances!" Shouted Al. "One of my Assets had to engage in criminal activities," said Al talking now only to Mr Mcguire. "And he is one of my best. The rest are experienced Special Forces and law enforcement professionals. The best this country has to offer." Al paused to calm down. "It makes no sense to keep them in the UK."

"You're right," Mcguire agreed. "It's a waste of resources keeping them at home."

He fixed a stare at the intelligence officer. "Look, I have little say in most things outside the UK but I know people who do. If this goes without a hitch I'll have words in the right places at getting you a small overseas deployment. From there we will see. Are we all in agreement?" He said still watching the officer to gauge his response.

"Agreed," said Al. "I can barely ask for more."

"Yes, agreed," said the intelligence officer hesitantly. "So, I think I know who you are going to use on this one."

"Well he's the obvious choice," said Al.

"I guess, where the hell is he?"

"At four in the morning. He's probably asleep."

"Well get him up then."

* * * * * * *

The jolt sent Cam bolt upright in his bed. He was soaked in sweat and could feel his heart beating through his chest. He looked around the room; he was home, safe in his flat in Edinburgh. He swung his legs over the side of his bed and felt for his alarm clock. The small, battered, old one pound alarm clock told him the sun would soon be up.

He rubbed his face in an attempt to clear his head, only then did he hear the ringing phone. He had wondered why the nightmare had been cut short. Looking at the phone Cam saw the familiar name flashing on the screen.

"Hello," said Cam standing up.

"Cam, it's Al."

"I know Al, what's up?" Cam had been working with Al now for over two years. The near disastrous Torness mission seemed like an age ago.

"I've got something for you, shouldn't take up too much of your time," Al said. He had been coming up with these little tasks for Cam to complete for a while now. Some had been a bit more complicated but for the most part he had been having an easy time of it.

"What is it?"

"We have a target that we have had our eyes on for some time now. Things have come to a head and he needs to disappear. I'm not going to get into who he is and what he's up to as you don't need to know and I'm guessing you don't really care either."

"No, not really," Cam said blinking and pulling faces in an attempt to wake up.

"I didn't think so." Cam was a seasoned operator, a veteran of many anti-terrorism tasks. He did what needed to be done without asking questions.

"What do you need me to do?"

"Simple really, he's local to you," said Al. "We need you to get close to him and place a GPS tracker on his car. We have information that he is going on a long car journey later today and we are going to arrange it that he won't get to his destination."

"No problem, how do I find him?"

"His name is Adam Harith. You will receive an email with his details shortly. Best of luck, keep me informed." The call ended and the phone bleeped with the incoming email. The email's subject was simply titled 'Adam Harith,' and had little else in the body of the email, only his photo, address, make and model of his car and its number plate. Cam didn't need much more.

Cam was growing bored with these simple tasks; he longed for something more exciting to come around. He made a coffee and watched the sun rise through the early morning mist. The cold white cloud stuck to the tops of the houses, at this time of the year the mist was a permanent feature of the city.

The sun was now over the rooftops and glowed like a bright red beacon, in the direction of Adam Harith's house. He finished his coffee, dressed and grabbed his charging phone on the way out the door.

The midweek traffic hampered his progress across town. On reaching the address, he drove past the target's house. He noted the car described in the email, parked half on the pavement outside the address. He turned in someone's driveway and parked up within view of the car.

He opened the glove box and took out the wire-bound notebook. Clicked the glove box closed and scribbled '09:30 target at home.' With the engine off, the air inside the car quickly cooled forcing him to zip up his coat. He rubbed his hands together and blew onto his fingers to warm them up. His breath was visible in the cold air.

It was only when he saw Harith leaving his house and walking down the path towards his car that he forgot about the cold. Harith opened the car door, got in and started the engine. Cam wrote: '10:20 target leaves house. Destination…' He left the destination blank, he would fill that in later. Cam went to start his own engine, but stopped when he saw Harith get out of his vehicle. Confused, Cam watched and waited. All was explained when Harith started to scrape the thin layer of frost off his windscreen.

* * * * * * *

Cam followed at a distance, keeping a couple of vehicles between him and Harith's car. When Harith pulled into a car park Cam drove past and stopped by the side of the road not far from the car park. From under his seat he pulled a number of signs and began flipping through them. He selected the 'Doctor on call,' sign and threw it on top of the dashboard and got out of the car.

It would be to hard too place the tracker in the car park; it was busy that time of the morning. Also, parking attendants milled around. It would take time to attach and hide the fact the device was there.

Harith walked down the street with Cam tailing. Harith was going somewhere; he was walking quickly with a purpose. Cam stopped when he saw him enter a high street bank. He kept out of sight in a doorway and wrote the target's destination in the notebook.

Usually patient, Cam grew restless. There was no point in tailing this man for too long as all he needed to do was place the tracker on his car. He decided to wait and see if a different way to place the tracker would present itself. He left the doorway and returned to his car. Cam didn't care what he was doing in the bank. Al hadn't mentioned anything about it so he assumed it would not effect his role in this operation.

Harith took his time in the bank but finally passed by Cam's parked car thirty-five minutes later. After another few minutes he appeared at the car park's entrance driving the same car. Cam was so close that he could see him looking left then right as he started his own engine. When Harith was sure it was safe to exit the car park he pulled forward. Cam saw his chance, it was impulsive but Cam had grown impetuous during his time as an Asset. He put on his seat belt, gritted his teeth and stamped on the accelerator.

The two cars slammed together. Cam hit Harith's car square on the driver's side front wheel. Once the vehicles came to a standstill Cam pushed against the airbag trying to deflate the cushion pinning him to his seat. The door creaked on being forced open against the twisted metal and Cam climbed out. Immediately he started to walk off in the opposite direction from Harith.

"Hey! You!" Cam heard as he strode away from the accident. "You fuckin' idiot, where the hell do you think you're going?" Cam had hoped to escape before Harith had managed to process what had happened. "You just going to walk away? Get your dumb ass back here." Cam stopped but didn't turn round.

He heard footsteps then felt a hand grip his shoulder and he was spun around face to face with Harith.

"Where the hell do you think you're going?" Said Harith taking hold of the centre of Cam's shirt. Cam winced, feeling the pinch of his skin.

"Take your hands off me." Cam said calmly.

"Or what, tough guy?"

"Look it was an accident, there's nothing I could do about it."

"So you were just going to run off? Shit, you don't have insurance do you?" Asked Harith with a look of contempt. "You people make me sick; everything you people do is a sin." Harith fixed Cam with a stare full of hatred. "Soon you will all pay for your sinful ways," he said after a pause. "But first you will pay for this." Harith motioned towards the wrecked cars with his head.

Cam didn't feel like taking any more abuse from the guy; he slipped his arm up and over the inside of Harith's, trapping his attacker's arm under his own. Cam lifted his enemy's elbow up, forcing it the wrong way.

Harith looked surprised at the flip of power. Cam delivered two hard punches to Hariths face, shocking him further. He blinked, a puzzled look on his face as the blood started to trickle onto his top lip.

Cam let go of his arm and intertwined the fingers of his left hand into the side of Harith's hair and pulled his head down towards the ground, bending Harith sideways on his right side, exposing the side of his face. Cam punched downwards with all his force on Harith's ear.

Harith was now incapacitated, rolling around in agony clutching his ear as it burned. Cam stood over the screaming man and looked around. Nobody was watching, he had time to condition the man, to put him in his place. He brought his foot in wherever he could: his back, his chest, his head it didn't matter. Only when Harith was a bloody mess did he stop and maybe only because Al probably needed him alive.

* * * * * * *

Cam stood by his window sipping a large whisky; he was waiting for a call from Al. He had sent a brief report about what had happened and was expecting a fast response.

"Do you want to tell me what went on a little earlier?" Al said without even saying hello. It was unusual for Al to forgo the pleasantries.

"He just pushed a few buttons," replied Cam. "But believe it or not it is all part of a plan."

"Go on then," said Al. " I'd like to hear this."

"Well, now his car is probably a write-off. And I don't imagine he'll get a replacement soon.

Just find out from his insurance provider where he will get his loan car from, get the GPS installed on it and we're all done here. You will have plenty of time to get it done whilst he's getting patched up in hospital."

"OK," said Al. "I hate to admit it but that is quite a good idea, well done." Al seemed pleased; Cam felt a huge relief that he actually thought it was all part of the plan. "Cam," Al continued. "Are you still having the nightmares?" There was an uncomfortable pause.

"Yeah, most nights," sighed Cam.

"OK, um, look. We have been given an opportunity to branch out internationally. How would you feel about a task abroad, you could treat it like a holiday?"

"What's the job?" Cam asked, interested.

"It's surveillance, just watching a foreign diplomat. There should be nothing more involved. We've only just been handed this one as a trial and if we do it well we could see ourselves moving more into the international arena. That's why I'm asking you, I know you'll get it done."

"OK. But how do I travel? I have no passport." Cam had not always been called Cameron Sterling; Al had changed it when he had forced him into the Asset program. Cam had been on a path of self destruction and Al had offered him a way out, he took it and ran with it.

"Leave it to me," said Al. "Check your drop location tomorrow; I'll sort it all out."

Chapter 2

This last minute training mission had taken the Tornado GR4 crew by surprise. Testing the new Enhanced Paveway mark II laser guided bomb in inclement weather was rare as it cost the Air Force a small fortune. What was more unusual was that they had been directed to drop the warhead onto Tain bombing range instead of Cape Wrath. Tain had been closed for live bombing for a good few years now, but orders were orders and the crew were happy to have the opportunity to drop a live weapon.

Mr Mcguire sat nervously next to the intelligence officer; in front of them a small monitor displayed the black and white static of an un-tuned television.

"So Al, what's the plan?" Asked the intelligence officer looking at the phone lying next to the silent monitor screen.

"Harith is on the move now in the hired car with the GPS tracker. In a few minutes a GR4 will drop a laser guided bomb from forty thousand feet onto Tain bombing range. We're going to hijack that bomb and drop it on Harith."

"Christ! Won't that make a hell of a mess?" Said Mcguire.

"The mark II is a general purpose, four hundred and fifty kilo warhead. So it will make a bit of a crater but he's on a remote road and nobody else will be hurt. I've also got my containment team ready to cordon off the area and the press release is already prepared. We're going to make out that it was a huge car bomb."

"Won't the Tornado crew know what's going on though Al?"

"No, we're going to break their feed and switch it from laser guided to G.A.I.N.S."

"Al, what the hell is G.A.I.N.S?" Asked Mcguire clearly out of his depth.

"Global Positioning System Aided Inertial Navigation System. In a sense it's the weapon's own GPS navigation. Basically we are going to give the weapon Harith's location and it will guide itself. We will simply debrief the crew that even though they didn't see the hit, they were right on the money."

"Impressive stuff," said Mcguire. "How do you do all this?"

"Anything is possible with the tech support I've got here, what we can do is only limited to our own imagination," said Al. "In fact, the weapon has just been dropped. I'll talk you through it in real time. Watch your screen." Mcguire and the intelligence officer turned their attention to the monitor that was still crackling away. "Any minute now my tech guys are going to hijack the bomb and break the crew's feed. There." The screen burst into life showing a gray image with numbers around the edge of the screen. The cross in the middle of the screen was similar to the images shown to the general public of the bombings during the Iraq war.

"What are we looking at here Al?" Asked Mcguire.

"That is a bank of clouds. The crew, when they realise there's a problem, will switch from their own laser system and activate the weapon's GPS, which we know to be Harith's car. Paveway missiles are mostly switched to GPS when there's strong cloud cover." The screen faded further into gray as the weapon entered the clouds. "There, they have switched it over. It's only a matter of watching the hit now." The monitor slowly cleared as the weapon punched through the base of the clouds.

Now the landscape was clearly visible, Mcguire sat open-mouthed, watching the ground come up to meet the camera in the nose of the weapon. The image on the screen began to twist and turn as the bomb's on board computer made the final corrections to the course of the weapon.

"There, is that him? I think I can see a car," said Mcguire pointing at a small car on a long, lonely road.

"Yes, that's him," Al confirmed as the car nearly filled the screen. "And… Impact. Problem solved."

"This is very impressive stuff Al, very impressive." Said Mcguire finally sitting back in his chair now the monitor had returned to static. "And nobody will ever find out?"

"No, like I said all that will be released is a car bomb attack on a man named Adam Harith. I doubt anyone will remember after a few days."

"Incredible, well done. Well done both of you," said Mcguire patting the intelligence officer on the back. "So, who's going to be your man abroad?"

"The same Asset that worked on this one, in fact, I think he's on his way to the airport as we speak."

* * * * * * *

"God damn airports!" Cam cursed under his breath, he could not stand these places. He wasn't fond of the general public, it freaked him out to be where they all congregated. He hoped the flight would be on time and that it would be over sooner rather than later.

Earlier that day Cam had checked his post and found a large envelope; he knew it was from Al. In it he found a passport under the name 'Cameron Sterling'. It had been two years since he had started using that new name; it was now normal for him. Also flight tickets and a collection of documents about the individuals he might observe whilst on the task were in the envelope. Cam was pleased to see his destination. Malta: he knew the island well.

"I'm sorry Sir; your bag is overweight," said the lady behind the check-in desk. "You're going to have to lose a couple of kilograms." He was sure he had the correct weight. Even though it was mostly heavy diving equipment he had been careful not to go over.

"It's OK, my carry-on is well under weight, you can weigh it if you like." Cam held up his backpack for her to see.

"I'm still going to have to ask you to lose two kilos from your hold baggage."

"What? You mean I have to get out of line and take two kilos out of that bag and put it into this one?" Still holding the backpack in the air he shook it to show it was half empty.

"Yes please Sir," she said quickly.

"Really? Even though it's all going on the same plane?"

"I'm afraid so Sir." After a long stare at the woman he lifted his luggage from the weighing scales and moved off to one side.

It had been a strange day. Only yesterday he was on one of Al's tasks and now he was flying off on what he considered to be a holiday. He almost felt like a normal person. Stood in the line for Security he looked around at all the people. He wondered where they where all going, what kind of lives they lead. He moved closer to the metal detectors and began to prepare himself. Whilst doing so he continued to watch the others in the queue. He wondered why they weren't preparing themselves too.

By the time he had arrived at Security he had removed his watch and put it alongside his wallet in his backpack. He took off his coat and waited for his turn. To his annoyance the couple in front of him seemed to be surprised when asked to do the same. Had they never flown before? How could they be oblivious to all the signs that lined the route to the security point? Cam found it incredible that some still turned up with bottles of water.

Cam managed to keep a hold of his patience. He shook his head as a man bleeped on passing through the detector. He was sent back through. Cam watched whilst he struggled to find the metal on his body. Finally he was beckoned forward; he dumped his backpack in the plastic tray, draped his coat over the top and walked through. On the other side he collected his belongings, wondering why others found this so complicated.

After being crammed on a bus, like cattle, and driven less than a hundred metres to the plane he took his seat. He sat next to the window and looked out at the ground crew loading the baggage and re-fuelling the plane. The aircraft filled up and inevitably someone sat next to him.

Things seemed to be going OK, it was an average take-off; the plane ascended into the clouds and the seatbelt sign flicked off. Immediately the person sat next to him opened up his bag and began what could only be described as a picnic, crunching crisps and slurping drinks. 'Annoying,' thought Cam.

With the picnic finished, the passenger next to Cam decided to read his paper. He unfolded a huge broadsheet and Cam moved even further to the left, his shoulder pressed firmly against the window. He concentrated on staying calm, the flight would end eventually.

"Do you want to read this?" Said the man finishing the paper, revealing an American accent.

"No," Cam said bluntly.

"It's got a lot about Egypt, you know the troubles."

"No thank you," Cam said, not even looking at the man.

"Well, I'm going there next after my stay in Malta. I know all about the Middle East and all those places."

"Egypt isn't the Middle East," said Cam still staring out of the window.

"They're all the same though aren't they? Have you ever been?"

"No," said Cam hoping to end the conversation before it started.

"Yeah, I could tell you haven't been to that part of the world." The American started to sound cocky. "I served during both Gulf wars." Cam thought it a strange thing to blurt out.

"Who with?" Cam said turning to look at the man.

"Yeah, yeah," said the man looking into the distance, as if reminiscing. "23 years, 152nd."

"152nd?" Cam searched his memory for the unit. "Never heard of them."

"152nd field kitchen, National Guard."

"Wow," said Cam turning back toward the window. "You must have seen some things." Cam tried not to sound sarcastic.

"Yeah," said the man stretching back into his seat. "Things you could never imagine."

Luckily the part-time egg operator didn't have too many stories and ran out of his kitchen adventures somewhere over the Mediterranean. There came an announcement that the flight had only an hour left and the cabin crew would be making yet again another pass selling processed food and overpriced duty free. Cam settled down and thought about trying to get some sleep. Unfortunately the person sat in front of him had the same idea.

Cam kept repeating in his head that there was less than an hour left and then he would be back on his own. He would concentrate on the job in hand and try to fit in some time to relax. Hopefully get some diving in. He had dived Malta and Gozo many times and looked forward to going back and revisiting some of the wrecks.

With the back of the seat in front of him inches from his face he attempted to force himself to sleep. The weight of the person had pushed the seat further back than it was designed to and Cam had virtually no room. He could not believe that he had the same baggage allowance as that huge person.

He loosened his seat belt and fidgeted in his seat. He pushed the man next to him, who was also sleeping, off his armrest and made himself as comfortable as he could. With the cramps setting in and his knees pressed hard against the plastic back of the seat in front of him, he risked the inevitable dream that was to come and drifted to sleep.

Chapter 3

"Good morning gentlemen, welcome to operation cave runner." The U.S Intelligence Officer stood at the front of the large briefing tent looking at the gathering assault force. Every last one of the soldiers was still speculating on the mission they were about to be given.

"Your area of operation for today is the Shawal Valley, north Waziristan," continued the intel officer. "Your target," he paused as if to increase the anticipation, "is Osama Bin Laden." He paused again to allow the muttering amongst the assault force to die down.

"Settle down, gentlemen," shouted the officer. The muttering petered out and the officer had his chance to continue. "OK, down to business. Shawal Valley is a rocky expanse on the border of Afghanistan and Pakistan. A mountainous region of vertical rock walls, crags and caves. It's these caves that we are interested in today. We have strong human intelligence from within these cave complexes that Bin Laden is in there. And it's your job to go in and flush him out."

"On the 3rd of this month we received another audio message from Bin Laden, this message referenced recent events confirming that it's relatively new. It was the usual garbled sermon containing messages of hatred of the west and the U.S. It is strongly believed that it was recorded in these cave complexes."

"His last ten messages have been audio only; the last video message was received in 2007 fuelling the rumours that he is ill or injured in some way. We do have information that suggests he is suffering from kidney failure but this can't be confirmed. Also there is some intel that he has undergone plastic surgery and shaved off his beard in order to alter his appearance. This may be why the last ten messages have been audio only."

"It will be one hell of a climb to the entrances to the complex and there are six in all. These have been designated Uniform, Victor, Whiskey, Xray, Yankee and Zulu. Three teams of S.E.A.Ls will take the first three and two teams of S.B.S and Charlie Troop will take the other three. A large force of Rangers will be inserted at the bottom of the hill and they will provide sustained fire from there during your ascent. There is artillery support in the form of the 101st Airborne and the Royal Horse Artillery and some limited air support, call them in if you need them, high priority targets only."

"Once you reach the entrances the Rangers will advance up the hill and as you clear the caves they will flood the complex and hold the ground. Move slowly in the caves, we learned a lot from Torra Borra. They will fight to the death. Bin Laden's bodyguards have been ordered to kill him, not to allow him to be captured. If you can capture him all the better. However, the body will do. I'll now hand you over to Major Preston who will brief you on the rules of engagement."

The intel officer picked up his notes and moved off to one side. Major Preston, the unit's lawyer, took to the podium.

"OK chaps," said Major Preston in his highly educated voice. "Listen in; I'm going to go over today's rules of engagement." The men sighed and grumbled, rapidly losing interest. "OK, OK, I know, but it has to be done." Major Preston looked like a man who knew he was talking to the wall; the men in front of him were too busy contemplating what was ahead of them.

"If everyone can look at their R.O.E card," he continued in acceptance that nobody was listening to him. "I must state that nothing in your R.O.E limits your right to take action in self-defence. You have the right to use force, both in self-defence and against the enemy. You may use force, up to and including deadly force, in response to a hostile act or hostile intent directed against you and members of your unit." Major Preston read directly from the rules of engagement card. "A warning is to be given before opening fire in self-defence, if time and circumstances permit." The murmuring increased in protest to the order of issuing a verbal warning. "If you have to open fire," Major Preston raised his voice to be heard over the rabble in front of him, "you must fire only aimed shots, use no more force than is necessary to neutralise the threat. Take all reasonable precautions not to injure anyone other than your target."

He put down the R.O.E card having delivered his required speech. "Having said that," he continued, "we are under no illusion who you are and what we are asking you to do here. People are going to be killed today; all I ask is for you to act in a dignified manner. Do not attack those who surrender. Treat all detainees humanely. Care for all wounded personnel no matter who they are and do not, I say again do not take war trophies." This last remark had managed to silence the men, all of whom now realised what they were about to undertake. "Your section commanders have all the information you need. We go in one hour. Best of luck."

Cam turned to face the other members of his team. Swanny had his hands in his pockets and a cigarette hanging out his mouth.

"Well mate, this is gonna be a big one." Cam said.

"Mmm," grunted Swanny. Probably missing the gravity of the situation, as usual.

"Put that out Swanny, try and pay attention," Cam said moving off back towards Charlie Troop's staging area. Swanny flicked the cigarette to the ground and followed Cam to where the Boss was talking to the rest of the troop.

"OK guys, we are going to keep this simple," said the Boss taking a seat on a nearby crate of ammunition. "We have been given cave entrance Xray, eight hundred metres up the hill. It's cold where we are going but dress light, we are carrying a lot of kit and we will have to move fast up to the entrance. We will be covered by the sustained fire from the Rangers who will move up to support us in the caves as we clear them."

"We are going to split into three fire teams. I will be with Glenn and we are Charlie One. Cam and Swanny will be Charlie Two and Spike and Buzz Charlie Three. If we come under fire we will fire and manoeuvre up the hill. Glenn and I will be in the middle, Cam and Swanny off to the left and Spike and Buzz take the right. You guys will provide cover for Glenn and myself and when you move we will provide cover for you. Remember Glenn will let rip with his S.A.W." Glenn smiled smugly as he cradled his automatic support weapon. He gave the weapon a few pats to reinforce his confidence in his shooting abilities.

"We don't know what to expect when we reach the caves, we can only improvise from there. The guys defending the caves are going to be desperate and they are warriors every last one of them; they have grown up fighting for what they believe." The Boss paused and sighed, he looked at each of his team. "We must never underestimate our enemy. Always assume they are better than you." The Boss paused again and looked at the floor. "I've seen the ground out there from the view of the unmanned drones. There's plenty of cover, use it and move fast." He looked up again. "That's it; kit up, normal assault gear: ammo, flashbangs and frags. In one hour we'll be on that Sea King." The Boss pointed over towards a Sea King being prepared by the ground crew. "One hour."

The group split and moved to their individual areas. Cam laid his assault vest on his camp cot. He checked each individual pouch, ammo and water mostly. Next he opened one of his small claymore satchels and loaded it with fragmentation grenades. The other one with a mixture of flashbangs and Gas grenades.

His day sack was full of extra ammo both for his use and also Glenn's S.A.W. He checked that his personal P.R.C radio was on the same channel as everyone else's and slid it into the assigned pouch on the back of his vest. Finally he placed on his cot his respirator, helmet and fast rope gloves, this completed his personal checks.

Cam looked over at Swanny's bed space. It was a mess with kit strewn about all over the place. He was sat on his cot cleaning his M4 carbine. Somehow out of all that mess Cam knew a soldier would emerge that he could trust with his life. He was an unlikely but very capable soldier.

The rotors of the helicopters began to rotate signalling the time was at hand. Cam donned his vest and slipped his grenade satchels over his neck hanging them comfortably under each arm. He swung the heavy ammunition-filled day sack onto his back and tightened the arm straps. He clipped his respirator to his vest and did the same with his fast rope gloves.

The final check was his weapon systems. His P226 pistol was in his leg holster and was accompanied by two spare 9mm magazines. His commando fighting knife was in its sheath and his M4A1 was then slung over his shoulder. Cam re-checked his radio was still on the same channel and placed the earpiece into his ear, a small strip of tape placed over the earpiece ensured it would remain in place. Cam took a deep breath in, closed his eyes and then blew out, putting the nerves to one side. He picked up his helmet and moved to Swanny's area. He was not ready and Cam helped him kit up after removing another cigarette from his mouth and flicking it to the sand.

The troop convened near their assigned helicopter, the down draft from the rotor blades swept the desert sand into the air and the smell of aviation fuel filled Cam's nose. No words were spoken, adrenaline was flowing. The troop climbed, laden with equipment, one by one into the helicopter with the help of the Loadmaster; Cam was last to enter the helicopter along with the Boss. He looked over at Cam as they stood near the side door, still under the down wash of the rotor blades.

"Do you know what Cam," said the Boss with the dust swirling around them, "this would make a great book one day." Cam said nothing; he nodded and climbed into the helicopter.

Chapter 4

The screeching of the aircraft tyres on the sun-scorched runway prematurely woke Cam from his dream. As usual, it took him a few seconds to clear his thoughts and return to reality. He had arrived into a beautiful early Maltese morning.

The old Royal Air Force base at Luqa was converted into Malta's international airport back in the early nineties. Cam knew it well; he had travelled back and forward to Malta, mostly on holidays, throughout his life. Malta was a place where he felt comfortable and it was an odd feeling to be there under those circumstances.

All seemed to have gone like clockwork: no delays, not half as many annoying people as he had anticipated and his luggage had not been lost. He thought back to all the travelling he had done on leaving the Army after Waziristan and was amazed that nothing had ever gone missing.

With his two-kilogram lighter bag slung over his shoulder he made his way out of the terminal, still unsure of how he was going to get to the hotel that Al had booked. He was more than happy to make his own way there. After all, the island was small enough and anywhere was walkable. He had done it before, but to his surprise Al had organised a car for him.

The driver stood holding up a cardboard sign with 'Cam Sterling,' scrawled across it in messy, thick felt-tip pen.

"I'm Cam Sterling," said Cam. The driver just beckoned with his head, turned and walked away. Cam followed him to his waiting car, threw his luggage into the boot and sat in the passenger seat. The driver started the engine and lit a cigarette before pulling out of the pick up zone. The smoke stung Cam's eyes as he took in the scenery.

Beautiful Mediterranean trees lined the smooth, black tarmac road. Buildings of all shapes and sizes sprawled out in every direction, made of the local sandy coloured stone. Cam missed travelling; the warm smells, the feeling of discovery and the relaxed attitude of the local people.

The journey took no time at all; soon the car pulled up outside the hotel located on the southern side of the island. He looked at the entrance and wondered if they were in the right place, it seemed far too grand for this to be for him. Without saying a word he looked at the driver, pointed at the large, golden entrance and then pointed to himself. The driver simply nodded. Cam thanked him and had only just enough time to retrieve his bags from the boot of the car before it drove off.

Cam turned to face the posh glass door.

"Thank you Al," he said to himself entering the building. Smooth marble covered the entire floor of the vast reception room, air-conditioned and spotlessly clean. He approached the reception desk and placed his bag on the floor. Feeling a little out of place and very underdressed he smiled at the receptionist.

"Hello Sir." She smiled back.

"Hi, my name's Cameron Sterling. I believe I've got a room for a couple of weeks."

"Just let me check," she said. "Ah, yes room 615." She typed some information into the computer. "Do you have your passport, Sir?" She said holding out her hand. Cam hesitated, not sure if he should hand over his passport to a stranger. Realising he was nothing more than a tourist to this woman he handed her his passport. She disappeared for a short time and returned, handing it back. She inserted a small credit card-sized keycard into the register and it bleeped as she removed it. "Here's your room key. Would you like some help with your bags?"

"No it's OK, I'll manage, thanks," Cam said picking up his bag.

"Sixth floor, the elevator is over there." She pointed to the other end of the reception hall, past some small gift shops.

* * * * * * *

His room, also air-conditioned, was more like two rooms in one. The larger of the two apartments had a kitchen area and a lounge. He had never been in a place like that before. He had four balconies to choose from and three beds.

He dropped his bag on the floor of the largest bedroom and headed straight for the kitchen. Opening up the refrigerator he saw a nice choice of drinks. Knowing that they were well overpriced, but also knowing that Al was picking up the tab, he selected a local beer and walked through the net curtains onto the balcony. The cold beer felt good as it refreshed his overheated body.

From his sixth floor corner apartment he could see the resort's swimming pool curving round the hotel building. The private beach was down a set of stairs from the side of the pool. On the beach, which was protected by high rocks on all sides, he could see some divers preparing for a morning dive. He had brought his diving gear with him and that was where he wanted to be, but not just yet, there was work to be done. He hoped he might find some time to relax later.

Al's instructions led him away from the hotel and towards the coast near a small inlet called the Blue Grotto. He was to meet his contact outside a café near to where the tourist boats came in and out. His contact was an MI6 linguist who was a native of Malta. Between the two of them, they were to keep the target under twenty four-hour surveillance.

The day was warming up and even at that time of the morning he could tell it was going to be a beautiful Mediterranean day. Cam stood opposite the café watching the street for his contact. He had studied the photo supplied by Al, and hoped he would spot him first. His contact was average looking, nothing striking about him, a similar height to Cam and either bald or balding. He picked him out immediately, walking through the early-bird tourists. He walked straight up to Cam as if he knew him.

"Good morning," said the local man. "Are you waiting for me?"

"That depends," replied Cam. "Who are you?" The man smiled at the awkwardness of first contacts. There were never any codes like in the movies but Cam thought sometimes it might be helpful to have them. "Al sent me," Cam said eventually.

"I'm Donald, so you're going to help me watch this Saudi are you?"

"That's right."

"Good it'll be nice having some help for once. I've got the observation post set up in the brush on the cliff edge; we should see the target coming in." Donald led the way up to the established observation point. "So, what do I call you?"

"Sterling," Cam said.

"Sterling," said Donald stopping in his tracks. "You are one of Al's guys aren't you?" He said smiling.

"What do you mean?"

"The name," laughed Donald. "He loves naming his operators and gets carried away sometimes." Donald set off again towards the O.P. "I've worked with Al on a couple of things before." Donald broke from the track and started to push his way through the bushes.

"Well call me Cam then," he said. "So, are we expecting any difficulties on this one?"

"This should be easy, we wait and watch. The target will most probably be arriving some time today. His yacht will anchor just offshore from our O.P and he's scheduled to be here for at least three weeks. During this time he will receive a number of visitors and all we need to do is photograph the visitors and document what we see. Simple."

"OK, but how do we know he'll be stopping right here?"

"He's done it many times, I myself have watched him before." He motioned towards the spot where he saw him anchored the last few times. "If it's alright with you I'd like to take the night shift, will you be OK here for the day?" Donald seemed to be in a hurry to get away, thought Cam.

"Yeah sure, I'll need some food and water for today if we're going to split this into twelve-hour shifts."

"OK, no problem. Give me a few hours and I'll bring you some supplies." Cam nodded in agreement. "Here is a file on our target, I'm sure Al has got you up to speed but it's all in here anyway." Cam took the file from Donald. "I'll see you tonight." Donald turned and speedily walked away through the thick bushes that concealed the observation point from view.

"Alright then," Cam said to himself as he turned to the covered position overlooking the bay. It had been prepared well. A small but comfortable looking canvas seat, in front of a set of high-powered binoculars on a tripod, sat beneath a camouflaged lean-to. A box of other surveillance equipment contained night vision goggles, various digital cameras and smaller less powerful binoculars.

Cam rummaged through the box making sure he was familiar with the equipment. When satisfied he stepped out of the shelter, holding the small set of bino's, into the increasingly warm sun. He took a couple of steps to the edge of the cliff and sat down, dangling his legs over the edge. Here he would wait, taking in the sun until the target arrived.

* * * * * * *

As midday approached, Cam took shelter from the sun under the lean-to. He was tucking into some of the rations that Donald had delivered to him, before rushing off again, when he spotted a medium-sized yacht entering the bay.

He looked through his binoculars then opened the file he had been given in the morning and pulled out a photograph and specifications of the target vessel. He confirmed that this was what they were waiting for.

The yacht was a beautiful looking and obviously expensive sun-seeker, big enough to have a crew just to drive the boat for the passengers. One of those passengers was the target. The stern of the boat was open-topped with a large seating area and a Jacuzzi. Attached to the back decking and at sea level were two jet skis ready to be disconnected and used.

Cam watched the vessel slowly enter the bay and weight anchor, right in the spot that Donald had indicated. Cam picked up the journal and wrote the time and that the target had arrived on location. He viewed the boat through the high-powered binoculars until he had gathered as much information on the passengers and crew as he could.

Cam disconnected the binoculars from the tripod and attached the better of the cameras. Now with a steady platform to take photos from he began taking full body shots and face shots of all on board. Each photo was documented in the journal as to who Cam suspected was who. The only person who could be positively identified was the target. He was easy to spot.

The Saudi Arabian foreign diplomat to Iran was an awful human being. He was suspected of almost all crimes that could be described as 'disgusting.' A truly vile man and one not to be trusted. He was known to be involved in human trafficking. However, this time the trip was more about making contacts and spreading his money thinly by investing in others companies, making it hard to trace the original source of his wealth.

Cam did not understand why they had been tasked with this man. He pondered on it all day until Donald re-appeared to take over for the night. Cam asked about the target and more specifically if he knew where his money was being spent.

"Well," said Donald. "We are really not sure where his money is going, we suspect that it's going to some terrorist groups. Perhaps not A.Q but maybe some others."

"That makes at least some sense," said Cam handing over the journal to Donald. "No visitors today, just some activity on the boat. Nothing unusual."

"They will start turning up tomorrow, they always do. It's the poor girls that I feel sorry for."

"What do you mean, girls?"

"Human trafficking, sex trade, you name it, it all goes on here. I'm sorry to say I've seen some terrible things from this O.P."

"Christ," Cam blurted out. "And there is nothing we can do about it?"

"No, hell no. We watch and photo all the people coming and going." Donald looked at Cam fully understanding how he felt. "Look I would love to put a stop to it but we can do more good by taking the photos and passing them up the chain. I just hope that he'll get what's coming to him one day." Cam exhaled and nodded in agreement.

"Yeah, I know the score. How do I go about sending the intel from today?"

"Don't worry about that," Donald said holding up a small netbook. "I'll do it from here. Get yourself away and I'll see you in the morning."

"OK, have a good night," Cam said turning away and carefully making his way through the bushes back to his hotel room.

* * * * * * *

The days passed and Cam slowly collected information on the Saudi diplomat. He witnessed many disturbing scenes on that boat as the visitors came and went. Girls arrived one at a time, spent a few hours on board and where whisked away again, always escorted. Most looked like they where drugged up and all were there against their will. Cam hated to think what was happening on that boat. Were they being sold over the internet to some fat, greasy prince or were they being abused? Whatever was happening it was not on and all Cam wanted to do was help.

Donald understood Cam's feelings towards the task. They talked about it every time they handed over, after their shifts. It was the only way to deal with what they were witnessing. Donald kept saying that the more info they gathered, the closer they were to ending the sick activities of this man.

After the fifth day Donald turned up to swap over. It was clear to see that it was getting to Donald as much as it was to Cam. The handovers where becoming routine, telling each other who had visited and what had happened to some scared girls as if it was nothing at all. This was not what Cam had planned for his trip to Malta, one of his favourite places to visit.

"It's hard to think that this goes on here," said Cam as Donald picked up the binos for a look at the boat.

"Your kidding right?" Said Donald. "Al-Megrahi was convicted on evidence found here; money laundering is rife in Malta. Even your own B.N.P. have a splinter group out here meeting up with known German terrorists, I could go on and on. Just look at what that bastard down there is doing." Donald pointed to the boat in the bay. "Remember we are the easiest route into Europe, they all get to you through us. My country isn't the same as it once was." The look on Donald's face was one of disappointment. "Have you been into Valletta yet?"

"Not on this visit, why?"

"I'll let you see for yourself, if you go, that is," Donald said snorting a laugh of disapproval through his nose. "Get yourself away. You need some rest."

"Yeah," Cam said sighing. He left Donald by the cliff and returned to his room. As he walked away he didn't see the small boat arrive with two figures on board. Donald sat down in the canvas chair and picked up the journal. He prepared his camera for a visitor to the boat. For the first time at night!

Chapter 5

Cam couldn't sleep; he didn't want the dream to return. He decided he would rather be tired than relive the story one more time. It was dark outside and the net curtains fluttered gently in the cool breeze coming in from the sea. Cam lay under the thin sheet transfixed on the dancing net, mesmerised. Due to fatigue his wide, open eyes were beginning to dry out.

The vibrating phone went unanswered; it slid slowly as it pulsed, towards the edge of the bedside cabinet. Cam only noticed it when it clattered to the floor. He sat up and swung his legs over the side of the bed. He looked down and blinked his eyes trying to bring back some moisture. The phone continued to vibrate on the floor, more high-pitched now as it buzzed on the tiles.

Cam reached down and picked it up. Al was calling! Of all things, Cam had not expected that.

"Cam, it's Al."

"Yes, I know," croaked Cam.

"There's a situation," continued Al. "Donald's watching another visitor as we speak."

"We've been watching them all week, Al."

"But no one's come at night though, have they"

"No!" Cam was now wide-awake, something didn't seem right. "Do we know who it is?"

"Yes, he's a marked individual, already under surveillance. He's a high-level target and I want to know what's happening on that boat." Al paused. "Can you do it?"

"Leave it to me, I'll do what I can."

"You have your diving gear I suppose?"

"Yeah, I'm on my way."

"Cam listen, there is an S.B.S operator on the island, he's been watching this guy but he lost him when he left the shore for the Saudi's boat. We've been asked to find out what's going on." Al paused almost like he was trying to decide how to word what he was about to say. "The Asset program is being closely watched on this, do me proud and we will get more responsibilities. Do you understand?"

Cam had already set the phone to loud, placed it back on the sideboard and was un-zipping his dive bag. "I'm on it Al, it's as good as done."

"Good, best of luck. I'll be in touch." The phone went silent as Cam pulled out his 5mm, black, short wet suit. He fished around in the bag for his boots and fins, all the time illuminated by the glow of his mobile phone screen. He struggled into the suit and boots, zipped himself in and crouched down to find his weight belt and mask.

The glow from the mobile faded going into stand-by mode as Cam found his weight belt and mask. In his mask box he found his thin gloves, he grabbed them without a second thought and stuffed them under the trouser leg, trapping them next to his thigh. Now with the room in darkness he left, closing the door behind him.

The hotel was deserted as he ran through the lobby, not even the counter staff noticed him leaving as Cam had found the best way in and out with the most cover, even avoiding the hotels cameras. Old habits died hard.

Now he was out and running through the night towards the jetty near the café where he had first met Donald. As he ran he fastened the weight belt round his waist, pulling it tight so the two, one-kilo weights would not bounce as he ran. The mask was pulled over his head and down round his neck, to where it should always be kept whilst not in use.

He approached the jetty, which was nothing more than a concrete ramp leading down into the water. The boat that he had to get to was no more than two or three hundred metres away, round to the left of the rocks. The ramp was slippery with wet moss and Cam was swept of his feet as he tried to get down to the waters' edge. He slammed down on his side and slid down the rest of the ramp into the water.

The water was cold, it seeped into his wet suit and hit his groin and armpits. He ignored the cooling water and put his feet into his fins and tightened the straps to hold them in place. He would soon warm up on the swim out to the boat.

With his mask on he ducked under the water and began the swim out of the small fishing harbour to the waiting boat. When he had gone as far as he could under water he surfaced and gasped in air. From where he was now he could see the boat bobbing around in the waves, lit up like a beacon. He began the front crawl to the illuminated yacht.

He had large fins and they powered him there in no time at all. He was up current from the vessel and found himself gripping the anchor line that held the boat in place. He began the ascent up the anchor chain.

It was quite a substantial chain and Cam could get his feet in between the chain links. With his feet like Charlie Chaplin he climbed the chain.

Completely aware he was under the watch of Donald from the shore he reached the top of the chain. He was now alongside a railing that ran the length of the yacht below the main deck. He noticed his hands coloured a reddish brown from the rust on the chain and pulled out his gloves from his suit leg. He slid them onto his filthy hands; he didn't want to leave any rusty smudges on that shiny metal railing.

Dangling from the lower rail he inched his way towards the middle portion of the yacht. Gripping with his gloved hands he slid his way along the railing. He began to hear voices on board the boat, but they didn't sound real. Tinny sounding, like through a small speaker. Cam wondered if they were watching TV or a movie. Could the two men be nothing more than friends?

Above his head now was a small hole in the hull where, if needed, a rope or chain could run through. Cam pulled himself up and rested his now tired arms on the railing and peered through the hole.

Cam had a good view into the main sitting area of the posh yacht. He could see the Saudi sat on the leather crescent sofa, watching a small laptop that had been placed on the glass centre table. Behind him stood a skinny man in what seemed to be a cheap black suit, watching, interested more in the Saudi's reaction than anything else.

Cam watched as whatever was on the laptop ran its course. When it was all over the Saudi stood up and slammed the laptop shut. He span round and began shouting at the skinny man. The cheap-suited man listened unmoved until the torrent of abuse was over. He then spoke, his voice clear, concise almost rehearsed. Whatever was said shut the Saudi up. The skinny man then picked up the laptop, said one more comment to the now quiet Saudi and left the sitting room. Cam wished he could understand what was said; perhaps Donald could have made more sense of what had just happened.

The skinny man was leaving the boat; Donald could watch the Saudi from where he was. Cam made the decision to follow the man in the cheap suit. He allowed himself to drop into the water; he just hoped the splash would go unnoticed amongst the commotion of the visit. Cam silently swam over to the skinny man's motor-boat and, whilst keeping as submerged as he could, gripped the mooring rope that dangled from the speed-boat.

The skinny man climbed aboard with one other individual whom Cam had not been able to identify and the speed-boat took off in the opposite direction from where Cam had entered the water. Cam struggled to hold on as the boat accelerated away from the yacht. He was also aware of the two men talking – probably discussing what had occurred aboard the yacht. Cam however, was too busy holding on to listen, not that he could have understood anyway.

After a five minute journey the speed-boat was heading to a jetty point where Cam could see a waiting car. When they were about fifty metres from shore Cam released his grip and let the speed-boat finish the journey without him. He sat treading water and watched as the speed-boat docked on the jetty and the two men got into the waiting car and drove off. This, he knew, signalled the end of this part of the operation.

Confused and not knowing if he had gathered anything of importance he finned his way to the jetty. He couldn't have been far from Birzebbuga, at least south of the town anyway. The weather was beginning to turn and the water was swelling next to the jetty when he got there. Looking under the water he could see jagged rocks and sea urchins, completely covering the area where he would be trying to exit the water. He would want to avoid both of these hazards as much as possible.

He removed both his swim fins and placed his hands in the foot wells making the fins now an extension of his arms. That way he could still fin towards the ladder that entered the water from the jetty. He swam with his fins to the ladder, and after a few failed attempts when he was washed back out, he got a foothold, let the fins drop around his wrists so that he wouldn't lose them, and grabbed at the closest rung. Once secure he climbed out onto the jetty.

Now out of the water and standing on the wooden jetty, he looked in the direction that the target had driven off, realising he was a long way from the hotel and Donald. It was going to be a good cross-country run back. With time running out before the sun would rise he started back to the hotel.

* * * * * * *

Cam enjoyed the run back, along the coast of that beautiful Mediterranean island. The silver moonlight was shimmering gently off the water as it started to kick up. Cam was glad he had exited the water before it got too choppy; he never liked sea urchins since he had been slammed into some in Greece. The little bastards had graphite like spikes that would break off inside you – he still had the scars.

Cam entered the hotel lobby, again unnoticed. He made his way up the few floors back to his room. He left nothing but damp, sandy footprints to baffle the cleaners the next morning.

He entered his room to find Donald helping himself to the minibar.

"Impressive stuff, quite the little monkey aren't you?" Said Donald as he snapped open an overpriced whisky. "Want one?" Offered Donald.

"Al's paying, so why the hell not."

"Al's footing the bill?!" Said Donald. "You should have said." Donald reopened the fridge and scooped out the rest of the whisky. He threw a couple to Cam keeping at least four for himself.

"He wants to speak to us. I think this is about to get big." Cam opened one of the whiskys and took it in one, all the time looking at the giddy Donald.

"I can't tell you how long I've been waiting for this. All I've been doing is watching these bastards polluting my country, now I might get a chance to make a difference." He was opening another miniature when his phone rang. He pressed the answer button and listened.

"It has been a while," Donald answered, involved in a conversation Cam could not hear. "Yeah he's here," he smirked. "Yeah, I have no idea where you got him from, he takes risks but gets the job done." Cam was unnerved by the excitement of the obviously unseasoned operative. "No, I've not found out," Donald paused, "sure." Donald put the phone down on the bed and pressed the loudspeaker mode.

Al's voice was muffled and incomprehensible. Cam walked to the bed, picked up Donald's phone and placed it on the sideboard next to the bed.

"Say that again Al, didn't get that." Al repeated, and Cam proceeded to tell him what had happened, he left out no detail, no matter how trivial.

"OK, this has the potential to be big." Al's voice sounded louder than normal, probably because of the slightly amplified sound of the phone on the sideboard. "Our operative in Valletta has been watching this guy for a few weeks now, he's the communications officer at the Pakistan embassy."

"What's so interesting about him?" Asked Cam.

"He has connections to someone of great importance. I'm not going to get into it on this line; it's not as secure as yours Cam.

I'm sending you some help. I've one of my best on their way to you as we speak. I want you to meet him Cam. Donald, get back to your bar, we will use it as a base of operations for this one."

"You have a bar?" Cam said turning to Donald who just nodded in reply.

"You will also be joined by the S.B.S operator in Valletta. His name's Rory."

"Rory! From Dorset?" said Cam.

"I think so, do you know him?" Said Al.

"Everyone knows Rory."

"Good that should make thing easier. He'll be at the bar soon, listen to him, he has a great deal of knowledge about the target." Al paused to collect his thoughts and then repeated the main points of the plan. "Donald, get back to your bar and meet Rory. Cam, meet the other Asset in Valletta; he will be there in a few hours. He has the full briefing and will fill you all in."

"How will I know who is the Asset?" Asked Cam.

"His name is Hasler."

"That doesn't help much Al, how will I recognise him?"

"You already know him."

Chapter 6

Al had instructed him to go to the main bus terminal at Valletta, the island's capital city, to meet up with the other Asset. He had not been able to get any sleep after the excitement of the night. He wondered what was happening and what information this new member of the team would give him.

The public transport system worked well in Malta and all buses tended to head to Valletta at some point. His contact would make himself known to him and he would deliver the brief. Not the best instructions but that's all he had.

The bus drivers were still as crazy as ever, they would fit their old nineteen sixties buses through the smallest gaps. The bus bounced along the potholed roads as it snaked through the old streets. Cam thought over what Al had said earlier; who was this Hasler? How did he know him? How would he recognise him?

The bus pulled into Valletta station. Situated at the gate to the town the stops ringed the central fountain. Between the stops, food kiosks sold sandwiches and warm bottles of coke. Always crowded with locals and tourists trying to find the correct bus to their destination, Cam had no idea how he would locate his contact.

He exited the bus and decided to take up a position near the bridge that led to the city's entrance. It had been a number of years since he had last been there and he didn't like the changes. He tried to remain inconspicuous and leaned on the wall near to the stone bridge that led to the city gates. He had a good look around taking in his surroundings.

The city hadn't changed since his last visit, just more tourists now being dragged around by city tour guides. Another change he noticed was the gangs of young Tunisians gathered in groups of two or three, watching the tourists. They seemed to be identifying ones not in the tour groups. One would point out an unsuspecting family or couple and the other two would start to follow them. The leader noticed Cam and the two made eye contact. The stare lingered and Cam thought he might have made a mistake by bringing attention to himself. However, the leader of the gang relented and ushered his cronies away to another location. It was sad to see but it looked like low-level organised crime had arrived on the peaceful Mediterranean island. It was now he realised what Donald had been referring to at the O.P.

Distracted by the obvious criminal activity Cam was surprised to hear a familiar Irish voice.

"Hello Cam." He spun round to see someone he recognised immediately.

"George?"

"How you been?" George asked.

"Good mate," Cam said. "You're Hasler?"

"Yeah," nodded George. "George Hasler." Cam thought back to the last and only time they had met. It occurred to him that he had never asked his full name or been properly introduced.

"It's been a while, what you been up to?" Asked Cam extending his hand.

"Since Torness, not much. You know how it is," said George shaking Cam's hand.

"Yeah, anyway good to see you. So, what's going on?" George suggested that they went somewhere a little quieter so they could talk without being overheard. Cam knew the perfect place. They jumped on the number eighty bus to Mdina, The Silent City.

* * * * * * *

The Silent City was the old Maltese capital, called The Silent City because no cars were allowed in; only a few dotted the streets, used for essential business. A walled city with narrow streets and beautiful churches and buildings. On the top ramparts overlooking St Paul's Bay and the old military hospital was a Café called Fontanella. Cam had been there many times for the famous chocolate cakes, there they could sit and discuss the task that Al had for them.

"Nice view," George said.

"Yeah, I used to come here all the time. I always wanted to own that small farm down there, where I could be left alone and be self-sufficient."

"Sounds good. I had a similar plan on a Greek island. Never works out the way you want it though does it?"

"No, not really."

"You look tired Cam, are you doing alright?" Cam looked back at George thinking that was a strange question to ask.

"Just been up all night, that's all."

"Al told me about Waziristan, I had no idea you were involved in all that," said George.

"It was a long time ago."

"But it's obviously still affecting you."

"Only recently, look it's just a passing thing. I'll be fine. Now what's this all about?"

"Right," said George clearing his throat. "This has a potential to be big. Bigger than Torness." Cam, relieved that George had dropped the subject, raised his eyebrows at the prospect of a more dangerous job than the attempt at blowing up a nuclear power station. "We have to find a dead Iranian military officer."

"Dead, how hard can that be?" Cam said tucking into his sticky chocolate cake.

"That's just it, we're not sure he is dead." George paused to take a big fork-full of cake. "General Abtin Pourali apparently died in an air crash six weeks ago. He was a well known psychopath, constantly causing trouble, ignoring orders and doing his own thing. He was under U.S. and British attention for his interest in chemical weapons, also known to be strongly involved in developing airborne delivery systems."

"Chemical weapons," Cam interrupted. "I know they are developing nuclear weapons but chemical?"

"Well they aren't developing them so much as acquiring them." George continued.

"What do you mean acquiring them?"

"Iraq! When the coalition went in last time to find weapons of mass destruction, Hussein hid them in the desert and they virtually disappeared. Back in the eighties the Iraqis declared they had produced just over three tons of blister agent. Then in the mid nineties this was reduced to two thousand eight hundred and fifty tons. Leaving around one hundred and fifty kilograms missing."

"Let me guess, they found their way into Iran." Cam said.

"Exactly, just like we all thought," exclaimed George shrugging his shoulders and raising his hands. "Only now we have the evidence that it was found by General Pourali, then he went missing and was declared dead."

"How do we know this guy's not dead?" Cam asked.

"We don't, we only suspect it. There is no real evidence for any air accident at the time he went missing and we think it's a cover story," George said with a mouth full of chocolate cake.

"You said something about Pourali having dealings with the delivery systems."

"Yeah, that's the clincher," said George pointing his fork at Cam. "Between 1999 and 2001, Ukrainian arms dealers smuggled around eighteen X-55 missiles out of the Ukraine and distributed them between China and Iran. Pourali was responsible for adapting them for chemical weapons."

"So we have a rouge Iranian General, lost chemical weapons and a missile capable of launching them. All missing."

"Yep. The X-55 has a range of two and a half thousand kilometres. They can be launched from long-range bombers, like the Iranian SU-24 and guess what type of aircraft Pourali was in when he died."

"And that's missing too, isn't it?" Cam asked, knowing the answer.

"Oh yes. And no wreckage has been found."

"Christ! How do we find him?"

"It's a long shot but we have tracked down Pourali's trusted radio operator. Pourali took this guy everywhere and we found him working in the Pakistani embassy here in Malta."

"Let me guess, the guy we caught on the yacht," said Cam jumping ahead. "But why the Pakistan embassy?"

"He's half Iranian half Pakistani. How he got the job of communications officer there we will never know. Sounds like someone high up got it for him. That's where we are going to start."

"Do you have a plan?" Cam said.

"Not yet, but we're going to meet up with the shooter and your linguist. He should know how we can get to him"

"OK, let's go," Cam said getting up. "Our linguist, has a bar in Bugibba called Donnie's bar. That's where we're meeting."

"Sounds good, I could use a drink."

Bugibba was a town that had turned into a holiday resort. A mixture of local's flats and tourist accommodation surrounded the small town centre that looked like a piazza and covered band stand. It was one of these local flats built above a garage that was Donnie's bar. Sometimes the locals turned their garages into small bars and sold bottled beers and an assortment of other drinks.

"Donald is an MI6 linguist," Cam said leading George through the winding streets of Bugibba. "He's a local who speaks many of the Arabic dialects; apparently he's one of the best."

"He's Maltese, but works for the British government?" Asked George.

"Yeah, the Maltese are natural linguists; they speak at least Maltese and English. Maltese is Arabic based, but best of all they are loyal to the British and perfect for intelligence gathering. I met him a week or so ago; he's alright."

"Who's the other?" George asked as they came into view of Donnie's bar.

"His name's Rory, he's S.B.S."

"Do you know him?" Said George.

"Yeah, we've worked together before. He's a damn good soldier but can be a bit of a joker." They arrived at the entrance to Donnie's bar and entered the small garage. A home-made bar had been built in the corner of what used to be a double car garage. Donald was stood behind the bar cleaning glasses. The bar was otherwise empty apart from one customer sat at the furthest table reading a newspaper.

"George, this is Donald, Donald this is George." Cam said introducing the two men.

"Hi, how was the flight?" Donald asked reaching out his hand.

"Good, on time at least." George responded shaking Donald's hand.

"Can I get you two guys a drink?" Donald said, sounding like a cliché bartender. George and Cam looked at each other and ordered two large Jack Daniels, clinked glasses and took a sip.

"Hey you!" Came a voice from the other side of the bar. "Didn't you used to be Robert Cameron?" The bar's single customer lowered his paper, folded it up and placed it on the table next to his local beer. Feeling shocked at hearing his old name, that had been dead for over two years now, Cam recognised the owner of the Dorset voice.

"Hello Rory," Said Cam. The man rose from his seat and walked over to the bar.

Rory was a tall, broad shouldered man who always had a huge smile on his face. He was one of Britain's elite soldiers, the S.B.S. And like most S.B.S. he had the look of a surf dude with sun-bleached light curly hair. He was from Dorset and had a thick Dorset accent to match. He had been involved in more secret missions than he could remember; he also had a wicked sense of humour.

"Cam," grinned Rory extending his hand. "How long has it been?"

"Don't know mate," Cam said shaking his hand. "A good few years."

"Must be, you look a hell of a lot older." Cam introduced Rory to George and the four men took their drinks over to a large enough table and began deciding on a course of action for getting into the Pakistan embassy.

"Look, I've been scouting out the embassy for the past few weeks now, and I've got a plan in place," Rory said. "The building next door is a beauty salon, that's our way in. Communications officer's office is next door to the waxing room of the salon, I've booked an appointment for two of us tomorrow."

"For a waxing!" Cam said. "Who's getting waxed?"

"You're the two hairiest." Rory said pointing at George and Donald. "Plus Donald can do the talking whilst you get into the office; the windows are very close together. You can just hop over."

"And that's your plan?" George said. "Just hop over!"

"It's all we got," shrugged Rory, still grinning. "The embassy's computer system was supplied by Hewlett Packard, so all the equipment should be standard." Rory reached into his pocket and retrieved a computer mouse. "I had Al make this up." He placed a computer mouse on the table amongst the drinks. "It's a flash drive, slash mouse. It will record everything on his hard drive, all internet activity and all passwords."

"Clever stuff." George picked up the mouse and inspected it carefully.

"All you have to do is switch them: simple," Rory said finishing his drink. "Your appointment is half twelve tomorrow. He goes for lunch at the same time every day and normally leaves his window open." Rory looked in turn at Donald and George. "OK?" George sighed and looked at Donald.

"I suppose so."

Chapter 7

"Cam, Rory, can you hear me?" George said testing the new communication system. These new almost invisible earpieces were virtually undetectable and also clear as a bell. They tapped into the nearest mobile phone repeaters and transmitted via the local mobile phone network. Even without a network to link into they would provide a good two hundred metres of communication. The Asset program had come on leaps and bounds in the two years since the Torness job. More funding and equipment made their jobs far easier.

"Certainly can," Cam replied. The two members of the team not tasked with entering the salon were sat in a locked up Donnie's bar. "Where are you guys now?"

"We're about to enter," George said. Donald led the way into the salon. He walked up to the receptionist and began to speak to her in Maltese. George could not understand but followed the gist of the conversation.

The modern salon was split over three floors. The waxing room was in the highest corner of the building. The building was air-conditioned and was over decorated with plants and artwork. The lady behind the reception was talking to Donald in a very pleasant manner; shifting her gaze between her two customers.

"I'm sorry, I don't speak Maltese." George said when the woman asked him a question.

"Oh, I'm sorry Sir; I was just asking who would like to go first?"

"Yeah, that would be him." George said gesturing towards Donald.

"OK, would you like to follow me?" The lady said, leaving the reception desk. "I'll introduce you to Kaya. She will be looking after you today." Donald and George followed her up the first flight of stairs. "Where are you from Sir? England?"

"No I'm from Ireland," George said.

"Oh, I'm sorry; I'm not very good with accents."

"That's OK, it's an easy mistake to make."

"Well I think it's great that you two managed to find each other." Donald and George looked at each other, their faces dropped when they realised what the receptionist meant.

"What! No, no!" George protested looking at Donald. "No, no!" He said again. Donald was lost for words; all he was aware of was the giggling in his earpiece.

"Um, well this is Kaya," interrupted the lady, embarrassed at her mistake, as they arrived at the entrance to what turned out to be the staff rest room. George had stopped listening to the receptionist by this time; all he could hear was the sniggering through his hidden earpiece. Rory was thoroughly enjoying himself.

"Hello gentlemen, I'll be taking you for your three-piece therapy today," Kaya said reaching out to shake Donald's hand.

"Three piece therapy," George said now back in the conversation. "What do you mean three piece?" The sniggering intensified in his ear.

"Don't worry Sir, I'll be very gentle," Kaya said compassionately. "Would you like to follow me up stairs?" She said showing them the way to the third floor.

"What have you done?" Said Cam interrupting Rory's enjoyment.

"It's called a back, sack and crack." Said Rory bursting out in more laughter. "I couldn't believe my luck when I made the appointment, I had to do it!" All George and Donald could do was try not to react to the two back in Bugibba who were clearly finding pleasure at their misfortune.

"OK, here we are." Kaya said opening the door to the waxing room. Donald and George peered over her shoulder into what they considered to be a torture room. "Now, there is a shower in here, so if whoever's first would like to get themselves ready I'll be back in five minutes."

"Where does the other wait?" George asked.

"Would you not want to be together?" Kaya said sounding surprised.

"Good God no!" Said George raising his voice unintentionally. He looked at Donald who was as horrified as he was. The two avoided eye contact and George had nowhere else to look but at the floor. "Christ," he whispered. "This is so embarrassing."

"George you go first, use that five minutes to get into the embassy." Said Rory directly into George and Donald's ears via the hidden earpieces. "Donald if she comes back, keep her busy till George is done." As Kaya had heard none of that, George informed her that he will be first and stepped inside the room and closed the door behind him.

"If you'd like to take a seat over there Sir, I'll be back in a few minutes." Donald sat down on the wicker seat and drummed his fingers on the armrests. He looked at his watch and started waiting for Kaya to return.

George looked around the room; in the centre lay a massage table with clean white sheets draped over it. The shower was in the far corner; he walked over to it and turned it on. He closed the door to the shower cubical and turned his attention to the only window in the room. The window was in the other corner of the room and could be opened fully, allowing him to lean right out.

"What's going on George?" Cam asked.

"I'm looking out the window and I can see the one for the office next door. It's about three metres from this one. It's open but I don't know how I'm going to get to it."

"The ledge, there's plenty of room to shuffle along it. Hold on to the guttering above," Rory said.

"What?" George said. "The ledge is tiny; I'll only get my toes on it."

"You'll be alright." Cam said.

"Hey, I'm not a monkey like you."

"You're going to have to hurry. She's on her way back with the wax." Joked Rory.

"For God's sake," George said as he climbed out onto the ledge. He gingerly inched his way towards the Pakistan embassy. Without looking down he took one hand off the flimsy, rusted guttering and reached out for the semi-open window. He had to lean right out over the street to allow the window to open fully against the outer wall of the building, putting him off balance. Once the window was open he crouched down and in a controlled manner fell into the Communications office.

"I'm in," he said. The two men listening from Bugibba sat in silence waiting for more updates. Wasting no time he went straight to the computer and picked up the mouse. He pulled out the one from Rory and compared the two. The new mouse was slightly different from the one attached to the computer. "It's different."

"How different?" Asked Cam.

"Not much," he held the two mice next to each other. "I think we'll be alright."

"Good, make the switch," said Rory. Before he had finished talking George had the new mouse connected and was back at the window.

"I'm exiting the office," George said, climbing out onto the ledge.

"Shit!" George stopped when he heard Donald in his earpiece. "You had better hurry," he whispered. "I think she's on her way back."

"Stall her. I just need a minute." George was scrambling back into the waxing room. He could hear Donald talking to Kaya outside the door as he hurriedly undressed himself. He took out his earpiece and placed it on top of his clothing so it wouldn't get wet while he took a shower. He stepped out after his shortest ever shower and began to dry himself. He paused momentarily when he saw and heard the room's door handle move. Donald's muffled voice could be heard through the door trying desperately to keep Kaya occupied. George picked up the earpiece put it to his mouth.

"You don't need to hear this," he whispered, then he flicked the tiny switch turning it off.

"Bloody spoil-sport." Rory said. "Alright Donald, you've embarrassed yourself enough. I think he's ready." Donald had run out of things to say and finally let Kaya go. She entered the waxing room to find George ready, face down on the table.

"OK, Sir. Just relax and this won't hurt a bit," she said closing the door. George just grunted in reply.

* * * * * * *

Donald made it back to his bar where Cam and Rory were waiting before George. He decided to leave before he had to go in for his turn. The three men waited for him to return. They just smiled as George appeared in the doorway.

"What the hell happened to you?" He said looking straight at Donald.

"Well I didn't see much point in hanging around. We had completed the task."

"You mean I completed the task," George said joining them at the table.

"Alright keep your hair on," said Rory trying not to snigger.

"Nice one," said George sarcastically. "What do we do now?"

"We wait for it to collect the information then we send it to Al for analysis."

"Tell me I don't have to go get it back?"

"No," Rory said. "It works like a Bluetooth device. I'll go to the embassy every day and from the other side of the street I'll download the information and pass it to Al."

"So does that mean we've got a few days to ourselves?" Enquired Cam.

"Yeah sure, leave it to me," said Rory. "When we get something from Al I'll be in touch. Keep your phones on."

Chapter 8

The Pakistani communications officer sat at his desk deep in thought. He felt the cool breeze of the swivelling desk fan as it turned back and forth. The old building had no air con; he was glad that he could open his window for some refreshing fresh air. This job was too much for him and he really felt out of his depth; he had had to take it when it was arranged for him. But still, he only had to be there for a few more weeks. Then they would be ready.

He finished up his last email and deleted any trace it had been sent. He was meticulous when it came to covering his tracks; no evidence would remain about what they were up to. That was General Pourali's orders. He would wait now for the reply, he knew it wouldn't take long. When it arrived he opened it with a click of his mouse and read the contents.

It was all coming together nicely; soon Iran would be hitting out at its enemies. Although the Iranian government did not know about it yet, they would have no choice but to follow through once the first strike had been launched or they themselves would be finished. He read it over and over until he had the information memorised then deleted it along with the rest.

He slid back his chair and stood up arching his back, stretching out the knots that had formed from sitting at his computer all morning. He picked up his pack of cigarettes and opened his window. He leant forward on the window-sill and lit his cigarette.

He dragged the smoke deep into his lungs and breathed it out into the warm Maltese air. It was a beautiful day, not a cloud in the sky. The air was warm but there was a pleasant cooling breeze. He looked out over the calm, clear water. He was enjoying the view so much that he failed to spot the man sat on a small wall across the street from the embassy.

* * * * * * *

Rory perched himself on the breeze block wall and balanced his small laptop on his knees. He had been there twice a day for two days now, gathering information from the communications officer's computer. The mouse was working well, collecting everything it could from the computer and sending it to Rory's laptop.

All he had to do was sit within range of the mouse and it would automatically download to his computer and be sent straight to Al for analysis. So far this job had been one of the easiest jobs Rory had ever been on. He wished they could all be like this.

* * * * * * *

Cam stood waiting for the boat to Comino, the island between Malta and Gozo. Every time he visited the island he would take a trip to Comino. It was a small, almost uninhabited island that had an air of peace and calm about it. The port of Cirkewwa at the northern tip of Malta was anything but.

It had changed beyond all recognition, from a small dock with a little café to a large ferry terminal where crowds of people gathered to catch the ferry or smaller crafts. The boat too, was over crowded; it seemed to struggle with the amount of passengers as it chugged towards the Blue Lagoon.

Cam stepped off the boat into what could only be described as a miniature Ibiza. He tried to comprehend what had happened to his little Mediterranean sanctuary. There were people everywhere. And with people came noise, rubbish and pollution. He looked over towards Comminoto, the even smaller island about one hundred metres off the beach.

The stretch of water between the two was crowded with private boats blaring loud music. He was disgusted to see cans and empty packets of crisps floating around the rocks. They had even created a seating area with deckchairs to be rented out and fast food kiosks that sold burgers and chips. The kiosks were powered by generators that burred and hummed, kicking out petrol fumes.

Cam just turned his back on it all and walked off in the opposite direction. He walked along the rocky coastline towards St Mary's Tower, a square, red building on the south side of the island. There were less people over that way. Cam looked down into the water as he walked; he could see a couple swimming in the bay. The water was so clear he could see past the swimmers to the rocks beneath them.

He hopped from rock to rock avoiding standing on the lizards that darted between the jagged rocks. Reaching the tower he climbed the wooden stairs and sat down at the top. The tower was between him and the sun giving some rest from the heat, allowing him to cool down. He sat for a good hour enjoying the shade and the peaceful view from this elevated position; pleased to find, at last, some peace and quiet.

The large car ferries passed by with regularity, transporting people from Malta to Gozo and vice versa. Smaller speed-boats zipped about taking divers to the main dive sites. He remembered back to his travelling days, after Waziristan. He himself had been a diver, working his way round the world. It felt like such a long time ago.

Perhaps he should go back to his simple life travelling around the globe aimlessly. Maybe he should try to get away from this lifestyle that he had found himself living. But how would he escape? Disappearing would be harder than ever now that he had become involved with Al and the Assets. It would take some serious cash, cash that he did not have. After Waziristan, Cam had made a promise, a promise he had to keep; he had vowed to use any extra money he came across helping the families of his lost colleagues. He had managed so far but it was never enough, no matter how much he gave they still struggled to get by.

He shook the thoughts of his lost friends' relatives from his head and looked back over to where the crowds of people were. It was time to go back, but first he would have a swim. When he made it back to the Blue Lagoon where the boat had dropped him off he slid into the water. Swimming through the cool water he felt free, he loved being in the sea. The cooling water had a way of relaxing him. He walked ashore onto the smaller island, stepping through the kelp close to the beach and made his way up the rocky slope. His feet were tough from years of blistering marches and resisted the sharp, stabbing rocks. He stood at the top, at the highest point and took in the island. He felt like he may never return here.

When the time to leave came he bid a silent farewell to the island and boarded the boat back to the mainland. The return trip took slightly longer as the captain decided to show the tourists the caves on the way back. Before long he was back in Malta and sat on one of the crazy buses heading to the hotel that Al had booked them all into.

The afternoon was hot and muggy; Cam was sweating when he finally made it back to the hotel. He entered through the back of the complex and headed straight to the pool where he found George sat enjoying a cocktail.

"Hey George," Cam said reaching the poolside seats.

"Cam, how you doing? Fancy a drink? My treat," George said raising his cocktail glass.

"Err, yeah sure. Whisky sour please."

"Back in a min," George said getting up. Cam dropped his bag on the floor and took off his t-shirt and jumped into the pool to cool down. He found a floating water noodle and put his arms over it allowing him to float freely in the chlorinated swimming pool water.

When George returned from the poolside bar with his drink, Cam climbed out of the swimming pool, dried himself off and replaced his t-shirt.

"Cheers," he said picking up his drink and taking a sip. He dragged over another seat and sat at the table with George.

"Where you been all day?" George asked.

"Comino. I go every time I'm here."

"Been to Malta before then?"

"Yeah, I was born here."

"Oh right yeah, from a military family aren't you?"

"Yeah, Dad was in the Air Force." He looked over at George and realised that after all they had been through, he actually knew very little about the man. "What about you, where are you from?"

"Well it's a long story, but originally from Youghal."

"Oh right, I've been through, nice place." Cam replied. "So, how the hell did you get involved with all this?" George seemed surprised by the question and looked over at Cam. He seemed reluctant to answer.

"Another long story," he said looking away.

"We got time," said Cam waving his glass around the pool area.

"Well, I used to be in the Irish Army," George said after a short pause. "Infantry. Then something happened and I ended up in a hell of a lot of trouble. I had to disappear and fast, that's when Al found me. That was back when the Asset program had just started; I was the first or at least one of the first."

"Any family?" Said Cam.

"No," George sighed. "Not any more. I was married back then but it was too much for her. She was," George paused to collect his thoughts, "wonderful. But she was in danger and at one point she was nearly killed." George looked back over to Cam who was nodding in agreement. "There was no way I could put her through a life of constant danger, and that was that."

"Yeah," Cam said agreeing.

"What about you, any family?"

"No, not like you had. Parents obviously and a sister. But no one special. Wasted too much time in the Army."

"So how did you end up here?" Enquired George.

"I got involved in some serious stuff and on one of our missions it all went wrong. I was the only one who got out and only barely. Left the Military, spent a couple of years travelling around the world then came back to finish something I started. And a bit like you, it all went wrong and Al got me. That's when I met you."

"Yeah, Torness." George looked like he was thinking back to two years ago. "That was a close call."

The conversation went on for another hour or so. Neither had spoken about how it all started for them, for a very long time. George had certainly never spoken about it. They had just ordered their third round of cocktails when Rory appeared by the pool.

"Hello Ladies," he said with his usual wide grin. "Look at you two having a heart to heart. Stay put while I get a drink, Al's got something for us." Rory went to the pool bar and ordered a drink. He returned with the most ridiculous looking tall cocktail glass with umbrellas, curly straws and slices of fruit.

"What the hell is that?" Said Cam pointing at the offending drink.

"It's an Electric Smurf," Rory said defending his choice of beverage. "It's refreshing."

"You don't normally drink that, do you?" Asked George.

"No, I normally have a Lindsay Lohan," smiled Rory.

"What's a Lindsay Lohan?" Cam said waiting for the inevitable punch line.

"It's a skinny red-headed slut with a splash of coke," said Rory trying to find the straw amongst the paraphernalia cluttering up his glass. Rory didn't look surprised to hear the moan that usually followed most of his jokes.

"OK, enough bartending for the insane," Cam said. "What's Al got for us?"

"The intel came back from the embassy," Rory said finally locating the straw. "He wants to call us tonight. My room in one hour, Donald knows about it."

"Do you know what it's about?" Cam said.

"No, I guess we'll find out tonight," said Rory spitting out the straw. "This is shit! Come on I'll get the Lindsay Lohans."

Chapter 9

Behind the door of room four hundred and ten, George, Donald, Rory and Cam gathered waiting for Al's call. Cam connected his phone to some small loudspeakers and placed it in the centre of the round wooden table. George stood from the table and went to the kitchen area of Rory's room.

"Does anyone want a brew?" He asked. Only Rory responded with a yes. "What do you want, tea or coffee?"

"Tea, Julie Andrews."

"What?" George said turning to face the table.

"He means tea, white, nun," Cam said, sensing George's confusion.

"Oh, right." George said pouring the water into the mugs on the counter. "Is it nearly time?" George barely had time to finish his sentence before the phone started to ring.

"There we go," Cam said. "Right on time." He reached out and accepted the call.

"Hello, can you chaps hear me?"

"Yes we can," Rory said leaning in towards his phone.

"Good, it's Al here."

"We know, Al," Cam said. "What do you have for us?"

"Well, the short version is we still do not know where the General is." Al began. "We have emails and fragmented messages collected from the embassy that lead us to believe that there are a number of supporters on the side of General Pourali. They are organising something. The intelligence we have suggests it will be a chemical attack, possibly multiple targets."

"Al," interrupted Donald. "How did you find the General's radio operator? I mean, he's our initial source of information, should we continue looking into him?"

"No," replied Al. "We are done with him; we will keep snooping on his emails in case we find anything more interesting. And it was luck we found him anyway, by accident really. Over the years it was noted by military intelligence that he has a particular way of talking on the radio. The same speech impediment allowed us to track Pourali wherever he went; our electronic warfare guys noticed the same impediment in some radio communications at the embassy. It was looked into and it was confirmed to be him. It was strange for him to be there so Rory was despatched to check him out. After a bit of digging it was still unclear how he got the job; we reckon the General got him in there. When you two guys found him on the Saudi's yacht we had to take a look at him in more detail. It was all we had at the time."

"Any more on the missing weapons?" Asked George handing Rory a cup of tea.

"They're still missing, this is all we know for certain. We're all well aware of the failed hunt for Iraq's weapons of mass destruction that was plastered all over the papers." Al's showed a slight hint of contempt in his voice when talking about the media. "Most people jump straight to nuclear when W.M.Ds are mentioned but chemical weapons kill more than one at a time, as the Kurds found out. Now, Hussein hid his chemical weapons in

75

the desert; they went missing and we have definite intel that they found their way into Iran."

George sat down at the table with his brew, "And you're sure it's blister agent that he has acquired?"

"We are positive about that," continued Al. "When he went missing he was flying in a long-range bomber and there is no evidence of any crashes or even an attempt by the Iranians of a search and rescue. Also, X-55 missiles found their way into Iran and he was tasked with modifying them for chemical warheads – these also went missing. Putting this all together he has a chemical capability and a method of delivering it."

"Rory mentioned he is unstable, just how dangerous is he?" Asked Donald.

"Extremely dangerous. He makes no attempt to hide his intentions; the Iranian military tried to put him to one side and limit the amount of influence he had, but it only fuelled his hatred. The west, the Arab League you name it, he is against it."

"OK," interrupted Cam. "How do we get to him?"

"The emails that Rory downloaded from the embassy point to a number of locations where it seems that Pourali has other sympathisers. They are all communicating via emails that are careful to give away very little. However, they all mention 'the compound.' Now, we are unsure what this is or where it is but we might have a way of locating it." Al paused to clear his throat.

"All of these other sites from the emails are sending coded messages that we can't intercept. They are well encrypted and are being sent by highly directional antennas." Al paused again. "So, this is where we are now gentlemen. Find the antennas at the sites, take a bearing that the antennas are firing off these messages and we can triangulate the destination. Hopefully that's where this 'compound' is and where Pourali is."

"What are the locations?" Asked Rory.

"I'm going to split you into two groups. There is a building in Dubai, George and Donald you're going there. Your flight leaves tonight. When you get there I'll contact you with the details of your task." Donald and George looked at each other and nodded accepting their task.

"Cam, Rory. You are going to infiltrate an oil-rig in the Maersk Al Shaheen field. You've both done operations like this before and I have every faith in you. I'm arranging your flight to Doha, Qatar now. Again you'll get everything you need when you arrive. This is the first time we are being used overseas. If we get this right we will be used globally. If we get it wrong this madman will strike out at us and the U.S. The Middle East will become more unstable and even more dangerous. We have been tasked with this because we accidently got mixed up in it, and we are deniable. If it goes wrong we are on our own; we have everything to gain and everything to loose." Al made one more dramatic pause. "OK guys, I'll be in touch with further details. Good luck."

When the line went dead the men began silently contemplating their tasks. Cam quietly tidied away his phone and the loudspeaker. They split into their teams, wished each other the best of luck and left to prepare for the next part of the task.

* * * * * * *

Before their flight left for Dubai, George and Donald received an email from Al. It contained everything they needed to complete the task. They were to head to a newly developed area of Dubai called Jumeirah Lake Towers. There they would find a huge building: the Almas Tower. This imposing sixty-eight storey building housed the Dubai Diamond Exchange. Most importantly it was sympathetic to Pourali's cause, although they would never admit to it.

George wasn't used to flying first class; his background had made him more accustomed to staying out of the way and not putting himself in the open. He sat in his personal cocoon watching television and thinking. He looked over at Donald who was fast asleep in his reclining chair. He wanted to sleep but couldn't. The talk he had with Cam had stirred up some memories that had long since been pushed to the back of his mind.

He remembered back to when he had a family, when he was happy, only to have it all taken away from him. He thought about his wife and son and wondered where they were and what sort of life they were living. She was a good person and deserved the best, more than he could give her anyway. Not after what happened. He looked at his surroundings and felt a million miles from when he had been running and hiding for his life, living in his car and stealing to survive. He took out his phone and re-read the email from Al. Al had saved him from that life and given him another chance. He had given him a new identity and George felt that he owed him.

Donald woke from his sleep and with tired red eyes looked over at George.

"Morning." George said.

"It's morning?" Replied Donald rubbing his dry eyes.

"Only just, we'll be landing in less than an hour. I thought we should head straight for the tower and check it out whilst it's quiet. What do you think?"

"Good idea. How hard do you think it will be to find the antenna?"

"We'll just have to find out when we get there." Donald agreed with a nod and a yawn. George looked out of his window and watched as the aircraft descended into Dubai International Airport. As the plane approached the coast he could make out the World of Islands on his left-hand side. He wondered how many celebrities were down there asleep or still partying into the night. If Donald weren't fast asleep again, he would be able to see out of his window the two Palm Islands that Dubai is famous for.

He was aware that he was now directly over the complex of towers that they had been tasked to infiltrate in order to find the directional antenna that was sending messages to Pourali. It would have been handy to see it from the air but it was a luxury that was not to be available that night. They would have to wait until the aircraft landed to make a quick trip on the Dubai light rail network before they could start formulating a plan.

* * * * * * *

The towers were an impressive sight. Donald and George felt like two ants looking up with open mouths at the skyscrapers towering around them like trees in a forest. The complex consisted of seventy-nine towers constructed around the edge of four artificial lakes. Their target was the Almas Tower, the centrepiece, built on its own island and the tallest of the collection of buildings.

"How on earth are we supposed to get in there?" Donald said.

"Don't know, let's get a closer look," George replied as they approached the Almas tower entrance.

"We're gonna have to come up with something. What goes on in there anyway?" Asked Donald.

"It's the Diamond Exchange. Everything in there has something to do with jewellery in some aspects."

"Of course, Al Mas is Arabic for diamond. Look at that security, we're going to need some help with this one."

"Yeah, I agree," George said, "I'll get on to Al and get him to do some digging around, see if he can figure something out for us."

With the message to Al sent, the two men made their way wearily to their hotel. Before they had a chance to book in, Al had replied. Through tired glazed eyes George read the message.

Dubai Diamond Exchange is having a grand event for its top investors tomorrow night. I have arranged an invite for you. Your invite and identifications for the names on the invite will be delivered to you tomorrow. One of the thirty-five elevators leads up to the Antenna floor on the outside of the building. I have attached a PDF copy of the building's schematics. Find the elevator and locate the antenna.

Good luck.

The next morning a messenger delivered a small package to the hotel entrance, Donald went down to pick it up and brought it straight to George's room.

"Ha, look at this!" Donald exclaimed. "I'm the executive and you're my bodyguard."

"What?" George sighed. "Well I suppose it makes sense. You can do the talking whilst I get the job done again."

"Yeah, just like the last one."

"Except this time I don't expect any hair to be ripped out of my arse." For some reason Donald was finding this far more amusing than George.

"Hey, this diamond place," Donald asked between fits of laughter, "does it say on the schematics where the vaults are?"

"Already had a look. They're in the below-ground basement floors. No chance mate."

"Oh well, never mind. Great minds think alike though."

Chapter 10

Doha, the capital city of Qatar, is one of the driest cities in the world: hot all year round and very little rain. It makes you feel like you're boiling in your own skin. Cam and Rory stepped out of the terminal at Doha International Airport onto the baking pavement. The usual taxi drivers tried their luck with the promise of low fares to wherever their prospective passengers needed to go.

"Over there, look," Cam said, pointing towards a waiting U.S. Army jeep. Rory nodded and the two walked over to the driver who was leaning on his vehicle. This was the first instruction in Al's email that they had received along with their flight details.

The driver was of average height but stocky and mean looking. He watched the two men approach through his mirrored sunglasses. He wore the typical U.S. Army off-duty clothes, had a medium length scruffy beard and arms covered in tattoos. Cam spotted the dirty looking tan and thought to himself that this man had spent some time on the ground mixing in with the locals. He remembered what he had been told by the intelligence team hunting Bin Laden: the longer the beard the more important the man, and this American must have needed to look important.

"You guys with Al?" The American man grunted in a gruff New York accent.

"Yeah," Rory replied, deepening his voice, trying to match the obvious toughness of the jeep driver. Cam looked over at him; Rory looked back and shrugged his shoulders accepting he had not pulled it off.

"Jump in; I'm taking you to the airbase." Cam and Rory threw their meagre belongings into the back of the jeep and climbed aboard.

"You might want to hold on, once we're off the main road it gets a little bumpy," said the driver. Cam was sat in the front passenger seat and went to rest his arm on the top of the door.

"Ahhh, shit!" He said lifting his arm away and rubbing it.

"Yeah, gets a little hot round these parts. You can burn yourself on pretty much everything."

"Al said he would have some equipment delivered. Has it arrived?"

"Sure has; I don't know who this guy 'Al' is but he's got you guys some good stuff," said the driver as the jeep bounced down the uneven road. "Also if you need anything more I'll do my best to get it to you."

"Who are you with, if you don't mind me asking?" Enquired Cam.

"My name's Bull, I'm with The Teams, but at the moment I'm attached to a number of different agencies." Cam got the message; he knew not to ask any more questions. "Who are you guys? Blades? Shakies?"

"We come from a mix of backgrounds." Bull nodded keeping his eye on the road.

"Well whoever you are, I've been tasked with making sure you get everything you need and that this thing goes off without a hitch."

"Cheers, Bull." Cam said reading the airbase sign that came into view through the shimmering glare of the hot desert.

"Welcome to Al Udeid," said Bull. The airbase, situated west of Doha, was owned by the Qatar Emiri Air Force. However, the Royal Air Force, U.S. Air force and the Royal Australian Air Force also operated out of the base. "There's an ISO container full of equipment from Al and a C-130 at your disposal."

The jeep skidded to a halt in a cloud of dust outside a sun-faded green tent.

"Drop your shit off here. There's some camp cots set up in the back. Two hundred metres that way, near the tower, you'll find your container. Meet me there when you're ready." Cam climbed out of the passenger seat and caught sight of a dust covered Rory trying to get out of the back. His seat in the back was slightly elevated and he was unprotected from the dust blowing over the windshield.

They dragged their bags from the back of the jeep and Bull roared off in the direction of the aircraft tower. Cam looked over at the sand-coloured Rory. He blinked his gritted eyes and cleared his throat.

"I'm uh," he coughed. "I'm going to take a shower."

* * * * * * *

Bull pulled at the metal locking mechanism of the ISO container. Rory gripped the other handle and they both yanked at the doors. The doors squeaked and creaked open.

"OK, let's see what we've got," Cam said, entering the container. The sun had heated the metal container like an oven. "Whoa," exclaimed Cam struggling to breathe in the hot air. "Right," he gasped. "We've got a selection of weapons, ammo, climbing equipment, diving kit, everything we need."

"And whatever you don't have, I'll find," said Bull standing arms folded at the entrance to the container. "But for now have a look at this." He reached into a bag, hidden underneath his driving seat, and pulled out a cardboard folder. "This is all we have on the oil platform." He handed the folder to Rory and jumped into his jeep, started the engine and slowly drove round into the shade cast by the ISO container. Rory opened the folder and spread the contents out on the jeep's bonnet.

In the cool shadow the three thrashed out a plan of how to get on the rig and off again without anyone noticing. All the men had experience of these types of operation before and it wasn't long before the details were finalised.

"So, let's re-cap," Bull said. "Drop from the C-130 at two and a half thousand feet as close as we can to the rig. We will then use the current to drift by the rig, attach ourselves to it wherever we can and ascend to the spider deck."

"The rig itself is a three platformed installation," Rory continued. "The installation consists of an accommodation block, the main working platform and the excess gas vent." He pointed to each platform as he listed them. "The platforms are connected via walkways."

"When we are on, I'll make my way to the accommodation block," said Bull. "I will secure one of their life rafts and wait for your signal for extraction."

"Whilst you're doing that, Rory and I will head to the helicopter landing pad. From there we can see the antenna array, and hopefully I will be able to spot a directional antenna and take a bearing."

"Once done," interrupted Bull. "Simply drop into the water and allow yourself to drift away. I will break one of the life raft's couplings and let it fall into the water; the crew will think it just broke free. Once you are far enough from the rig turn on your light beacons and I will pick you up in the raft. Nobody will ever know we were there."

"Any problems, just get off the rig," Rory said. "We want to remain undetected. We will arm ourselves but we don't want to be shooting on the rig."

"Yeah," Bull interjected. "Let rip in the wrong place and it could all go up. There are a lot of volatile gasses all over the place. So, I suggest low velocity rounds; there's fewer sparks from the primers and propellant." The three men looked at each other and nodded in silent agreement.

"When?" Asked Rory.

"Sooner the better," Cam said.

"The weather looks good tonight," Bull said. "Airframe is waiting, we got everything we need. Let's just get it done."

"OK, tonight then," Cam said. "I'll get on to Al and let him know what we're going to do."

* * * * * * *

The heat of the day faded as the sun set. Although still hot, the rest from the burning heat felt like a huge relief. The sky turned from red to orange and finally a stunning purple dotted with bright stars. Cam walked from the tent, where Rory was sleeping half in and half out of his cot, across the airfield. The C-130 was waiting near the runway in the distance. Bull was leaning on his jeep smoking a cigarette, the lit tip could only just be seen poking through his bushy beard.

"Al's approved it." He said.

"Good, let's kit up," Bull said blowing out smoke. He stamped the cigarette into the sand putting it out. "Get in." Bull drove Cam back over to the tent. They drove right up to the opening, shining the headlights into the tent. "Dude, we're up!" Bull shouted waking Rory with a start. Rory tried to block the blinding light with his hand as he got up out of his cot. He put one leg into his trousers, but dazzled by the headlights he caught his foot in his sleeping bag and fell face first onto his cot which folded up around him pinning him to the ground.

"Help!" Rory said, muffled by the face full of sleeping bag. Cam looked at Bull who leaned forward resting his forearms on the steering wheel. He could swear that he could see a slight smile barely visible under his beard.

Chapter 11

The party was in full swing when the Maltese representative for Swarovski arrived. The guests were the top executives in the field of jewellery, rich and well dressed. They were making their rounds and mingling, waiters weaved in and out with silver plates laden with entrées and champagne.

The function room was on one of the upper floors of the tower giving a spectacular view of Dubai. The room was decorated to the highest standard with marble flooring, golden trimming and a giant diamond chandelier. Two wide polished wooden staircases led to the upper mezzanine deck, one on each side of the function room.

Each party goer was dressed as sharp as the next, the men in black tuxedos and the women in expensive looking cocktail dresses. They sipped champagne and talked shop, hoping to make business connections and expand their empires. The low music just about drowned out the conversations of the elite members of the diamond industry.

Glass panelling ran the length of the room and the lights of the city sparkled like stars. In the distance the coast and the ports could be made out as the city lights dwindled and the scattered ships' red port lights and green starboard lights took over.

The other buildings in the Jumeirah Lakes Towers, dwarfed by the Almas Tower, allowed an unobstructed view from the function room. The view was hypnotic and the majority of the guests were stood by the window talking and staring, pointing out areas of the city that were important to them.

Above, on the mezzanine area, the Swarovski rep looked down on the crowd below. Behind him stood his bodyguard, an unnecessary precaution but one most of the guests had taken, probably as a show of their own importance. The bodyguard approached the railing and joined his employer in looking down on the sea of penguin suits.

"Well then, shall we mingle?" The rep said turning to his bodyguard. He nodded in reply. Slowly they made their way down the curved staircase to the ground floor with the occasional polite nod or an 'excuse me.'

On reaching the floor the bodyguard adjusted his black tie and swiped a flute of champagne from one of the waiters as they passed by.

"No," whispered the rep and plucked it from his bodyguard's hand. "You are working." He then took a little sip, smiled and turned away from his disgruntled employee. "Follow me."

The pair took a couple of steps towards the crowd.

"Not too close, remember your place," said the Swarovski rep turning to his bodyguard.

"Be careful, Donald," said the bodyguard.

"That's Mr Allegritto to you," smiled Donald.

"Be very careful," said the bodyguard in a more menacing tone. Donald took another sip and led the way into the group of people. They made a quick circle of the room and came to rest at the large glass wall overlooking the city.

"OK," said Donald. "I don't think anyone gives a shit that we're here. Why don't you go find the elevator to the roof?"

"Yeah, that was easier than I thought it would be. Sit tight, I won't be long."

"Keep me updated on your progress," Donald said tapping his earpiece. George turned and walked away. "Oh, wait," Donald said calling him back. "Get me another one of these on your way back." He held up his empty champagne flute. George said nothing, ascended the stairs to the function room's entrance and entered the elevator that would take him back down to the tower's main entrance.

George stood in the elevator and watched the numbers of the floors go down as the elevator descended the long journey to the ground. The sounds of pan pipe classics filled the elevator. After a good two or three minutes the doors opened to an audible 'bing.'

George stepped out of the elevator and the metal doors slid shut behind him. He looked around; the corridor on his right led to the door that would give him access to the service elevator. To his left was the main vestibule area that housed the buildings reception and the security desk.

Donald and George had paid particular attention to the security as they entered the skyscraper and presented their faked invitations. The security was tight; armed guards, metal detectors and regular patrols could all be potential problems.

From his position, near the bank of elevators, he could see a deserted vestibule. He was free to enter the service corridor. He gripped the handle and went to turn it, but it would not move, it was locked. Looking at the door it seemed unremarkable, nothing special. The handle had no keyhole or keycard slot and George wondered how the staff accessed the corridor.

He had no choice but try to check out the reception and security desks in the foyer. Looking around for inspiration on how to do this he spotted a clipboard slotted behind a couple of fire extinguishers. Checking the coast was clear he stepped over to them and slid out the clipboard. Inspecting the attached sheets of paper it appeared that this was the record of the buildings fire checks.

The checks seemed to be done on a daily basis. Not today however. George decided this was his quickest and possibly only chance to gain himself entry to the service corridor.

He strode across the foyer towards the reception desk; his route took him past the security post manned by two switched-on looking guards who watched him pass by. He needed to look like he belonged there; he must act the part of someone of importance. He assumed a role of authority like putting on some sort of uniform. He concentrated on looking forward avoiding eye contact with the security team; he did not want to invite any questions on his presence. Using the clipboard as some sort of shield he approached the receptionist sat behind the desk.

"Who is responsible for the daily fire checks?" George demanded of the receptionist slamming down the fire safety clipboard on the desk top.

"Oh, I'm not sure, I think it's my supervisor but she's not here right now," said the receptionist, taken aback.

"Well they have not been done tonight," George paused to judge the girl's response but she just looked back unsure of how to respond. "Fire safety is the responsibility of every one of us. Have you completed the checks before?"

"I have yes but…"

"No excuses," interrupted George. "I want it done now. We have the world's most important figures in our industry here tonight and I don't want anything to happen on my watch."

"Yes Sir," said the girl jumping up and heading off to begin the checks.

"Good," George shouted after her. "I'll be right here, I'll watch the desk until you get back." George made sure the security guards overheard him. Through the corner of his eye he saw they were more interested in their paper work than the obviously annoyed and grumpy executive giving the receptionist a hard time. They seemed to want to avoid his wrath and they ignored him as he moved round to the reception station.

George scanned the desk for any way through the locked service door but there was nothing standing out. He knew he might not have long until the receptionist returned; he sat down in her chair and continued his search. The door he wanted to open had no key or card slot, no keypad and no combination lock. This meant that someone would have to let the maintenance personnel through. He felt under the desk, groping around until his hand touched a hidden control.

He ducked down and saw a button with the printed label 'service corridor,' placed next to it. He quickly pressed the button and stood up and started on his way back to the door leaving the reception chair spinning behind him. Realising it may be on a timer he quickened his pace attracting the attention of the guards who were both now watching him move speedily through the open space towards their desk.

George sensed they were about to challenge him; he decided to pre-empt them.

"Did you not realise this hadn't been done?" He said holding up the clipboard.

"No." Came the simple reply.

"Well it's nearly midnight; this should be done daily. When were you planning on doing it?" George did not wait for a reply he just moved passed the security desk and back to the corridor. When he reached the fire extinguishers he slid the clipboard back behind them in its original place and jogged toward the hopefully un-locked door. "The old ones are the best ones." He said to himself. Nobody questions someone with a clipboard.

George reached out and held his breath as he turned the handle. The door opened with little effort and he slid inside allowing it to close behind him.

"Donald, can you talk?" George said tapping his hidden earpiece, activating it.

"Yes, nobody seems to want to talk to me," Donald said turning towards the large glass window and partially hiding his mouth with his champagne glass.

"I wouldn't take it personally," George said walking down the service corridor. "Have you thought of changing your aftershave?"

"Hmm," Donald said. George realised that Donald would have to only speak when he could as it would be hard for him to have a conversation with himself in a crowded room. "Where are you?" Mumbled Donald.

"I'm by the service elevator," George said pressing the call button. The elevator door immediately opened. This was good thought George, if it had been on another floor it would be definite proof that there were still maintenance personnel on site. With it opening straight away it meant that the last person to use it got off at this level.

From studying the schematics sent to him by Al, he knew that this lift should take him to the top floor, which would open on the outside of the building; this outer floor was the communication and antenna field. George pressed the top button and the lift jerked into action and began ascending to the roof-tops.

"Bloody Pan Pipe Classics," George said, complaining about the same elevator music that he had endured on the trip down. He tried to ignore the tune; he didn't want it to get stuck in his head.

George watched the floor counter steadily rise as the elevator took him towards the roof of the tower, up and up until it stopped. George immediately noticed a problem. The elevator had stopped one floor short. He pressed the top button again but it refused to take him there. Examining the control panel his attention was brought to a keyhole adjacent to the top floor button.

"Shit, Donald I need a key to access the top floor."

"Is there no way you can get to it?" Donald said through an almost closed mouth.

"No, I've stopped one floor short." Donald didn't reply. Looking around desperately for inspiration he saw there was a hatch in the roof of the elevator. He raised his hand; it was only a few inches short from the hatch. He jumped and pushed it with his fingertips, it moved, it was un-locked.

"There's a hatch," he said.

"Good, it's a way into the elevator shaft. Get up there."

"Not as easy as that in these trousers." George said, climbing on the metal railing that passengers would hold on to steady themselves. He lifted away the hatch and hauled himself up with lots of huffing and puffing.

"What the hell's going on there?" Asked Donald.

"Nothing, I'm in the lift shaft," George said slightly out of breath. "The next floor up is a few metres above me but there is a ladder in the shaft." George stepped over onto the ladder and started to climb towards the closed elevator doors. Once at the same level he leaned over and began to prise open the metal sliding doors. It took some effort but they could be pushed open.

With a good handhold on the side of the elevator shaft and the ladder, he stretched out his right leg feeling for the narrow ledge by the now open doors. It was further than he thought and he had to stretch wider and wider, straining the well-fitting trousers of his suit. Just as he found a decent foothold his trouser seams gave way with an audible tearing sound.

"Oh for Gods sake." George said.

"What is it?" Donald asked.

"Nothing, don't worry about it." George said avoiding the inevitable fatty jokes that would be sent his way. He pulled himself out into the open air and onto the cluttered antenna field. "I'm out, I can see the antennas. Starting the search."

George searched the antenna field but it was so cluttered and disorganised that it was hard to tell which antennas might be directional. Without much experience of communications, George had to take bearings on all the antennas that he suspected of being the one planted for communicating with Pourali. George calmly walked around with his small digital compass that he had hidden in his belt buckle to get it past the metal detectors.

Donald stood in the crowded function room and as each minute went by he felt more and more uneasy and out of place. He was beginning to worry that somebody might spot his awkwardness. He kept hoping to hear through his earpiece 'task complete' and then he could leave.

"Donald, I've done what I can. Let's get out of here," George said.

"Good, this party's starting to bore me," Donald said. "Meet you out front." He snaked his way through the groups of people and started up the stairs, entered the lift and pressed ground floor.

George re-entered the lift shaft and dropped down into the elevator. Replacing the hatch was made easier with the extra give from his ripped trousers. He too started down to the ground floor.

* * * * * * *

The two men met at their pre-arranged meeting place outside the Almas Tower.

"Did you get it?" Asked Donald.

"Yes and no," said George. "Had to take a bearing on a few antennas but I'm pretty sure one of them is the one Al's after."

"Good, what's next?"

"Well, I'll give Al this info and we wait to see what Cam and Rory come back with."

"What bearings did you get?"

"The majority of them are facing between 280 degrees and 340 degrees. There was another at about 315 and a few more. We will have to let Al work out which one is more significant. But most point towards the Iranian mainland."

"I suppose it's just a waiting game now," said Donald. "Look what I got," he said, lifting his jacket and revealing a magnum of champagne. "This is the expensive stuff, come on, lets celebrate a mission well done."

Chapter 12

Cam, Rory and Bull stood in front of the ISO container. The C-130 Hercules aircraft, only one hundred metres away, was being prepared to drop them into the Persian Gulf. There they would climb aboard their target oil-rig and find the second antenna that would point them towards the hiding General.

The three men stepped into their fire retardant emersion suits or F.R.I.S. These would keep them warm in the water and also protect them from flames if something should go very wrong. The tight rubber seals around their wrists and necks felt constricting and uncomfortable. All three had spent far too much time in these suits in the past. Cam could remember an exercise that had lasted for over one week and he had been in his F.R.I.S for almost the entire time.

The feet were all in one and had to be forced inside their combat boots; most soldiers opted for old style jungle boots. These boots were mostly made of canvas and would allow water to seep out through eyelets and not collect as it would in leather boots. The jungle boot however, had a metal strip in the sole to protect the wearer from sharp sticks buried in the ground by the enemy. This strip would get cold in the icy British waters, especially when stood on a cold metal deck of a ship, and conduct heat away from the wearer's foot. Today though, in the relatively warm waters of the Gulf, it should not cause any problem.

After putting on their boots they stepped into their climbing harnesses. They tightened the waist and leg straps, stowed away the attached skyhooks used for difficult climbing, wrapped the velcro pistol holster straps around their legs and inserted their silenced pistols.

Also, connected to their climbing harnesses were waterproof demolition bags, normally used by water-borne troops for keeping respirators dry. This time it would be used to keep each of the men's individual mission-specific equipment dry and operational.

Then it was time to zip up the suits, assisting each other they stood with their arms outstretched and helped each other close the zip on the rear of the suits, making them water tight. They then squatted down and broke the seal around their necks allowing trapped air to escape; this would stop them from floating like the Michelin Man once in the water.

Kitting up was always a strange time before each mission. People's minds buzzed with information. What to do if this happens, what to expect if that should happen. It is a time of mental preparation and each man would handle it differently. Most could think of nothing else except the task in hand.

Rory picked up his black assault vest filled with extra ammo and his own personal items that his years of experience had taught him he might need. Cam and Bull did the same. Zipped to the top of their assault vests was a life-jacket folded in a small hood-like pocket. This was attached around the back of the neck and around the collar and stopped a few inches down the front of the vest. If they had trouble in the water it could be inflated and keep them above the waves. Cam preferred these new ones, he had some awkward moments with the old style.

Last but by no means least they picked up their weapons; they had opted for MP5s, silenced for stealth. They knew they could only be used as a last resort. The three men, now fully kitted up, stood looking at each other, checking their equipment. Almost invisible against the night sky in their dark blue immersion suits they turned and walked towards the C-130 waiting on the runway.

Bull found one last opportunity to spark up a cigarette during the walk to the aircraft and their waiting parachute equipment. They had prepared the parachutes earlier and given them to the Royal Air Force Loadmasters to look after. They found them on the rear ramp of the Hercules aircraft. On top of the parachutes were their swimming fins and their plastic caving-style helmets with attached strobe lights.

The swim fins were open-toed black split fins. They placed the toes of their boots through the heal straps and raised the blades of the fins to their shins and taped them in place. They would stay there securely fastened until they landed in the water.

The parachute had been individually checked by the user and marked up with the name of the jumper. A small cylume glow stick was taped to the reserve parachute handle so it could be found quickly in an emergency. Before donning the parachute this glow stick would be snapped, illuminating the handle in a soft colourful light.

The chutes were lifted on and given a final check. They picked up their helmets and put them on and clicked the buckles under their chins securing them in place. The flashing strobe lights on the top of the plastic helmets were turned on momentarily to be sure they were working. These flashing beacons would be used later to locate the men in the water for extraction.

Under the weight of their equipment the men walked up the ramp and into the C-130 aircraft. They found positions to sit on the floor and watched as the rear ramp closed and sealed them inside the transporter. Cam wriggled in his parachute harness trying to find the most comfortable position for the flight to the oil field. Everything was digging into him, his climbing harness, his assault vest and his weapon that had been slung by his side. It was just something that had to be endured; nobody found it comfortable. Bull however, seemed unfazed. He sat leaning against the seats, one knee raised with his arm resting on it. Cam was surprised that he wasn't smoking.

The noise inside the C-130 began to increase as the engines were brought up to power. The aircraft strained against its own wheel brakes stopping it from being pulled forward under the power of the propeller blades. The Air Loadmasters moved around the back of the aircraft performing final checks, then the plane lurched forward.

They were underway; there was no turning back now. Cam wondered how it was going for George and Donald. Had they completed their task yet? Had they found the antenna in the tower? He tried not to think about their task and focused his mind on his own.

The aircraft gained speed as in bumped along the runway then it lifted off the ground and the bumping stopped. The whirring of the landing gears being stowed away could be heard against the loud hum of the four engines.

Once airborne the transporter began the short flight to the oil field. Cam had time to remember how much he hated parachuting; it always made him nervous. He used to enjoy it when he was out of the aircraft, but the actual act of jumping was the hard bit. He tried not showed his nerves, but got on with what had to be done. It was never something he was going to take up as a hobby.

The plane banked left and right as it navigated its way towards the oil platform. Cam sat uncomfortably, sweat beading on his forehead and dripping down his back. Rory was on the other side of the airframe completing some of his own personal kit checks.

Bull stood up under the weight of his equipment and walked as if he was carrying nothing at all to the front of the cargo hold area. The toilet was not much more than a metal funnel under a flap like a swing lid bin. Bull did his business and was on his way back to his seating area when the Air Loadmaster grabbed him by his shoulder and shouted something into his ear.

Bull replied with a thumbs up and walked over to Cam.

"Five minutes!" Bull shouted showing him five fingers. Cam struggled to his feet with the help of Bull pulling him up. Cam repeated the five minutes symbol to Rory who began the process of standing up.

The three parachutists stood on the Port side of the aircraft under the static line; this would open their parachutes for them once they were safely out the back and free of the aircraft. They handed their static line hooks to the Loadie who connected it for them. Each man checked it was on visually and by giving it a good pull to make sure it was secure.

They checked that their helmets were done up by following the straps to under their chins and checking the buckles were clipped together. They checked the buckles of their parachutes, centre and leg harnesses making sure they were secure.

"Two minutes!" Shouted the Loadie holding up two fingers. The last check was their reserve chute. Attached on their chests, they checked it was securely fastened to them and made sure the handle was free and visible with the small cylume stick lighting it up.

"One minute!" The Loadie held up one finger and the rear ramp began to open. The dark night slowly came into view as the ramp came down. The night was clear and looked peaceful compared to the noise and buffeting of the aircraft.

"Three OK!" Shouted Bull from the rear of the line. He reached out whilst shouting and pounded Rory on the shoulder to reinforce he was ready.

"Two OK!" Rory shouted to Cam who would be first out the door. He gripped Cam's shoulder in case he hadn't heard him over the noise of the aircraft.

"One OK, stick OK!" Shouted Cam to the Loadie who then beckoned the parachutists forward close to the edge of the ramp.

Cam could now see down and small wisps of cloud were all that was between him and the water below. In the corner of his eye his attention was drawn to the red light that came on; he took a deep breath in and let it out slowly through clenched lips.

"Thirty seconds!" Shouted the Loadie as he held up his index finger bent at the knuckle indicating only half a minute till the jump. He motioned them forward again, Cam was now right on the edge of the ramp. Only two and a half thousand feet of warm clear air and he would be in the calm waters of the Gulf.

His eyes were now fixed on that red light; he could make out the unlit green light below it. He was waiting for the red to go out and the green to replace it. The Loadie held Cam still on the edge of the ramp; his eyes too were on the lamps.

For Cam the wait felt far too long and his mind wandered back to the last time he was inserted into an operational environment. That one however, was not a parachute jump; he had fast-roped out of a helicopter and into a battle that would prove to be the last fight of his military career. It was also what kept him up at night.

Chapter 13

Shawal Valley, June 2008
North Waziristan

The flight had not taken long until the Loadmaster signalled five minutes. Cam struggled against his assault gear and turned in his seat and looked out of the round porthole window. A fleet of helicopters filled the sky, each one full of troops desperate to get on the ground and underway.

"One minute," the Loadmaster shouted above the sound of the engines; he held up one finger signalling to the troops they were close.

The helicopter buffeted as it descended towards the landing zone, but it didn't drop all the way. Cam felt something was wrong. The Loadmaster made his way to the Boss and shouted something in his ear. They both headed to the front of the helicopter. The Boss spoke to the pilots then turned to face the troops in the back.

He tapped his radio and pointed to his earpiece. The men fumbled for their own radios and turned them on.

"We can't land," said the Boss directly to each of the men via their radio earpieces. "The grounds too uneven, we're going to fast-rope down." Each member of the team unfastened their seat belts and unclipped their toughened gloves and put them on ready to go. The Loadmaster opened the side door, attached the rope to the winch and threw out the thick green rope and watched it fall to the ground.

"OK, one on the rope," shouted the Loadmaster. The Boss was first. He gripped the rope and waited. The Loadmaster waited for the signal from the pilots; when it came he smacked the Boss on the shoulder and he spun out of the helicopter and disappeared down the rope. The Loadmaster watched the Boss as he slid to the ground.

"One half way," shouted the Loadmaster. "Two on the rope." Glenn reached out for the rope and readied himself. On the command, he too spun out of the helicopter. The Loadmaster watched. "Two half way, three on the rope." It was Cam's turn; he felt the slap on his back and threw himself out under the rotor blades. He held the rope lightly and almost free fell towards the ground. He looked down over his left shoulder and saw Glenn and the Boss moving to cover. On approaching the ground he gripped the rope and pulled his elbows in to his ribs attempting to slow his descent.

Cam smashed into the ground and under the weight of his day sack fell onto his back. Looking up he saw the soles of Swanny's boots heading straight at him. He quickly rolled out of the way as Swanny crashed down on top of him.

"Jesus Christ! How fast did you come down that rope? You fat bastard!" Cam said as he struggled to his feet under the down-wash from the rotor blades. "Come on, push left." The two men ran for the nearest cover. Once safe Cam saw Buzz and Spike doing the same over on the Boss' right hand side.

With the men down, the rope was detached from the Sea King and it banked away as the rope fell to the ground. The noise disappeared with the helicopter, leaving a peaceful calm behind it. Cam saw in the rear distance the Rangers disembarking from their Chinooks.

Cam turned and looked up the hill towards their objective. Just then the whistle of the artillery rounds sounded over their heads. The barrage was devastating, the shells slammed into the hillside destroying anything out in the open. After a few minutes the barrage started to dwindle, that signalled the Rangers to open up with their sustained fire weapons.

The tracers flew overhead, lighting up the areas around the cave entrances.

"OK, it's now or never. Let's get moving," said the Boss. The troop stood up under the weight of their equipment and began weaving their way up the hill. Cam could see in the distance the other sections moving like ants towards their caves. The S.B.S on their right flank and the S.E.A.Ls on the left.

The troop edged closer to the mouth of the caves. Slowly they approached the line of fire from the Rangers. At less than two hundred metres from the cave entrance they were hearing friendly fire hitting the ground just ahead of their position. The Boss signalled for his men to take cover. Cam and Swanny found a set of boulders that would protect them and also give them a good view of the entrance.

"Sunray this is Charlie One, over," said the Boss through his radio.

"Charlie One this is Sunray, send your message, over."

"Charlie One, we are at the impact point from the sustained fire, shift fire, over."

"Sunray, roger out." Within seconds Cam could see the impact of the rounds from overhead shift either side of the cave entrance, opening up a corridor for the troop to advance through.

"OK guys, move up," Cam heard through his earpiece. The team moved cautiously forward up the hill, identifying possible cover that they could use if needed. All the time the Boss was watching through his binoculars for any sign of activity. It was not long before the Boss stopped and knelt down.

"I think we have movement," said the Boss. "They're coming out of the cave, take cover." In an instant the three fire teams found separate cover and took aim at the cave entrance. Through his magnified sight Cam could see small heads bobbing about. Then muzzle flashes as the distant figures started to fire.

Rounds pinged off the rocks around Cam and Swanny; ignoring them the two men took aim and returned fire. Soon Glenn had joined the fight and Cam could hear the rattle of the S.A.W automatic rifle drilling away at the enemy. Every few rounds that Glenn fired was a tracer round that glowed as it flew at the enemy. These tracer rounds showed that there was a strong wind whipping along the entrance to the caves. The troop's fire was ineffective and the enemy knew they were safe as they rained down fire on the three two-man teams.

The Boss' voice filled Cam's earpiece again with a request for air support.

"Sunray this is Charlie One, our fire is ineffective requesting close air support on objective Xray, over."

"Charlie One this is Sunray, wait out." Cam looked up from behind his rock to see a flight of F16s circling overhead. "Charlie One this is Sunray, C.A.S inbound on your position now, out."

One of the F16s broke from the circling pattern and turned in on the caves. The sound of the jet engines grew louder as the fighter-bomber approached.

"Charlie One this is Ogre one, inbound on Xray now, out." The roar of the engines along with the radio static nearly drowned out his message.

"Ogre one this is Charlie One, be advised we are danger close, over."

"Roger that Charlie One, keep your heads down, out." The jet swooped in on the cave entrance and released its payload. Two freefall bombs detached from the aircraft and gently fell to the ground.

The destructive blast seemed far too close for comfort; the deafening explosion covered the teams in a blanket of dust and small rocks. Cam looked up over his cover, his face caked in dust, to see nothing but a cloud in front of the cave entrance. Swanny joined him.

"Wouldn't want to have been on the wrong end of that," said Swanny coughing through the dust cloud.

"Bloody right," replied Cam.

"Charlie One this is Ogre one, call my rounds, over."

"Ogre one this is Charlie One, good hit, good hit, thanks for your help, out." The Boss took a look through his binoculars again, then stowed them away. "OK, let's get up there before they come back out," said the Boss over the air. The three fire teams pepper-potted their way up the last hundred and fifty metres to the now smoking entrance, each providing cover for the others.

Arriving at the entrance, which was now nearly twice the size it was before the air strike, the troop split into two sections and took up positions either side of the cave.

"Sunray this is Charlie One, we are at objective Xray. Send up the Rangers, over."

"Charlie One this is Sunray, roger that, hold your position, assault will commence in three minutes, out."

Cam looked down the hill to see the force of Rangers that had provided sustained fire support heading up the hill.

"OK guys, ammo check, everyone alright?" Asked the Boss. All five replied they were unhurt and reported their ammunition status. The ammo was re-issued around the teams so everyone had the same amount; more was passed to Glenn with the support weapon. Swanny leaned on the rocky wall and sparked up another cigarette.

"Hello all call signs this is Sunray," cracked the radio. "Commence assault now, out."

"OK, this is it," said the Boss. "Swanny, Cam you're first, nice and slow." Swanny brought his M4 up into his shoulder and with a cigarette hanging out the corner of him mouth, slipped into the cave. Cam followed the smell of Swanny's smoke and entered the cave. The cold air inside cooled the sweat that had formed on his back during the assault up the hill. Cam shivered as he left the light behind him, his eyes slowly adjusting to the darkness.

Chapter 14

"GO!" Cam was brought out of his daydream by the Loadie pushing him in the direction of the night sky. He took a giant step forward out the back of the aircraft. He adopted a position like he was sitting in a large armchair, arms out stretched as if he was resting on the arm rests. He was riding the slipstream and was being buffeted by the air current of the C-130 aircraft. The seating position allowed him to almost sit in the slipstream and safely ride it away from the aircraft.

The static line was unfolding out the rear of his parachute but he couldn't feel it due to the noise and the buffeting pushing him around. When it had unravelled as far as it could he felt a jolt, as the parachute was pulled open. Then the noise disappeared as the aircraft went on its way having delivered its passengers to the oil field.

Cam looked up to make sure his chute had deployed correctly. He saw a full square canopy above him; he also inspected the risers up from his shoulders to the edge of the canopy making sure there were no twists. He had made a good exit and with the favourable weather conditions he had encountered no problems. Breathing a sigh of relief he reached up and pulled the control handles from their velcro holders. He tugged on the left and he turned slightly left, he tugged on the right and he turned slightly right. Next, he pulled them both down at the same time and he flared slowing his descent.

Happy his chute was deployed and correct he looked around and located his team. They were above and behind him, exactly where they should be. The two other parachutes were being put through their own tests and Cam could see them doing small turns and flaring.

The sudden change from the noisy aircraft smelling of aviation fuel to the peaceful tranquillity of floating like a feather was a pleasant contrast. The aching and uncomfortable pains from the constricting parachute and equipment was gone and Cam was now sat in his harness in the warm night air.

Looking down he saw the lights of the oil platform that was his destination and he began banking towards it. Remembering the briefing by the meteorological section, he followed the changing air currents at the different altitudes to a good position north of the platform.

The others followed his lead and they were all coming down towards the sea so the water current would slowly wash them past the oil platform. From where they were it would not be more than one and a half or two kilometres swim to the platform.

Cam was now on his approach to the water; he was mindful of the phenomenon of ground rush, when the ground or water seems far away until it rushes up to meet you and you hit it far too fast. This was more common on night jumps. Cam was looking down over his right shoulder watching the ripples of the water come up to meet him. Just at the right point he pulled both controls as far down as he could and flared the canopy slowing his descent then he touched down softly into the water.

Cam disappeared under the water and after a second he bobbed back up on the surface. He grabbed the harness release and yanked it, disconnecting the right hand risers, collapsing the canopy into the water. Floating now he watched the other two coming in within a few metres of his position. Rory in good S.B.S style disconnected his harness well above the water and free fell the last five to ten metres into the sea. Bull did the same, neither one wanted to be dragged through the water by an un-collapsed canopy.

Each man wriggled out of his parachute harness and swam away from it. The harnesses slowly sank below the surface to wash up on some distant shore and give the finders some free silk for their home-made boxer shorts. Cam broke the tape holding his swim fins to his legs and fitted them to his feet and finned his way, on his back, to where Rory was doing the same. Cam reached Rory and saw Bull front crawling his way over.

"You guys OK?" He said in his New York drawl.

"Yeah, no problems." Cam replied.

"Cool. Shall we?" He said motioning towards the lit up platform on the horizon. With that they started finning towards the distant lights.

* * * * * * *

It took no time at all to reach the rig; the current did most of the work for them. The only effort they had to put in were small course corrections so that they would drift past one of the platforms legs. During their drift they secured themselves to one another with a pre-prepared line with three karabiners attached, one on each end and one in the middle.

As they approached, bobbing up and down in the swell, they all reached out and grabbed at the rungs of the ladder that ran vertically up the length of the support leg and disappeared under the surface. It was Bull that got the best handhold and gripped the slimy metal rung.

Once on, they climbed a few body heights up and unclipped themselves from each other. Now free, they ascended the ladder to the first of the oil platform's spider decks. Used by maintenance personnel, those criss-crosses of walkways and stairs can be found all around the underside of these types of installations. Tonight they would be where the trio of intruders could organise themselves before separating.

"You good to go Bull?" Asked Cam attaching his swim fins to his climbing harness via another karabiner.

"Yeah, how long are you gonna need?"

"Give us two hours."

"OK, see you in two," said Bull turning to leave the group.

"Wait," Rory interjected stopping Bull short. "Can it be three?"

"Why? We won't need that long," Cam said looking at Rory.

"It's just…" Rory paused. "I have this thing." He looked at Cam and Bull in turn. "I know it sounds strange but I have to do things in odd numbers."

"What, everything?" Said Bull.

"Yeah, it's some kind of O.C.D thing."

"So we either do this thing in one or three hours?" Asked Cam.

"Or five."

"Is he serious?" Bull said looking at Cam for confirmation.

"It's difficult to say," said Cam feeling sorry for Bull's confusion. He wasn't used to Rory's strange sense of humour.

"Look, enough," Bull said changing the subject. "Earpieces in and stay in touch." They each opened their own waterproof demo bags and took out their communication devices and slipped them into their ears. "I'll see you in three hours." Bull said rather sarcastically whilst looking at Rory. He then turned and ran off up some metal stairs towards the rig's accommodation block.

* * * * * *

The accommodation block took up one whole section of the installation, it was where the crew ate, slept and spent their off-duty time. They generally had twenty-four-hour galleys and a recreation room with pool tables and rows of computers with internet access constantly available. It was an area of the rig that would be busier during these twilight hours than during the day when there would be more activity on the working end of the platform.

On the far side of the accommodation block from the working platform the emergency life rafts could be found. These were Bull's objective. He was to locate and steal one for the extraction, whilst making it look like an accident.

* * * * * * *

Bull crept up the final flight of stairs underneath the first of the main walkways. He poked his head up above floor level and waited; he looked and listened. All he heard was the wind whipping through the holes in the metalwork that held the rig together. He climbed the last few steps and began making his way to the life rafts.

This level had plenty of hiding places, the pipes and support structures left many nooks and crannies. If he were to be surprised he could easily duck into one of them and disappear quite nicely into the shadows. As he walked cautiously along the walkway he was conscious of voices on some of the floors above him. They could be heard entering and exiting doors, the large metal doors slamming shut behind them. Bull thought that this was perhaps the entrance to the recreation area.

Bull encountered no one on his way to the bank of life rafts. When he reached them he studied them and the way they were being held to the rig. The rafts were encased in a white plastic casing. When dropped into the water they opened up to form the base of the raft, then the rest automatically inflated around it to complete the craft.

They were secured to the rig via some metal couplings that were operated by a lever on the walkway. When the large red metal lever was pulled, the couplings detached the raft. It could either be lowered by some attached ropes, as it would in a non-emergency situation or be allowed to free fall into the water if more urgent.

Bull decided he wanted to see how the ropes that would lower them into the water were attached to the structure of the rig above him. To do this he had to walk back along the walkway that he had just came and climb the set of stairs that would lead him up one more floor.

Once on this upper floor he found it far less cluttered than the one below him. If he were to be disturbed he would be hard-pressed to find a hiding place. He sneaked along the metal walkway his feet squelching the sea water in his boots. He was still aware of the movement that seemed to be above him; as long as it stayed there he would be OK.

He reached the motors that the ropes were attached to; these motors would be responsible for lowering the rafts into the sea. There was not much he could do with these sturdy motors; it would be far too obvious that they had been tampered with. Whilst looking down on the rafts below, he heard some voices and metallic footsteps approaching from the right hand side.

Without moving he looked in the direction of the voices. He saw nothing, but his ears didn't lie, they were close. He had no choice, he flipped himself over the edge of the railings and lowered himself hand over hand until he was hanging off the side of the walkway. His strong fingers were all that was stopping him falling onto the rafts' casings twelve metres below him. After a few seconds he heard the small group of workers pass by without noticing him.

He looked down over his shoulder to see the rafts lined up below; one of the sets of ropes was by his side. He reached over and grabbed one and slid down onto one of the raft casings. Bull decided to just cut away at the ropes to make it look like one had simply fallen away.

He pulled his diver's knife from its sheath and began to fray the ropes. He used a scraping motion instead of a cutting motion to make it look like natural damage as opposed to someone cutting the ropes. When the time came he would simply finish the job enough to allow the raft to slip into the sea. To allow the raft to fall he would pull the release handle then return it to its original position, confusing whoever would be tasked to investigate the incident.

Once he had frayed the ropes as much as he dared he looked along the row of other rafts. A thought occurred to him that it wouldn't happen to just one of the raft's ropes; it would, most probably, happen to more if not all. So he began the long job of fraying all the ropes so that it would look like an accident that one had broken free.

Bull swung from one raft to the other, diver's knife in his teeth as he Tarzaned himself over the ocean below. His movements were masked by the dark shadows of the oil platform between him and the shining moon. Maybe he would need the three hours proposed by Rory.

Chapter 15

"What you got left to do?"

"Week and a half."

"Are you taking a break then?"

"Hell no, not part of the plan. After here I'm off to the States. Three months there then back to the UK for four weeks then back here. Then I'll think about it."

"You're gonna burn out mate, you should take it easy like me. Enjoy your money whilst you're young."

"I will once I've got my house and car."

"Well just be careful. If they find out they will be more hesitant to take you back."

"Yeah. Hey, did you hear the plane flying past?"

"Mmm, probably just having a look around, must look pretty stunning up there on a clear calm night like this."

"Bet it does, but now for us, it's back to it. Come on they'll be wondering where we are."

The two oil platform workers made a move from their position on the gantry that connected the two platforms. One tapped his finger on the handrail as they walked off towards the accommodation block. The tapping of his finger was eclipsed by the sound of their work boots clanking along the metal fretwork walkway.

Neither of them spotted the small hooks on the edge of the walkway, but they had no real reason to suspect that there were two men dangling beneath their feet.

Cam and Rory had been sky hooking their way along the underside of the gantry when the two workers had stopped on it for their break. They had decided that under the walkway would be more covert than simply bumbling across, and it had been a good decision. If they hadn't, they would have been discovered.

Now alone, they continued towards the middle platform. The skyhooks were attached to their climbing harnesses with black cord. To move along they held a hook in each hand and swung hand over hand under the metal gantry.

Cam looked down into the sea. It was smooth and lit up in the moonlight. He tried to judge how high they were; he thought maybe a couple of hundred feet. High enough to be injured if they fell. Cam made a conscious effort to be more careful with his hook placements.

They inched their way to the work platform leaving the accommodation block and Bull behind them. Cam hoped he was organising the extraction. They swung along under the walkway making good progress, then Cam heard another set of feet clanging along the metal gangway.

Cam stopped in his tracks and listened. Were the footsteps heading for them? Of course they were, he thought. He hooked his way to the side of the gantry and Rory followed his lead making his way to the opposite side. There they waited and listened as the footsteps approached.

Silently the two figures hung, swinging slightly from side to side as the oblivious individual walked past their position. Cam looked over at Rory who was adjacent to him. He looked back and slung him a look as if the two were work acquaintances passing each other in the local super market.

Cam replied with a rather nonchalant 'hey,' look and then resumed hooking towards their objective leaving the surreal moment behind him.

On reaching the working platform Cam stopped and swung in the cooling breeze high above the sea. The small waves crashing into the rig stanchions would comfortably mask any noise the pair might make as they climbed from the underside of the gantry up onto the rig. Rory waited for Cam to make his move.

Cam had waited less than a minute when he made the final move from the gantry to the working platform. It was a struggle to move from the freedom of swinging along on the skyhooks to clambering around the metal framework, but it took him no time at all to find a safe position where he could wait for Rory. Rory followed suit after watching every move he had made.

"If you can get yourself to the heli pad," Cam said looking around, "I'll make my way to the antennas, and you can let me know if anyone is coming."

"No problem, consider it done." Said Rory sounding confident.

Cam remained in the same position and watched as Rory climbed round the exterior of the installation until he was below the helicopter landing pad. Above him was a mess of pipes and metal supports that held the heli pad high above the rest of the rig. Under the Cam's watch he began his climb. He would have to climb well over forty metres up to the landing pad and from there he would have a good view of the oil-rig's antennas.

Once Cam saw that Rory had hidden himself in the shadows of the landing pad he too began clambering around the outside of the rig. He wanted to stay off the walkways as much as possible but this could not be done. He would at one point have to make a dash across some open ground to reach the communication tower.

"OK, Cam. What you have is part of the main working platform to cross," Rory said after bleeping his earpiece into action. "From where you are," he continued, "you will have to negotiate the floor for fifteen or so metres to reach the tower."

"OK, sounds easy," Cam replied as he hid out of view below the edge of the railings that surrounded the platform.

"Well it is and it isn't," Rory said with a hint of apprehension. "There are a number of workers milling about and it looks like someone has locked up the tower's ladder."

"What do you mean 'locked up'?"

"It's got one of those cages around it that can be padlocked, blocking the ladder. That's what you're going to have to get around."

"Do we need to find another way up the tower?" Enquired Cam.

"Na, shouldn't be a problem for someone of your abilities, just avoid being seen by the workers."

"What are they doing?"

"You have a group of three stood around chatting and at least two working together on something. Every so often one gets up and goes to check on some pipes across the other side of the rig. There are plenty of places to hide, I'll tell you when to move. Are you ready to go?"

"Sure, on your word." Cam remained out of view but started to find a good handhold ready to spring over the railings on Rory's signal.

"Stand by, the mobile one is moving away. Stand by." Cam waited trying to imagine the scene only metres from him. "Go."

Cam swung out and over the railings in one swift move. He vaulted the metal rail and landed as quietly as he could on the metallic flooring. He crouched, attempting to hide his presence from the workers as he looked around and tried to take it all in. Rory had described the scene well and he made his first move.

Keeping as low as he could he darted for one of the many hiding places dotted around the work space.

From his new hiding place he could clearly see the three men chatting, only one was facing his general direction but was hardly going to notice him if he was careful. The men working on something had indeed split and only one was visible to him, again he would be easy to avoid as he was engrossed in what he was doing. The only possible problem was the one wandering around. Where was he and when would he show up?

"Cam, from where you are, about six metres to your eleven o'clock there is a set of metal containers. Go now." Cam moved instinctively trusting Rory's judgment, knowing that from his elevated position he had a better view. "Good, stay there," Rory said seeing Cam move to the new cover. "Now, I don't want to worry you but the three guys who were chatting have split and two are walking right towards you," Rory said without any hint of concern. "As you are looking at the containers now, move to the left hand side and be ready to move round as they approach."

Cam did as he was told. He waited for the next command. He could hear the men close in on his position, their footsteps clanging on the metal flooring. "Now!" Instantaneously Cam slipped round to the other side of the containers blocking him from the view of the two threats. "Wait," Rory said and Cam waited, crouching silently in the shadow cast by the containers. After a moment or two Rory instructed Cam to go straight to the tower and he followed his orders and made a dash for the locked up ladder.

Cam found himself on the far side of the communications tower from the workers. He looked up and studied the obstacle stopping him from getting to the antennas. What he saw was a padlocked metal cage surrounding the ladder starting three metres from the ground and designed to stop unwanted climbers messing with the communication equipment.

"Is the coast clear?" Asked Cam.

"Yes, go for it." With that Cam reached up and jumped. Grabbing hold of the bottom of the cage he pulled himself up inch by inch until he could swing up his leg and get a foothold. Now clinging to the side of the cage he found it easy to climb up and get to the ladder.

"Stop!" Rory said, "don't move." Cam froze, he wanted to look but even the smallest movement would draw unwanted attention. "The wanderer is back," Rory continued. "He came out of nowhere and is almost below you." Cam remained as still as a rock, he could now hear the man below him. In his peripherals he saw him walk right by completely unaware of the black figure high above him.

"OK, get up there," said Rory, finally happy Cam was in the clear. He began his climb towards the communication equipment high up on the tower. Now looking down he could see the workers going about their duties and was glad he had Rory on over watch, it would have been far more risky to have done it unaided.

Cam climbed past many differing antennas, none looking highly directional. Near the top he spotted what he was looking for.

"Think I got it mate," he said. "Taking a bearing now." Cam hooked his left arm through the rung of the ladder and unzipped his waterproof pouch. He fished around and eventually pulled out his electronic compass. He leant towards the small modern-looking antenna and took a bearing. "One hundred and thirty-five degrees," said Cam.

"Hundred and thirty-five, what's out that way?" Asked Rory.

"Um, not a great deal. Maybe U.A.E or south coast of Iran but that's it."

"Not for us to worry about, we've done our bit so lets get the hell off this thing."

"You don't have to tell me twice, I'm on my way down." Cam started to climb back down the ladder stopping short of the cage.

"OK Cam, you're clear." Cam jumped down to the floor, landing hard on the metal deck. Hidden from view by the tower he peeked in the workers' general direction. He could clearly see they were busy and shouldn't notice him if he did this right.

He broke from the shadows and kept low; moving from cover to cover he reached the oil platform's railing.

"OK, see you in the water." Cam vaulted the railing like a ghost and plunged into the sea below. He free fell the sixty or so metres into the calm, clear water of the Persian Gulf entering with a loud splash. Rory watched making sure nobody heard and raised the 'man overboard' alarm. When he saw no reaction he descended using the stanchions and pipes to a more sensible height. Before dropping from the installation he sent one more message.

"Bull, Cam is in the water and I am exfilling now."

"Roger that," said Bull who had been listening all along. "I will be with you once we are clear of the rig." The second splash of Rory hitting the water also went unnoticed and the two men floated happily away from the platform.

The small amount of air trapped in his dry suit was keeping Cam comfortably above the small waves; he had no need to deploy his life vest. He looked back at the rig as it slowly disappeared into the distance.

Meanwhile Bull had cut the final strand of rope holding one of the life rafts in place and fell with it into the sea. The raft automatically opened once it hit the water and Bull sat on top waiting until he was a safe distance from the platform. He gave it a good twenty or thirty minutes until they had drifted into the vast black sea and only then did he turn on the engine. As the motor smoothly came to life he saw two small flashing lights appear in the near distance. Bull set a course for the closer of the two.

"You guys OK?" Asked Bull.

"Yeah, no probs," said Cam reaching for Bull's hand. Bull hauled him aboard the craft in one powerful movement. "Where's Rory?"

"Over there, hundred metres or so," said Bull steering the raft in the general direction of the second flashing light. Rory slowly came into view bobbing up and down in the waves.

"What the hell's wrong with you?" Said Cam noting the look on Rory's face.

"My bloody dry suits leaking! I'm soaking in here."

"Chopper will be here any minute now," said Bull helping Cam haul Rory aboard the raft. "There are a couple of your guys waiting for you in Dubai."

Chapter 16

George and Donald stood looking up into the night sky waiting for the helicopter. Al had instructed them to meet the other half of their team at the Al Minhad Air Base.

"So this is Camp Mirage," George said looking around.

"Camp Mirage, what's that?" Asked Donald.

"Well, it never officially existed," George said taking it all in. "It's a U.A.E facility but the Canadians used it from about two thousand and one for operations in Afghan. However, they never acknowledged its location. They were supposed to have shut it down in two thousand and ten but obviously not completely."

"Obviously not," agreed Donald. "Could that be them?" Donald said pointing into the distance.

"Maybe," replied George straining to see if he could hear rotor blades through the breeze. "Yeah, that's them," he confirmed as the helicopter drew closer.

The yellow CH-149 Canadian search and rescue helicopter flew over the heads of the two men on the ground joining the landing pattern as directed by the control tower. It turned side on to its original direction and skidded to a holt in mid-air, then slowly drifted over the landing pad descending as it did so.

George turned as the helicopter cushioned under its own rotor wash. The down-force from the blades blew dust and debris along the ground and into Donald's eyes. He turned away as George had done. The door of the aircraft opened as it touched down and three passengers exited and ran crouched over to the waiting men.

"Hey guys," said George turning back to face the trio. "How did you do?"

"Good mate," said Cam. "One thirty-five degrees," he shouted above the noise of the rotors. "Did you get yours?"

"Yes and no," said George. "I'll give Al your info, see what he finds."

"Cool," said Cam noticing that they were wondering who their new member was. "George, Donald, this is Bull. Bull, George and Donald. He helped us out on the rig."

"Pleased to meet you," said George extending his hand.

"You too," said the Bull shaking his hand.

"And what the hell happened to you?" Asked George after seeing the soaking wet Rory.

"Suit leaked," said the unimpressed Rory who was starting to shiver slightly.

"Anyway," interrupted Bull. "I gotta go, it's been a pleasure."

"Cheers Bull, maybe we'll work together again," said Cam.

"You never know." With that said, he spun around and returned to the helicopter that had been waiting on the pad. Once he was aboard, it lifted off and faded into the horizon.

"Come on," said George. "Lets get this guy some warm tea before he catches a cold."

* * * * * * *

"Hello chaps, it's Al." Al's familiar voice filled the state-of-the-art operations room in Camp Mirage. The room had kindly been loaned to the team of Assets by the Canadian Air Force.

"Yep," said Cam unenthusiastically.

"I know it's late, or early depending on how you look at it, but I've got an update for you." The four men sat scattered around, George had his feet up on a desk and Rory sat snivelling, holding on to his second hot cup of tea.

"Right," continued Al. "We have plotted the lines from the antennas and they are obviously pointing to the southern coast of Iran. But, without an accurate shot from the towers we can't zero it down."

"So are you saying we need a third bearing to triangulate the exact spot?" Said Cam.

"That's right." Said Al cheerfully. George removed his feet from the desk and leaned forward listening, waiting to see where they were off to next. Everyone was wondering the same except Rory who sneezed spilling his tea.

"What was that?" Asked Al.

"Nothing," said George. "Just Rory being weak." Rory couldn't be bothered to react.

"Anyway," continued Al. "Where was I? Oh yes, Yemen. You're off to Yemen. It's the best of the other locations that should help us narrow down the General's location on the Iranian coast."

"What's the target?" Asked Cam.

"A building in Ataq, a small town surrounded by desert. Not entirely sure what the building is but we think it's government controlled at the moment, possibly a police station. The antenna's on the roof."

"And Yemen, what's the state of that place at the moment?" Asked George.

"Civil war, A.Q training camps you name it. There have been some suicide threats against western embassies recently and lots of kidnapping, many ending unhappily. You can do this however you want. I suggest you tool yourselves up and go in hard, aggression might be your best option on this one."

"A good old shoot out eh?" Said George sounding excited.

"Yes, I think it's probably the only way, with the state of the country that is. Anyway, get some sleep because in the morning the Canadians are going to kit you out and you will be inserted on the Saudi side of the boarder around midday. I've got you a good vehicle. Get yourselves as far into the desert as you can and hide up during daylight hours. It might take you two or three nights driving to get to Ataq depending on terrain and how you go about avoiding the locals. After that you're going to have to make it up as you go along. I'm sending you as much info and intel as I can and we will be in touch throughout via sat phone. Apart from that best of luck."

Once Al had signed off, the four tired men slowly rose from their seats; it was time to get their heads down for a while before it was all to start again.

"All this to find a dead man," said Cam stopping at a huge wall map of the Persian Gulf. The rest of the team gathered next to him and began to mentally zoom in on the area that they had already pin-pointed. "Where the hell is he?"

* * * * * * *

The full moon glinted off the rippling water by the jetty and the palm trees swayed in the background. As the wind started to pick up, indicating a storm was on the horizon, the trees had started to release the sweet warm smell familiar in that part of the world.

The lone figure stood on the jetty and looked out to sea, the reflective water merged into the sky seamlessly. He could see no signs of anything apart from the lights of a ship in the far distance, probably belonging to a cruise ship. They passed by here every so often taking the fat, lazy westerners from place to place so they could spend their excess money.

He turned to face back inland and saw the trees starting to bend in the now growing wind, the storm was not far off. As had been his regular nightly ritual, he had been conducting his tour of his base of operations, that he had been secretly creating for the past few years, checking all was in order.

Although these storms were normally short-lived he decided to make his way back to some sort of shelter. He stepped from the wooden jetty and trudged across the sand towards the main open door hanger. He passed the hut used as a rest room by his security guards and nodded a silent good night to the team responsible for his security.

It had been much easier than he had anticipated to recruit the manpower that he needed to pull off his plans. The people he knew in the Iranian military were easy to select. He knew who shared his views and theses people he trusted. He had also found many civilians that he needed such as electricians, chefs, engineers and builders easy to recruit. The people of Iran were ready to fight for what they wanted.

Now off the beach and weaving his way through the trees a large structure started to come into view. The structure had been built under the noses of the Iranian government and the western world. To keep it hidden, the hanger had been heavily camouflaged with local foliage concealing it from the air.

Situated on the far side of the hanger was his crowning glory, a runway of over two miles disappearing further than the eye could see. It was ingenious, almost a work of art. It had been cut through the trees and rocks, painted in the most up to date disruptive pattern paintwork ever used on a runway, it was nearly indistinguishable from the landscape on either side of it. This technology had been developed during the second world war but had largely been forgotten about and had not been used since.

Entering the hanger he stopped, taking in his work that had taken him years of planning and preparation. The aircraft that he had supposedly gone missing in, sat in the middle of the hanger. Far from being destroyed in an accident it was ready to carry out his orders when the time to strike arrived.

He wandered out of the aircraft hanger and entered the one next to it. In the far corner of this hanger, there was an area he had ordered to be under constant guard. This area housed the weapons he had acquired; he had them ready to go, hidden from view underneath a large heavy tarpaulin cover. The two armed guards, accustomed to his many visits nodded to him as he approached. He stopped and reached out a hand and felt the objects that were hidden beneath the tarpaulin. They gave him power.

Soon it would be time for the glorious nation of Iran to take its place as the leader of the world's super powers. Soon he would lead the way. Soon they would strike out at their enemies, but first he would make them pay, they would all pay. Even if they did they would not be safe, their fate had already been decided.

He turned and walked away under the watchful eyes of his guards. He made his way to the edge of the hanger to where the storm was now in full force. He felt as strong and as powerful as the act of nature that was in front of him. He was going to bring a storm of his own.

For a dead man, he had never felt more alive.

Chapter 17

The Canadian C-130J Super Hercules created a huge sandstorm as it landed in the southern Saudi desert. Four turboprop engines churned up the dry topsoil as the aircraft spun round a full one hundred and eighty degrees ready for a quick getaway.

The rear ramp of the aircraft opened and scraped the ground under the watchful eye of the crew chief who had positioned himself just inside the fuselage, near the deploying ramp. When the speed was slow enough he turned to look into the belly of the aircraft, made a hand signal and purposely pointed out the back of the plane.

Within seconds, a four-by-four all terrain vehicle drove out of the back of the Hercules, down the ramp and into the dust bowl. The vehicle slammed onto the ground as it transitioned from the moving aircraft onto the static desert floor. The vehicle put some distance between itself and the aircraft before hand brake turning to face the departing Herc.

The four occupants of the sandy coloured four-by-four watched through the already dirty windscreen as the Herc picked up speed and lifted off the ground and soared upwards into the clear Saudi sky.

"That was pretty cool!" Said Rory from the front passenger seat.

"Was a bit intense, wasn't it?" Replied Cam answering Rory's question with another question. The team had spent the entire night preparing for the next part of the operation. They had been supplied by the Canadian Air Force with everything that they could have needed: vehicles, supplies, specialist equipment and weapons, all readily available on Camp Mirage as it never officially existed. When the Special Forces who had been stationed there pulled out, they simply left behind most of their equipment.

Rory cracked open his window; the smell of aviation fuel filled the vehicle and sand swirled into the cab of the vehicle.

"Shut that bloody window until we are underway," said Cam as he put the vehicle into first gear and set a course for the boarder of Saudi Arabia and Yemen.

"Sorry, just like the smell of aviation fuel, find it comforting." The four men were tired; it had been a long night of planning and preparing. They had packed for any eventuality and had liaised with the Canadians about the logistics of getting them as close as was reasonably practicable to their target.

It had been decided between the aircrew and the team that the safest way would be to fly them to the edge of Saudi airspace and deploy them near to the boarder of Yemen. From there they could drive across the desert to the Yemini town of Ataq.

"OK, keep this bearing," said George looking down at the sat nav from behind Rory's seat.

"How far does it say?" Asked Rory.

"Just over four hundred Ks," said George. "As the crow flies that is, but we're not going to be able to do that out here." George repositioned his Heckler and Koch SL8 semi-automatic rifle onto his lap as it was starting to dig into his torso.

Al had given very little information on the target; they knew if the intel wasn't there to give, that's it. They had to get on with it regardless. It was as simple as it could be, a quick covert in and out, if not it would be an old-fashioned smash and grab. General Pourali had a man in the old police building in the centre of the town. The directional antenna that would point the way to the general would most probably be on the roof of the police station.

With their mission set, the team had worked all night with the Canadians. 'Just get to the old police station, get a bearing from the antenna and get away.' That was all that swirled around Cam's head. To that end, they were kitted out to look as much like local Yemenis as possible. Traditional Arab clothing hid tactical vests full of ammunition, grenades, flashbangs and emergency rations. Their four-by-four vehicle packed full of state-of-the-art equipment and extra ammo, weapons and food would take them south across the boarder and through the desert.

With red, bloodshot eyes, Cam peered through the windscreen, the vehicle bounced across the sand away from the landing site. His three passengers sat holding on as the vehicle nearly became airborne as it slammed from dune to dune. All the men looked tired and drained from their previous tasks, their faces gaunt and scruffy, with nearly a week of growth. However, this aided in their attempt to blend in with the locals.

"You OK?" George said looking over at Donald gripping on to the door handle whilst bracing himself against the seat in front of him.

"Yeah, why so fast?"

"We just have to put some distance between us and the drop-off point, in case anyone saw us coming in." George was concerned about Donald's lack of experience in the field. He was an excellent linguist and would surely be of use but this was his first possible combat op. "We'll stop soon and sort ourselves out, then we will move more tactically." Donald's language skills would be instrumental in keeping this low-key and covert but if it went the other way he might prove to be a liability.

"See those rocks ahead?" Shouted Cam stealing looks over his shoulder at the passengers in the rear.

"Yeah." Replied Donald peering into the distance.

"That's where we're going, we can find some cover there, get our heads down and wait for dark. We'll move at night." Donald looked as if he was trying to calculate the time it might take to get to the rocks.

"Maybe an hour or so," said George guessing what Donald was thinking. They were all tired and needed some rest but they couldn't just stop, not so close to the border and in the middle of the desert.

In the front seats the driver and passenger squinted against the sun that sat bright in the southern sky. The heat began to warm the cab through the windscreen and Cam tried to shield his eyes by lowering the sun visor. He fumbled for the air con switch as Rory opened the glove box on his side of the dashboard.

Rory found what he was looking for and with a smug look on his face placed a set of sunglasses on his face. He looked over at Cam smiling his normal, pleased with himself smile.

Cam kept glancing over as he negotiated sand dunes trying to make sense of what he was seeing.

"What the hell are those things?" he said.

"What things?"

"Those," he said pointing with his nose. "On your face."

"Sunglasses," replied Rory, his smile slowly dropping.

"They're huge! You look ridiculous," said Cam returning his attention to the drive.

"They're expensive, cost me a bloody fortune."

"You look like Jackie Onassis!" Rory turned in his seat when he heard the giggling from the rear passenger seats.

"Jealous, the lot of ya!"

* * * * * * *

"Got a road," Cam said loudly.

"The 556, it runs mostly north to south but on this north end it has a strange u-bend," said George staring at his handheld sat nav. "I think that's what you're seeing." He looked up from his navigating equipment and located the feature on the ground. "I suggest we take it slow."

Cam brought the vehicle to a halt, the road still in the distance.

"Rory, check it out," Cam said without breaking his gaze on the entire road.

"Sure, I'm the only one who can see in this sunlight anyway," he said as he opened the door and stepped out. Placing his foot on the front tire he climbed up onto the bonnet and then to the roof avoiding the extra fuel cans strapped all over the vehicle. Standing on the roof he viewed the road through his binoculars, from left to right once, twice then a third time before he issued the all clear.

Rory lay down on the roof of the vehicle and peeked inside the cab, his head upside down through the open passenger door.

"Hi," he said surprising the other occupants of the vehicle who looked over to see his upside down, sun glassed face. "Keep it slow, I'll stay up here, I'll bang on the windscreen if I see something." Cam nodded in silent agreement and Rory's head jerked back up towards the roof. As he did so his glasses slipped off his face falling into the sand. "Whoa, hold up!" Shouted Rory from his prone position on the roof. But it came too late; Cam drove off leaving the glasses buried in the sand from the churn of the tires.

A small grin on his face.

Rory sat up and spun his legs over the front of the roof of the vehicle dangling them in front of the windshield. He stretched his leg over the side and slammed the passenger door shut with the heel of his boot.

"You owe me hundred and fifty pounds!" He shouted finding himself a comfortable position sat on the roof. He kept his binoculars up to his eyes and used the spare tire on the bonnet to steady himself on the bouncing vehicle.

Cam kept the vehicle to a crawl to avoid kicking up the sand; he wanted to maintain a low profile in case of any activity on the road. Rory scanned the road constantly as they approached. All remained quiet. The back seat passengers looked towards their respective sides for movement along their aspect. Cam watched as the edge of the road emerged through the haze of the heat, it was a metalled road, single carriageway slightly elevated with large smooth pebbles on either side.

Cam stopped the vehicle a few metres before the stony rise.

"We cool up there?" He shouted above the hum of the hot engine fan.

"Yeah, I got nothin." Cam slipped the gearbox into four-wheel drive and began to climb the rocky rise towards the road surface. The vehicle bobbed side to side until it reached the flat tarmac track. The engine whined at being left in four-wheel drive as it crossed the flat road but it was only for a few second before they began climbing down the other side to the desert floor.

All the time Rory scanned the road that snaked off into the distance, turning to watch it disappear behind the vehicle as they resumed their course to the rocks, now closer than before.

"OK, I think that's far enough," Cam shouted reaching across the cab opening the passenger door. "Get in." Cam pushed the door open and Rory slid himself into the cab stepping on the door's armrest.

"Hit it!" Rory said closing the door behind him; he snapped his fingers and pointed towards the upcoming terrain. Cam carefully accelerated watching the mirrors, he didn't want to make too much of a dust cloud until they had some ground between them and the road they had just crossed.

* * * * * * *

It took another hour of cross desert driving to reach the low level mountains south of road 556. The three passengers watched all round in three hundred and sixty degrees as the vehicle slowly drove into the rocks. There were plenty of passages weaving through the foothills of the range.

"This looks good," Cam said leaning forward on the steering wheel looking up at the hide he had found. He had located a small outcrop of rock to reverse the vehicle under ready to drive out and escape down one of the three passages if trouble should arise. "Everyone out, take a passage each. I'll go to high ground and have a look about. Come on guys."

Cam pressed his earpiece to activate it and soon after heard the low bleeps of the others doing the same. Their earpieces would give them a good few hundred metres of communications with one another. Everyone exited the vehicle and closed the doors softly without slamming them shut, avoiding unnecessary, metallic noise that would travel long distances over the desert terrain.

Cam felt the cooling effect of the rocks as he made his way up the slope. He stopped every so often to look around for anything unusual. Below he could see the other three cautiously moving away from the vehicle to check their possible escape routes. George made eye contact with Donald and motioned towards the passage they had entered the hide from. George felt it safer to send the less experienced Donald down the already cleared passage.

From higher up Cam could see far enough that he was satisfied the area was clear. He had now lost sight of his colleagues as they cleared the valleys leading away from the hide.

"Clear above," said Cam into the open mic that was part of his earpiece.

"Clear to the north," came a reply from the northern ravine.

"Clear east."

"Um, clear the way we came in," said Donald unsure of what to say.

"Cool, come back in and secure the area, prep the vehicle. I'm going to stay up here and provide cover."

"Roger that," said George.

"Coming in," informed Rory.

"Me too," said Donald.

"Rory," said George. "Get some trip flares out, one down each ravine."

"Sure, no probs." Rory replied going to the rear of the vehicle where all the supplies were being stored.

"Donald mate, help me refuel the truck," George pointed towards one of the jerry cans of fuel strapped to the side of the vehicle. "Pull that down, I'll get the funnel." The vehicle had used more fuel than George thought and the tank took another half a can to fill.

"Thirsty beast isn't it?" Said George.

"Big engine," Donald replied strapping the second can back on the side of the truck. "And what with it driving on the sand an all."

"Yeah, suppose," muttered George looking around the hide location. "Donald mate, go swap with Cam. We need to contact Al, then he'll need to get some sleep before the sun goes down."

"OK, on my way." Donald climbed the rocky slope up to where Cam was on over watch and let him get back down to the vehicle. Rory was returning from securing the site.

"Trips out, if anyone comes within a hundred and fifty metres we'll know about it."

"Good," Cam said looking at his watch and then up to the sun. "We've got three or four hours of light left. Lets get on the blower to Al and then we can get our heads down."

"Does anyone know how this Sat Phone works?" Asked Rory dragging the toughened black container out the back of the truck.

"Whoa, thought you said you did?" Said George.

"Yeah, I did," said Rory rolling his eyes in an attempt to remember if he did or not. "It's err, pretty straightforward," he said trying to bluff his case. He opened the box and pulled out a folded up satellite dish. "Right, it's simple," he said whilst trying to un-concertina the dish. He gripped at the dish but it remained folded in its transportation position. Rory looked over his shoulder at his audience. "Do you know what," he said returning his attention to the dish, "I'll do that bit last," and placed it on the roof of the vehicle.

Cam and George stood back both with arms folded as Rory took out the contents of the box one at a time and pretended to know what each part was for. Each item was met with a nod and a grunt of understanding.

"Does he know what he's doing?" Asked George.

"No, I've known Rory for years," replied Cam. "He'll never admit he hasn't got a clue." Rory, aware he was under pressure, resorted to jamming components together in the hope they might somehow connect. "I mean look at him," continued Cam. "I feel like I'm watching the ape at the beginning of that space odyssey movie."

"Yeah, I can almost hear the crescendo of drums and horns," said George as Rory put down the components and put his hands on his hips. Unsure of what to do next, Rory ran his fingers through his hair. "Oh look, a technical scratch." Cam nodded. "Look mate, just get your head down this might take a while." George turned to Cam. "Go on, you need some sleep. I'll update Al. When numb nuts is done that is."

"Cool, make sure Donald gets his head down. Guy's knackered." Cam walked over to where the vehicle was tucked under the rock overhang. Out of the back he found one of the two ponchos and attached it to the side of the truck, creating a lean-to.

He crawled under the makeshift tent and took off his grab bag satchel; he laid his head down on it and shifted the contents around until it was as comfortable as it could be. He laid his rifle on his chest and closed his weary eyes. Knowing sleep was bound to come, he awaited the continuing dream.

Chapter 18

Cave Complex Xray
Shawal Valley, June 2008

Cam advanced into the cave, his right shoulder almost touching the wall of the tunnel. Swanny was just ahead, on the left side of the cave. The stale fetid air filled Cam's nose; this rotten air mixed with the dust cloud from the air strike blast made it hard to get in enough oxygen.

"Stop," Cam whispered to Swanny. He could barely see him any more as the dust cloud was sucked into the tunnel. "Can't see much Boss," Cam said into his radio mic.

"Hold there guys," said the Boss. "Glenn set up just inside the entrance." Glenn got down in the prone position and set up his S.A.W, then he connected his night vision goggles to his helmet and snapped them down over his eyes. He switched them to thermal mode to see through the dust-filled tunnel and carefully scanned the tunnel ahead.

"No heat sources," Glenn said.

"OK, keep moving," said the Boss. Cam moved forward, rifle in his shoulder. He tried to see through the gloom but all he could see was the small orange dot from Swanny's cigarette bobbing along a few metres ahead of him.

The team moved deeper into the cave complex. Swanny led, followed by Cam. Spike and Buzz took the middle position and the Boss and Glenn covered the rear. Glenn removed his goggles as the dust cleared. Cam blinked and peered over the top of his weapons sights. The tunnel ahead seemed to end abruptly. Thud, Thud. Swanny let off two shots. The team braced and lifted their weapons into firing positions.

"What was that?" Said the Boss.

"Saw something." Replied Swanny.

"What did you see?"

"Movement, looked like a head peeking around a corner."

"Are you sure?"

"Yeah, definitely," said Swanny, cigarette still hanging out of the corner of his mouth.

"OK, stay put, cover that area. Cam take a look." Cam advanced, placing his feet carefully as he moved. He crouched, keeping his knees slightly bent, his M4A1 tucked tightly in his shoulder. He approached what appeared to be the end of the cave only to discover that instead of ending, the tunnel split. He stood just short of the corner and knelt down. He could see the two impact points from Swanny's shots. He carefully looked around the corner, choosing the direction that the mystery head would have looked around.

"Clear," Cam said. "The tunnel splits." The other members of the troop closed in on Cam's position.

"Right, we'll split up," the Boss said. "Cam, Swanny take left. Spike, Buzz go right. Glenn and I will stay here. If you need support we'll be right behind you. Keep in radio contact. Get going."

Cam and Swanny moved deeper into the complex, they stopped every few metres to listen for movement. The tunnel twisted and turned and they entered an area that had been hollowed out to form some kind of a store room. The walls of the store were lined with wooden weapon racks. They all were empty. That meant the rifles that should be stood upright in the racks were being used. Metal crates with Arabic writing on them lay on the floor, some locked some not. Swanny opened one of the unlocked ones.

"Whoa! Careful Swanny," whispered Cam. "You know better than that." Swanny realising what he had done hesitated, then peeled off the Styrofoam cover revealing the contents of the crate. Inside were rows of frag grenades. Swanny picked up two and clipped them to his webbing. Cam caught Swanny's gaze and he motioned towards a closed wooden door at the far side of the room.

The two took up positions either side of the door. Swanny reached over for the door handle. Cam took aim through the door ready to clear whatever would be on the other side. He looked at Swanny through the corner of his eye and gave the signal with a slight nod.

BOOM! The complex shook and small shards of rock fell from the ceiling. Screams bounced down the tunnel and filled the room echoing around making it difficult to identify who was making them. Random gun shots rang out and the screams stopped. Cam and Swanny stood rock still; the door would have to wait.

Swanny went to move in the direction of the now silenced noise.

"Wait a minute mate; give us one of those grenades." Swanny unhooked one of the explosives and tossed it to Cam. He then kneeled down, pulled the pin and placed it on the ground against the door. On top of the grenade he laid a piece of fallen rock; the rock held the safety lever in place. "There if anyone tries to come through the door they'll get one hell of a surprise." Said Cam.

"Yeah, as long as we remember it's there too," said Swanny removing his now burnt down cigarette and flicking it to the ground.

"Shh, do you hear that?" Said Cam standing up and taking control of his rifle again.

"Yeah, voices. And not one of ours," replied Swanny as he lifted his M4 and aimed at the entrance to the store room.

"Cover!" Ordered Cam. The two men took shelter behind some of the stacked metal crates. "Watch the entrance." Swanny leant on the top of the crate to steady his rifle. "Charlie One, this is Charlie Two, over." Silence. "Charlie One, this is Charlie Two. Sitrep over." Still nothing. "Charlie One, this is Charlie Two. Boss are you there?"

The short silence that followed lasted an eternity. Thoughts flowed through Cam's mind as he tried to make sense of what could be happening and tried to come up with a plan of action.

"Cam, we gotta check this out," said Swanny cutting Cam's thought process short.

"Yeah, I know," sighed Cam. "Come on." Cam readied his rifle at the entrance to the store room and moved round in a wide semi circle, covering the entrance. Swanny waited, until he was in a good L shape with Cam on the cave entrance, then went for the tunnel in the direction of the voices.

The two men retreated back to where they left the Boss and Glenn. Neither of the two could place where the voices had come from as they echoed around the cave complex. The familiar smell of cordite and explosions wafted around at the fork in the tunnel. The Boss and Glenn were gone.

"They must have gone to back up Spike and Buzz," said Swanny.

"Let's check it out, move up." Swanny moved down the tunnel that bent round to the left. Slowly more came into view as they snaked further into the complex. The voices had started to disappear and Cam became worried that they were walking into an ambush.

"Charlie One, this is Charlie Two, over," Cam repeated with no response.

Like the other tunnel that they had started to clear, this one opened up into a larger room. Bunk beds and lockers filled the hollowed-out cave.

"A barracks." Swanny said. Cam didn't answer he was too busy wondering where the men who occupied this barracks were. A small fireplace, cut into the wall, flickered, casting shadows across the room. The fire was still strong, the men who started it couldn't be far. Just like the store room, a wooden door blocked their way out of the other side of the room. This door however was nearly hanging off its hinges. Cam and Swanny moved in on the damaged door. The smell of battle hung in the air, the furniture in disarray.

"That's blast damage," Cam said softly. The two men took up positions on either side of the door.

"It's far too quiet in there," Swanny whispered. Cam took out a flashbang from his satchel and made sure Swanny saw it. He nodded in agreement and readied his weapon; he would be first in after Cam posted in the flashbang. The spring-loaded safety lever spun to the ground with a clink and Cam dropped the pin. He waited a few seconds then in an underarm motion rolled the flashbang into the room.

The grenade tumbled along the ground creating a metallic rattle. The ear-splitting bang was followed swiftly by Swanny forcing open the door almost wrenching it off its hinges. Cam watched as he entered the room. The second unexpected explosion caught Cam off guard. The wooden door swung into Cam's face and slammed him against the wall. He took hold of the door and forced it to one side just in time to see an enemy soldier appearing in the doorway.

Cam's rifle was slung down by his side; with the soldier too close for him to raise it he instinctively drew his pistol from his leg holster. The enemy fighter took two rounds to his chest and he fell back through the doorway. Cam reached for the door, he needed to find Swanny. As his fingers made contact with the door it was kicked open, Cam's pistol fell to the floor and dangled on its lanyard as the door hit his arm.

The enemy soldier tried to aim his AK47 at Cam but was stopped by his close proximity. The rifle was easily brushed to one side. He swung his right fist at Cam but he dodged and trapped the soldier's elbow under his armpit. Cam heard the crunch as he forced the limb to bend in the wrong direction. He then grabbed the man's throat, digging his fingers and thumb either side of the trachea and squeezing. The enemy fighter gurgled trying to breathe. Cam guided him backwards to the ground, drew his fighting knife and plunged it down between his enemies clavicle and neck. Face to face with his victim he looked into the man's eyes and could smell his breath as he struggled to breathe. He felt the warm sticky blood soaking into his clothing as it spurted out of the severed artery. As the gurgling stopped he heard shouts and screams coming from the other room.

Cam threw the enemy's lifeless body to one side.

"Swanny!" He shouted. The screaming continued whilst Cam tried to get to his feet. Only then he saw the grenade rolling towards him followed closely by a second. Eyes wide with fear he hit the deck and grabbed the lifeless body lying next to him. He shielded himself as best he could, gritted his teeth and waited for the blast.

The two explosions occurred almost simultaneously, throwing Cam against the metal legs of the bunk beds. All he could hear was the buzzing in his ears and his vision seemed to be in black and white slow motion. He could barely move but managed to arm himself by dragging his pistol towards him by its lanyard.

The buzzing turned to a high-pitched whistle as he started to hear what was going on around him. The screams and shouts had continued throughout his ordeal. He could hear Swanny desperately shouting for help.

"CAM, WHERE ARE YOU?" He heard but was unable to think straight let alone move from behind the enemy's body. Another enemy soldier ran through the blast-damaged doorway. Cam fired his pistol shooting him to the ground. Another, followed by another. All shot as Cam blasted at the blurred figures. He fumbled to reload as even more piled into the room. Shot by shot Cam barricaded the room with the bodies of the enemy fighters, only when no more could climb over their dead comrades did one toss in another grenade. Cam watched unable to defend himself. This was it, he waited to die.

Chapter 19

So real was this recurring dream, Cam was surprised to wake. He lay under the lean-to and tried to slow his raised heart beat. He could feel the sweat on his back and around his neck as it cooled in the evening air. Over to his left he could see Donald and George. The sun had set over the rocks and he could make them out chatting in the dim light.

Cam crawled out of the shelter and untied the quick-release straps keeping the lean-to taught. With the tension released the poncho snapped to the ground and Cam rolled it up and replaced it in the back of the truck.

"Hungry?" Asked George as Cam approached.

"No, not really." He knew they were on rations and what to expect.

"Are you sure?" Said George holding up a silver foil packet. "We heated you up a pasta and meatballs." George waved it in front of Cam in an attempt to get his attention.

Accepting that this offer was probably the best of a bad lot, he took the packet from George and started to tear it open.

"Ta mate," he said. "Did everyone get some rest?"

"Aye, Rory's up top. We were just waiting for you to wake up."

"Are the trips in?"

"Yeah, we're just talking over some drills, you know in case it don't go as planned." Donald stood between the two men and nodded, clearly nervous about the possibility of something happening. "We've decided," George continued. "To keep Donald at the back, number four. If we're in a contact he'll watch the rear as we move forward."

"Yeah, I'll tell you if I see anything," Donald chipped in. "If it's all clear I'll keep telling you."

"Cool," said Cam taking out his plastic spoon from the top pocket of his old faded green jacket. "Just keep your grab bags with you and stay with us. You have both with you right?"

"Yes," replied Donald. "One with ammo and frags and one with flashbangs and some supplies." They had been over their standard load out before deploying. Each man had their main weapon and a sidearm, two shoulder-slung bags with spare ammo and various grenades. Some of the more experienced operators had some of their own equipment and some extra kit they had scrounged from the Canadians.

"If we need you to do anything or go anywhere, trust me you will know about it," said Cam tucking in to his boil-in-the-bag meal. "We will be in communications the whole time." Cam pointed to his earpiece. "So if you are stuck, just shout up."

"Yeah, OK." Donald nodded, taking it all in.

"Remember, one tap on the earpiece will keep the mic open until you stop speaking," Cam said with a mouthful of pasta. "Double tapping it will put you on open mic."

"Yep, got it," Donald confirmed.

"We won't have the range we had back in Malta though," said George. "The earpieces link in with mobile phone masts, but out here," he said looking around, "they're hard to come by."

"So, what's the range?" Asked Donald.

"Only a few hundred metres," said Cam finishing his pasta. "But if we have the sat phone set up it'll connect us all, no matter the range."

"Also to Al as well," added George trying to comfort Donald.

"Don't worry," said Cam. "We're going to try and keep this one simple, nobody needs to know we are here, let's keep it like that."

"Oh yeah, I'm happy with that," said Donald.

"We all are," said George taping his earpiece. "Rory mate, we're off, come on in."

"Roger," said Rory from his look-out post. "Coming down." Rory slid down the rocks to the clearing bringing a small rock slide with him. "Shotgun!" He shouted as he climbed into the front passenger seat.

"Suppose it's time to go then," said Cam squeezing the last of the meatballs and pasta out of the packet. He opened the driver's door and stopped when the interior light came on. "We'd better disable these bloody lights."

"Yeah, that wouldn't be good in the middle of a pitch-black desert," said George opening the rear door. "Is there an on/off button in there Mate?" Rory had a good look round for anything that resembled a control for the interior lights.

"Not seen," he said. "Just jam the switches in the doors with some black nasty, that'll do it." Cam and Donald found some black tape and made their way round the vehicle taping up the door switches, the interior light went out as they secured the last switch.

With the light out, the contrast of light to dark was more pronounced.

"We better get going," said Cam climbing in the driver's seat. The new vehicle's engine turned over beautifully and hummed away, raring to go.

"Make your way out and go left, south east," said George turning on the sat nav, creating the only dim light source inside the blacked-out vehicle. The headlights would not be turned on as they needed to stay hidden for as long as possible.

"OK, south east it is. Did Al have much to say for himself?" Asked Cam.

"Na, not much," said George. "Well you know, when we finally got the sat phone working that is."

"It's working isn't it?" Defended Rory.

"There are no changes, no new intel," said George. "We're to update him when we hide up and before we move off."

The four occupants of the vehicle got their first view of the desert landscape at night as they exited the canyons. The moon was waxing, moving from the new moon to a full moon, this period would last for well over a week so they knew they still had plenty of dark nights left to work in.

"At one point we might have to cross that road again," said George.

"When?" Asked Cam.

"Before we hide up, we should try to parallel the road only to cross it before sun up to use the rocks for cover."

"Sounds like a plan," said Cam shifting in his seat trying to find a comfortable position, not made easy with his rifle laid across his lap. His grab bags with his extra kit sat next to him, ready to be slung over his shoulders if anything untoward should happen. The others had a similar arrangement.

Cam checked the side door compartment for his door pistol. This extra pistol would be used then discarded in the event they had to escape out of the vehicle. His sidearm, a Glock 17, would remain in his leg holster.

Cam followed George's directions from the sat nav, he would keep them a safe distance from the road. If they followed the route of the road it should take them to Ataq. This should take them a further two nights of driving.

"Bored already!" Stated Rory. "Does this thing have a working radio?" Rory started to press random buttons. "Typical! Expensive new vehicle like this and the radio doesn't work."

"Wow, I guess the Canadian military gets ripped off just like ours," said Cam.

"Maybe, or they've disabled it," said George from the back seats. "Or you just can't get that to work either."

"OK, OK. I admit I don't know much about sat phones. But I'm sure I can get a bloody car radio to work. And this one isn't working."

"I don't suppose anybody brought any cds with them did they?" Said George.

"Last thing on my mind mate," said Cam.

"We're gonna have to come up with some driving games," said Rory.

"I spy, with my little eye," said Cam.

"Something beginning with 's'," said George finishing Cam's sentence.

"Funny," said Rory sarcastically. "Someone must know some driving games." A few games were mentioned but most relied on other vehicles or road signs. So the four men entered a competition of burp tennis. George beat Donald in the finals and earned a round of applause from the others.

"Feel sick," said Donald.

"Me too," added George. "What about embarrassing stories. There must be some awesome ones between the four of us."

"Yeah, tell us about some of your marriages," said Cam looking over at Rory.

"Some! How many have there been?" Asked Donald.

"Four or five, can't really remember," said Rory. "And they ain't that funny, trust me."

"You must have something."

"Um," said Rory thinking hard, back into his past. "Well, ahh!" He laughed. "This is funny. When I was a kid, we had this dog; it was pretty old but it loved chocolate spread…"

"No!" Said Cam. "Christ no! I feel sick enough after the tennis I don't need to hear about you abusing the family pet."

"What! I thought we were sharing," Rory said still laughing.

"That's not sharing, that's just wrong!"

"Alright! Bunch of prudes," protested Rory. "I got another one!"

"No," added Donald. "I think we need another game."

* * * * * *

The thin sliver of moon afforded very little ambient light on the dessert floor. The flat mixture of sand and gravel land had a dark silver tint as the vehicle carried its passengers towards the town of Ataq, nearly three hundred kilometres away.

"We got about an hour or so till sun up," said George. "We should probably look for a place to hide up." The comment broke the long silence that had followed the earlier conversation. Tiredness had set in and the banter had ceased but they remained vigilant, watching for movement on the road that lay just out of sight.

"Right, looks like there are some rocks up ahead. I'll try in there," Cam said steering towards the rocky outcrop. It looked good and Cam found a narrow track that took them deep into a ravine with a decent sized clearing. "This will have to do."

"Not sure mate," Rory said. "Only one way in equals only one way out."

"It's cover."

"It's obvious cover."

"It's all we got, it's this or a flat desert," Cam said manoeuvring the vehicle to face the exit. Rory climbed out of the vehicle followed by Donald and George.

"Check this out," said George kneeling down. "Looks like goat shit. All over the place." Rory rounded the vehicle to George's side.

"It's fresh," he said looking around. "And there's lots of older shit. I reckon some herders use it as a pen."

Cam still sat in the driver's seat opened the door and turned to face his colleagues.

"What do you think?" He said. Rory sighed as he contemplated the situation.

"It's the best of a bad lot," he said. "Looks like there's a good period of time between visits, probably as the herder takes his goats from one place to another."

"So we stay?" Asked Cam.

"Yeah, we stay," said Rory after a short, thoughtful pause. "You look knackered," he said turning to see Cam's tired eyes. "Get your head down, we'll secure the area."

"Keep a sentry out, we can't get caught out here."

"We know what we're doing mate, go on, get some rest." Rory was right, he was done, and he desperately needed to grab a few hours sleep before the next night of driving. He closed the driver's door sealing himself in the car and climbed through to the back seats. Settling down on the back seats he could hear Rory's voice, muffled through the window, giving instructions on how to secure the area.

Cam turned onto his side and placed his G36 rifle in the passenger foot wells. He fidgeted around moving his equipment in his belt kit and tactical vest to a more comfortable position.

He felt cold, the sun was about to rise over the rocks hiding them from view and Cam was looking forward to some of the new sun's rays warming him through the glass of the car's doors.

He curled up into the foetal position and slid his hands between his knees for warmth. Closing his eyes he sighed after taking in a big lung full of air. He doubted his ability to get any quality sleep; he hadn't for many months now, nearly a year. However, exhaustion sent him to sleep, transporting him from one set of rocks in the middle of this desert in Yemen to another set of rocks many miles away.

* * * * * * *

Cam saw the soldier running at him with hatred burning in his eyes. He pulled his Glock 17 pistol from his holster breaking the safety clip securing the weapon to his thigh and brought it to bear on his target. He spun onto his back and took up the slack on the trigger. Extending his legs he braced himself on the closed door of the vehicle.

With his eyes now open he blinked in the light that was streaming through the window. The light was shielding the enemy soldier from view. Had the hide been over run? How could he have not heard anything? He had not had a decent, deep sleep for a long time now. Then reality began to return. There was no enemy soldier; he was safe in the back of the vehicle.

He sat up, still a little jaded by his dream. He had a cursory look around before re-holstering his sidearm. Stretching his back from an uncomfortable few hours of curled up sleep, he saw Donald and George sat by a small fire a few metres away from the truck. It was afternoon; his watch said it was nearly five.

"I slept all day?" Said Cam yawning approaching the two guys by the fire.

"Yeah, we thought you could do with some beauty sleep," said George.

"What's with the fire?"

"Come on Cam, it's broad daylight, smokeless fuel," George said reaching into a pot hanging off a tripod. "Take your pick, we got corned beef hash, chicken mushroom and pasta and Lancashire hot pot." George looked over at the Cam, still yawning and wiping his eyes. "Three of the best mate."

"As long as there's no fruit dumplings in butternut sauce; that stuff's shit."

"Would I do that to you?" Said George throwing him a corned beef hash. Cam caught the pack and wiped it dry.

"Got any Tabasco sauce?" No sooner had Cam said it when a bottle of Tabasco flew through the air, which Cam struggled to catch, almost dropping. "Ta," he said ripping open the packet and dropping in a few drips.

"Rory up top?"

"Yeah," said Donald. "We've been doing two hour stints. Is he really on his fourth marriage?" Asked Donald after carefully considering if it was his place to pry into someone's personal life.

"Third or fourth," smiled Cam. "You know how it is," he said catching a glimpse of George. "Marriage and this type of existence don't go hand in hand."

"Mmm," said Donald. George dug into his own ration pack pretending not to hear the conversation going on next to him.

"I been looking at the sat nav," said George changing the subject. "We're going to be damn close to Ataq after tonight's drive."

"Yeah?" Said Cam answering in a positive manner yet as if shooting a question right back at George.

"Well, has anyone thought up a plan before we get close up?"

"We got the U.A.Vs. I'm gonna speak to Al now and get an update, but when we get close enough we'll send over one of our unmanned aircraft, get a look at what's going on and try and sneak in the back door."

"Ask him more on the building, where the antenna could be. We don't want to be hanging round for too long. Those towns that far out are like the wild west."

"I heard it described as very Beau Geste, surrounded by desert. You probably expect to see a section of Foreign Legion running around or buried up to their necks in sand or something."

"Still we better be careful, it's a dangerous place. A.Q are all over this area. Kidnappings are common and I don't want to be used as a bargaining chip or end up a Youtube clip."

"George mate, we'll be fine," Cam said trying to make Donald who was listening feel better. "We'll get a good recce before we go in, that's what the unmanned air vehicles are for."

"Just I don't think we got enough intel from the Canadians. The maps looked like they were printed off Google Earth."

"I think they were," smiled Cam finishing off his spicy corned beef hash. "It's an old desert town. Mostly one or two floored buildings so our target should be easy to spot being the only three storey one. The towns got an airfield to the north east, not military and we're going to slip right past it, that's about all the town has to it."

"Just used to getting more to go," said George opening the black bin liner being used for the rubbish. Cam dropped the empty silver foil ration packet into the black bag.

"I'll see if I can get any more out of Al. Lets all stay chilled, it's all cool."

Chapter 20

"I understand Cam," said Al through the sat phone receiver. "But I don't have any more info to give you."

"Sure," Cam leaned back on the tail end of the truck. "We just don't like running into situations we know nothing about," said Cam looking over at where Donald and George were sat around the fire.

"The information lifted from the Iranian embassy in Malta highlighted Ataq as one of the locations of the scrambled communications. After a bit of digging around we found a long-time acquaintance of General Pourali had turned up at the old police station. You can call me crazy but it's too much of a coincidence."

"So much for my easy holiday."

"I know, sorry, I had no idea this was going to happen. But trust me, things are happening back here. We are getting a lot of interest with this one." Al sounded excited.

"Interest, what kind of interest?" Asked Cam.

"From the international community. We are being carefully watched and if we can pull this off we can be sure to get funding like we have never seen before."

"What do you mean we? If we can pull it off."

"OK, if you can pull it off. The Yanks know about us now and are looking to cross train. A site for a training complex is being mentioned."

"Wow."

"Like I said, it's all happening."

"Right, well, we'll be in contact at sun up. We got a lot of ground to cover tonight."

"OK, get going. So can we expect tomorrow night, to be the night?"

"That's the plan. We'll get close to Ataq tonight hide up, during the day. We'll send over a U.A.V to check out the town, find a way in and to the antenna and be out of Dodge before anyone even knows we were there."

"That's why we send you on these things. Cam, one more thing." Al paused. "The Americans have asked for us to be on the look out for one of their guys."

"Who?"

"A C.I.A Colonel. Went missing a couple of days ago."

"What the hell was he doing out here?"

"God only knows. The area around Ataq is crawling with A.Q and all sorts of other undesirables. Be on the look out but also be careful. You're more important. However, it would be good to get some more positive PR with the Yanks."

"OK, no problem. Speak to you soon." Cam pressed the disconnect button and replaced the handset into it's housing on the sat phone. With no answers from Al that he needed, he began to pack away the phone.

* * * * * * *

"Sun's going down," Rory said returning to the two men keeping warm by the fire.

"What you doing down here?" Said George. "You're supposed to be keeping an eye out."

"Come on, we've seen nothing all day. What's the chances of anyone stumbling in on us now? Anyway it must be time for us to get going."

"Yeah," grunted George struggling to his feet. "I suppose it is." Donald followed suit and helped George stamp out the fire. Cam approached his team returning from his conversation with Al.

"Anything?" Asked Rory.

"Not much, same as before." Cam wasn't surprised to see some visible sighs from the three men. "From the intel he's almost certain it's the right place."

"Oh, thank God for that," Rory remarked with his usual sarcasm.

"Just been warned about movement around Ataq."

"Movement?" Said Donald.

"Yeah, A.Q and other groups. All over the place, so we have to be on our guard the closer we get."

"Aren't we always?" Said George.

"Also," Cam continued. "Al has got intel that a group of pirates are holding a C.I.A agent nearby. If we come across them we can have a go. If we want to that is."

"Damn," said George. "Wouldn't want to be him right now."

"Hell no," said Cam. "Always keep a bullet back for something shit like that." Rory broke from the group and headed towards the vehicle managing to change the subject with his movement.

"Right then, now we know we are heading to the right place," he said sarcastically. "We should get a move on. And before anyone else says it, shotgun."

"Son of a bitch," said George. "You can't have the front seat every time."

"Well, get better at shotgun," said Rory making himself comfortable in the passenger seat. The other doors of the vehicle closed quietly and Cam drove out of the canyon pausing at the entrance to allow everyone to have a good look around for movement. The surrounding desert was as clear as it had been for the previous few nights.

Cam continued towards the destination as directed by George with the sat nav. The men remained vigilant mindful of the information provided by Al. The hours passed like the miles of sand and as the night came closer to sun up, the conversation moved from topic to topic.

"So you're telling me, it's possible to travel through time!" Said George.

"Yes," replied Rory. "Like I said it's all to do with the speed of light." There was silence in the cab as everyone attempted to get their head around what Rory was proposing. "And the fact that you can't travel faster than it." He added.

"You can move faster than it," said Cam.

"How?" Challenged Rory.

"Well, if we were travelling in a train going the speed of light and I walked from the back of the train to the front, I would be moving faster than the speed of light."

"Um, OK. If this car was travelling at the speed of light," said Rory after a short think. "And you turned on the headlights, what would happen?"

"Nothing?" Said Donald in a puzzled voice.

"Exactly," said Rory pleased to have proved his theory. "You can't travel faster than the speed of light."

"No," interrupted Cam. "That just proves that light can't travel faster than itself. But I can, hence my train story."

"But if you are travelling faster than the speed of light, you are time travelling."

"How do you work that out?"

"If I stand still and look at a face of a clock, then travel away from that clock at the speed of light, it will appear to stand still, agreed."

"OK, I agree to that. But all you've done there is prove that time can appear to stand still."

"Just like this conversation!" Said George to Donald who tried to hide a snigger.

"Ah, but if I move back to that clock, from a distance, at the speed of light the hands of the clock will just move normally. Right?"

"Um, hold on a minute, I need to think about that."

"Well it would. So now if, while moving towards the clock, I go faster than the speed of light, the hands will speed up faster than normal." Rory holds up his hands marking his point. "Time travel!"

"What! That makes no sense," said Cam.

"It makes every sense," protested Rory.

"You even said you can't move faster than light, so how can time travel be possible?" Cam said, voice raised.

"Can I suggest a change of subject," shouted George from the back seats. "Albert Einstein is turning in his grave round about now."

"Fine, but I'm right." Rory sulked, returning his attention out of his window to the left hand side of the vehicle.

"I've got a question for you guys," said Donald.

"Go on then," said Cam. "As long as it isn't about string theory or anything like that."

"Is Al's real name Al?"

"Mmm, doubt it," said Cam.

"Why's that?" Donald replied.

"Well, as you know, none of us use our real names. Only you and Rory use yours, cos you aren't part of the Asset program."

"And Al still chooses al the names?"

"Yeah," said George. "Al makes them up, presumably we're named after British war heroes."

"Except he spells them wrong, God only knows why," added Cam.

"What about Bull?" Said Donald. "I wonder how Bull got given his name."

"Are you kidding me!" Said George. "Put a metal ring through that man's nose and that's what you've got."

"Guys!" Rory said staring out of the window into the night of the desert. "Sun will be up in less than an hour, shall we think about hiding up?"

"Yeah. George, how close are we to Ataq?" Said Cam. George lifted the cover of the sat nav. The glow of the screen lit up the back of the vehicle with a soft light.

"We made good distance. We are…" George examined the screen attempting to judge the time it would take to travel the remaining distance. "Probably two to three hours away. He closed the cover extinguishing the light and waited for Cam to make a decision on what to do.

"OK, we get into cover, get our heads down. Before the light fades we'll send up the U.A.V, have a good look at the police station, try to find out what we're up against." Cam altered the direction of the vehicle towards the rocks that they had been paralleling throughout the night, scanning the rock face for signs of life.

"There's not much in the way of cover," said Cam. "We packed the nets didn't we?"

"Yeah, if we tuck right in close to the wall we can shield ourselves from view." Rory pointed over to a section of wall. "There, that's the best we can do." Cam manoeuvred the vehicle as close as he could to the rock face and the passengers piled out. Rory went straight to the back of the truck and pulled out a canvass bag containing the camouflage netting.

They covered the vehicle with the netting and from a distance was barely visible. Cam was first to get some sleep and curled up on the back seats waiting for the sun to rise and warm the cab. George assembled the sat phone and from under the netting called Al to check in.

* * * * * * *

"Cam. Cam, wake up." Cam woke with a start and his body jumped an inch off the seats as his muscles tensed in reaction to the voice. Instead of seeing a filthy, cave-fighting enemy soldier he saw George standing over him. He looked past George to the sun-filled sky. It was still daylight, it must be his stint on watch.

"Cam, we got a problem," continued George. "Al has told us they found the location of the missing C.I.A guy." Cam sat up and shielded his eyes from the bright sun behind George. "They are close by our position. The Yanks want us to go in."

"Christ! What time is it?"

"Early. Way too early." Cam climbed out of the back seats and followed George round to the back of the vehicle to where the others were waiting. Rory was sat on the open tail end of the vehicle and Donald was stood leaning next to him.

"What do you guys think?" Asked Cam with a just woken croaky voice.

"Well, we were just discussing that whilst you had your beauty sleep." Said Rory.

"And?"

"Al Shabaab, about twenty-five or thirty of the little bastards. Camped not too far from here." Rory motioned the direction with his head. "The Agent was captured over here doing something dodgy, and the Septics want us to get him back."

"Septics? What the hell's a Septic?" Asked Donald.

"Septics, septic tanks." He waited for a note of understanding from Donald. "Yanks! Not mastered cockney rhyming slang yet then?"

"Alright," said Cam trying to change the conversation back to the matter in hand. "I thought Al Shabaab were Somalian? What the hell are they doing here?"

"They're good mates with the Yemeni rebels; they have been identified taking hostages before," said Rory. "But this time they are only moving the hostage from one location to another."

"Some other group nicked him and handed him over, that's how the Americans located him," said George. "And we're the closest."

"Can we take them?" Asked Cam.

"Fuck yeah! Bunch of bloody sand monkeys," said Rory jumping down from the vehicle. "We'll hand 'em their ass on a plate."

"But," said George. "It will give our position away. And do we really want to be doing that at this moment, so close to Ataq?"

"Can we live with ourselves if we let these guys keep the U.S agent?" Said Cam. "What does Al want?"

"Al's up for the international recognition. However, he's said it's up to our assessment," said George. "Your lead on this one mate, it's your choice."

"Damn it," sighed Cam. "Why now?" Cam thought for a few seconds; he looked at the faces staring back at him waiting for direction. "We can't," he said. "We must stay undetected. It's against my instincts and I know you probably feel the same. I'd love to take them on and get that guy out of there. But, what we're here for takes priority."

Cam waited for the reaction to his statement, for an argument. They all wanted to do what they could and would have expected an American squad to do the same for them. But they understood that when getting into work like this, they were taking a risk. They all knew that some missions are too important to put into jeopardy. Sadly, sometimes people are left behind.

"You're call mate," said Rory.

"Don't dwell on it Cam," said George. "You're right, we have to stay on track, tough call." Cam nodded, thankful for their understanding.

"Right then, we'll hang here for a few hours then move off before the sun goes down. Get the U.A.V up and take a look at Ataq." Cam looked at the three guys who were visibly still tired. "Get your admin sorted, tonight's the night."

Chapter 21

Nobody could sleep. Their heads were full, thoughts of the C.I.A agent being held only a few miles away clouded their minds. They sat in silence waiting for the light to fade.

"It would put us behind a full day," said Cam. The others, wrapped up in their own thoughts, didn't answer. Cam looked over at them; he knew that they would never question his orders. "The whole area would know we're here," he said feeling the need to explain his actions. Still nothing from the other three.

Cam looked down at the floor avoiding any eye contact that might come his way. Rory sat still, leaning against the front of the vehicle. He gripped his Minimi, belt-fed automatic rifle. Donald fidgeted, looking uncomfortable with the situation. He kept an eye on the others around him unsure of what was going to happen next.

George opened the cover to the sat nav for the third time in half an hour. Cam watched him flick the switch on and allow it to boot up. George studied the screen of the navigation device and then looked towards the rocky wall, making passing eye contact with Cam.

Cam took a deep breath then exhaled, sighing. He knew what George was looking at. He hauled himself to his feet drawing the attention of the other two men. He dropped himself down next to George who angled the screen so he could see the display.

"We are here," George said pointing to the top left of the display with the nib of a pen. "And they are over here."

"We're that close?"

"I'm surprised we can't hear them." The others listened intently to what was going on. "We've got so many options on how we could do this. We can have the high ground here, for comms and sustained fire power." George pointed to a ridge line that would allow them good sight down onto the hostage takers camp. "We can send two round the side to infiltrate the camp. Get the guy out." He looked first at Cam then the others. "Well, I figure that's the best way."

George looked around the group one last time, for approval. Donald unsure of his place in the decision making process, because of his lack of experience, sat watching and waiting. Rory cradled his rifle and stood up as if ready to be given his task.

"OK. Prepare the vehicle," said Cam joining Rory on his feet. George, pleased to be doing something towards helping the agent, hurriedly tidied away the sat nav before he to stood up at the same time as Donald. "You're driving," said Cam pointing at Donald. "I want you on covering fire from the ridge," he said shifting his gaze to George. "So take Rory's Minimi." The two men swapped weapons.

"I'm gonna want that back." said Rory taking George's HK SL8 scoped rifle.

"I'll take care of it like it's my own," said George. "We'll drop you two guys off near the camp then take one of the paths up to the ridge. Comms should work between all of us and Al if we set up the dish."

"Yeah, good. Once we are in, listen for our shots, then let rip with the Minimi," said Cam.

"Take out as many as you can, there aint gonna be any survivors with this," said Rory. "We can't allow any to get away. If any do, we are in the shit."

There was nothing more to say, the team prepared the vehicle and themselves whilst the sunlight began to fade. Ammo was packed into pouches and grab bags; the two who were going to be infiltrating the camp added more grenades to their satchels. Once packed and ready to move they climbed aboard the vehicle, Donald replacing Cam in the driving seat. He started the engine and instinctively reached for the lights and turned them on.

"Woah, no!" George who had positioned himself in the passenger seat lunged over Donald as the side of the rock face was lit up by the headlights. "Lights, lights, lights!" He shouted.

George grabbed the stalk on the side of the steering wheel but instead of turning off the lights he pushed it forwards, activating the main beam.

"No!" Shouted Cam as the desert around them was lit up like day. George tried to correct his mistake by pulling the stalk in the opposite direction. He released the stalk and the main beam disappeared as Donald who realised his mistake gripped the end of the stalk where the headlight controls were, knocking on the indicator.

"Fuck! Come on guys!" Shouted Rory reaching through the gap in the front seats. The stalk clicked twice, turning off the lights, and was returned to the central position taking out the indicator. "Really! Why don't you just beep the horn?"

"Sorry, sorry." Said Donald, the wind knocked out of him by his error.

"Shit! No, my fault," said Cam. "Should have disabled the headlights when we done the interior lights." The occupants of the vehicles blinked, the dim light of the afternoon seemed even darker now they had destroyed their night vision. "Let's get a move on, anyone could have seen that."

"Can't really see where I'm going," said Donald still dazzled.

"Hit it Don," said Rory. "We better put some distance between us and the light show. Just don't bloody crash." The vehicle moved off in the direction of the camp where the C.I.A agent was reportedly being held.

The distance between the pirate camp and where they had been was not far; it took no time at all to get to the drop-off point. Cam was concerned that the pirates in the Al Shabaab camp may have seen the flashing lights from earlier. There was no other choice but to proceed. There was no turning back now.

"Here," said Cam. "Drop us here." The vehicle slowed to a standstill. "Comms, open mic." Cam double tapped his earpiece activating the permanent send function of the earpiece. The others followed, creating three sets of soft-sounding bleeps in Cam's ear. Rory and Cam exited the vehicle and drew their pistols.

"Stay soft until we go loud then give 'em the good news, OK?"

"OK." Replied Donald.

"Get yourselves up top and open a line to Al," said Cam attaching his silencer to the barrel of his pistol. "Hopefully Al can see us and give us a hand guiding us in. George mate, open up with the Minimi on my shots – no survivors." Cam nodded to George who returned the gesture in acknowledgement. "Donald, you're on comms duty. Keep our link to Al open and watch George's back; we don't want anyone sneaking up on you to up there. OK?"

"Yeah, no problem."

"Good," Cam tapped his hand on the door. "Get going and we'll see you when we got this Yank."

"Christ knows what we're gonna do with him," said Rory. "Has anyone thought of that?"

"Come on mate," said George leaning over so he could see Rory through the open driver's window. "No one ever asked us to think for ourselves."

"Go on, up top," said Cam.

"See yah," sang George as they drove off in the direction of a rocky path leading the way to the summit.

"So much of this could go wrong mate," Cam said. "They could have people out watching for a rescue."

"Mmmm," said Rory screwing his sound suppressor onto the end of his side arm. "Especially if he's important to them."

"That path could be booby-trapped, or anything."

"Nothing's perfect," he said sliding his pistol back into his thigh holster and clipping up the safety strap. "We just got to get on with it. Come on, it wont take them long to get to the top."

Cam and Rory broke into a jog and took a position hugging the rocks, which would lead them round to where the camp was. Alert and weapons at the ready, they moved in.

* * * * * * *

The vehicle bounced from side to side as it slowly clawed its way to the top of the outcrop. There had been no signs of movement on the path and nothing to suggest that anyone had been up there in a while. George assessed where the moon would be in relation to them and the camp.

"At least we won't be skylined." Said George. "The moon's gonna cast shadows in the wrong direction."

"I think we're nearly there," said Donald.

"OK, stop here and let me out. I'll take a look on foot." George climbed out of the vehicle and slowly made his way towards the spot where they presumed they would be able to see the camp. Donald watched from the cab as his passenger neared the edge.

As he did so, he assumed the prone position and crawled to a vantage point.

"It's good mate, I can see the lot," whispered George.

"What have we got?" Asked Donald.

"Only what appears to be a makeshift camp. They must be in transit. Got a couple of old style canvas tents, some kind of lean-to and a few vehicles."

"Must be why Al wanted us to get him out now and risk our necks."

"Cause they're gonna move him and the further down the chain they go the harder it is to keep a track." George paused to count the number of enemy in the camp. "About eleven or twelve well-armed guys down there. Maybe more asleep in the tents. Cam are you getting this?"

George waited for a reply but nothing came back. He didn't expect one; he knew they were probably out of range for their earpiece communications.

"Don mate, bring the vehicle close to me but don't get skylined, we've got to get the link up to Al going. That'll boost the power and we will all be singing off the same song sheet." George stayed with eyes on the targets while Donald positioned the vehicle, providing good cover to George whilst staying out of sight to the gunmen below. He removed the sat phone from the back of the vehicle and began setting it up placing the phone part on the driver's seat and the dish on the roof of the cab.

"Don, are you keeping an eye on anything sneaking up on us? We don't know if they've positioned any sentries out. We have to keep a watch."

"Sure, yeah. I don't see anything," said Donald peering out into the darkness. Once set up Donald pressed the on button and the sat phone bleeped into action.

"Al, this is Donald. Can you hear me?"

"Yes Donald, I've got you." Al sounded as close as George was, not like someone on the other side of the world.

"Al," said George. "We are getting your boy out, we have an over watch on the cliff top and Cam and Rory are closing in on the camp."

"I know, we have been watching. Cam, Rory can you hear us?"

"We hear you," whispered Cam barely audible.

"Just so you chaps on the ridge know, they are whispering because we see them prone, not far from one of the Somalian sentries. Isn't that right Cam?"

"Mmm Hmm," hummed Cam obviously concentrating on something else. "We count eleven Al Shabaab milling around the camp and there are some heat signatures in the tents. One of them is bound to be our American."

"I thought there were more than that," said George.

"So did we, but there is a vehicle missing from their group. I just hope we haven't missed them moving him away."

"Well, if we have, all this is a waste of our time. We do have other things we could be doing tonight."

"We may also never see the American agent again as well," said Al. "OK, they are in position. Stand by this is about to go loud."

Chapter 22

From Cam's concealed position he could clearly see the sentry. The guard was sat elevated on a rock, drifting in and out of consciousness. The Somalian wasn't expecting any complications with his night's duties; he certainly wasn't expecting to die.

Cam watched the sentry's eyes close and his head bob up and down as he tried to stay awake. He lent lazily on his AK47, unaware of the danger closing in around him. He wasn't even facing the right direction. Back towards the camp, not out in the direction of threat. Cam and Rory had no problem here.

Rory kept eyes on the others that were visible while Cam crawled into contact distance of the sleeping guard. Cam was prone, his rifle slung on his back, as he knew it wouldn't be necessary with this one. He needed to decide whether to use his knife or silenced pistol.

The sentry was lucky, before he knew what was happening it was over. He was grabbed from behind and pulled to the ground. His sleepy eyes were never to open again as he took a silent 9mm round through the side of his head. To make sure he was dead Cam sent two extra shots through his chest, barrel pressed against his torso.

Rory saw, through his peripheral vision, Cam hiding the body behind the rocks that the guard was using as his seat. Once the task was complete Cam turned to Rory who acknowledged with a slight nod, all the time never losing sight of the enemy camp.

The remainder of the Al Shabaab pirates, unaware of the predators moving in for the kill, carried on with their nightly activities. Cam and Rory slid silently across the ground invisible, so low to the ground that they blended into the silver shadows cast by the slither of moon above. They reached the optimum position, never perfect but the best that was available. The two men didn't need to say they had reached it, they instinctively knew.

Rory had a good view of the camp and the people milling around. He took aim on one man who was standing having a conversation with another. He pulled the butt of the rifle into his shoulder and steadied himself ready to let off a shot. Cam was ready with his pistol, near to the two tents, ready to move in and find the American. George was on over watch. High on the ridge, he had everything under surveillance, ready to let rip with the Minimi

"Can I say chaps," said Al. "I think your best bet is the tent on your left. There are two heat signatures in there, more in the others, possible about four or five sleeping, it's difficult to say. I recon it's the Yank and a guard only on the left."

"K," said Cam quietly. It was time. Cam rose to his feet and advanced on the tent on the left. Keeping low he pulled out a nine-bang flash grenade from his grab bag and readied it for use. One last glance over at Rory, maybe only for reassurance, and he opened the flap of the tent and threw in the nine-bang.

The flashbang exploded cracking off nine explosions in quick succession, temporarily disorientating the two people in the tent. Rory fired off a well-aimed shot into the head of one of the Somalians, followed by another hitting the second man. So fast were the shots that the first had barely hit the floor before the second took a shot to the back of his head.

Cam burst through the tent flap and immediately identified two targets, both Somalians illuminated by a Tilley lamp hanging from the apex of the tent. Two double taps took out both men rolling on the floor, hands over their ears hollering in pain from the effects of the nine bang. He scanned the tent for the American hostage, his eyes settling on a figure with tied hands laid face down in the corner of the tent.

"Got the Yank," said Cam in between random shots being fired by Rory as all hell broke loose in the camp. The odd burst of AK47 fire erupted in the background amongst shouts from the remaining hostage takers.

"Confirm you have the right guy!" Shouted Rory picking off targets that presented themselves to him through the scope of his HK SL8. Cam crouched next to the still body; he reached out and rolled him over. He didn't need to investigate any further. It was him.

"That's confirmed; it's him."

"Al," continued Rory. "There are no other friendlies on site are there?"

"That's right, everyone is now a target."

"We are sure about that?" Asked Rory again.

"Positive." Answered Al.

"George, rip that second tent to pieces." George followed his order without acknowledging. From high up on the ridge the Minimi opened up and began tearing into the canvas of the tent and into the occupants within.

Cam felt for a pulse knowing the result. Now he knew why there had been only two heat signatures in the tent and not three. The body was cold, there was no obvious gun shot wound, he had simply been beaten to death.

"Cam," said Rory standing up still on aim. "Are you OK in there?"

"Yeah," sighed Cam. "We're too late, he's dead."

"Damn it!" Exclaimed Rory as he started towards the area where the remaining enemy were cowering. Hunched over he crept forward using whatever cover was available. Always on aim he swept the area for targets, when one popped out he smoothly slid into cover and fired well-aimed shots eliminating the enemy one at a time.

Cam stood in the tent surrounded by the bodies of the American and the two Somalian pirates. He rubbed his forehead and sighed wondering if they hadn't hesitated would they have been in time. Out of the corner of his eye he saw slight movement from one of the bodies. Using only his peripheral vision he raised his silenced pistol out to the side and fired a muffled shot into the moving body, which fell limp to the floor.

Cam searched the body of the C.I.A agent finding nothing on his person but discovering a holdall style bag near to the body. He unzipped the bag and rummaged round. Inside he found a number of passports all of which had the photo of the dead American agent but all under different names and nationalities. Cam stuffed these into his tactical vest's pocket with a wallet full of various credit and bank cards he also found. He wondered if any of the names in the passport were his real name.

"Area clear," announced Rory through the radio having finished off the last of the hostage takers. Cam apologised silently to the American agent and turned to leave the tent. As he walked past the two guards he fired more shots into the still bodies. Once out of rounds he pressed the magazine release catch and allowed the empty magazine to fall to the floor.

"Fuckers!" He said as he reloaded his pistol with a fresh magazine taken from a pouch on his tac vest. He threw open the tent flap and stepped out into the night air to meet Rory who had returned to the tent area. Cam looked at the other tent to assess any danger that it may still pose. It was decimated; the Minimi had shredded it to pieces along with anyone who was unfortunate to be inside.

"Was it a stray shot?" Asked Rory poking his head inside the tent.

"No."

"So it wasn't us then?"

"No," said Cam. "Looks like they had beaten him to death. It's not a pretty sight in there." Cam holstered his reloaded pistol and retrieved his slung G36.

"Shit. That sucks." Said Rory closing the tent. "We shouldn't leave him but we can't lug a body round with us."

"Yeah, lets get the hell out of here," said Cam.

"Lead the way." Said Rory. Cam broke into a jog away from the wrecked camp site back the way they came.

"Um guys," said Al through their earpieces. "I don't want to add to your problems but there is vehicle movement coming towards Donald and George's position."

"What?" Shouted George. "Christ, must be that missing vehicle."

"Well there's two of them now guys," said Al. "They will be on you in a minute or two, the speed they're going." Cam and Rory stopped running and looked up at the ridgeline.

"What direction Al?" Asked Rory.

"From the north." They shifted their gaze to the north but seeing nothing they burst into a fast sprint towards the path that their vehicle took to provide them with cover from the ridge.

"We'll be with you in a few minutes," panted Cam as they raced to the top of the ridge hardly slowing as they hit the incline.

"Better hurry guys," said George fixing another box of ammo to his Minimi. "I can see dust clouds on the horizon. I think they're pissed at us."

"Just hold on we're on our way," shouted Rory gasping for breath as they ran up the path under the weight of their equipment and weapons.

"Donald mate, take cover and get ready to engage." Donald tucked himself in by the cab of the vehicle near to the satellite dish he had placed on the roof. "No mate, by the engine block," said George pointing towards the front of the vehicle. Donald moved into position resting his MP5 on the bonnet. George lay on his front using the rear wheel as cover. He opened the tripod on the Minimi and took aim in the general area of the approaching dust cloud.

"What's the plan, George?" Asked Donald unsure of when to open fire.

"I'm going to try and stop the vehicles before they get to us. I want you to pick off the targets when they present themselves. OK?"

"OK," replied a nervous Donald. "So you're going to fire first?"

"Yeah, wait for my shot," said George. "Is this your first contact?"

"Yeah, it is."

"Just relax, squeeze the trigger, good aimed shots. Take your time. Here we go." The first vehicle came into view and George opened up with the Minimi sending round after round of 5.56mm into the front grill of the engine. With a grinding crunch and a thick black smoke screen from the engine the vehicle ground to a halt.

"Shit! Can't see a thing!" Said George trying to see through the smoke that obscured the view of the other vehicle that was fast approaching. He could clearly hear doors opening and being slammed shut and the voices of someone barking orders.

George, knowing the enemy was now out in the open, continued to fire, guessing where they would be as they exited the vehicle. In a well-aimed but estimated direction he fired short bursts of automatic fire into the dark smoke.

"Magazine!" Shouted George as he ran dry. He quickly reloaded with a fresh box of 5.56 that he had placed by his side in anticipation of needing more ammo. "Ready!" He shouted to let Donald know he was reloaded. Donald waited, anxiously.

"What's going on guys?" Asked Cam breathing heavily.

"Contact from the north," reported George. "One vehicle so far. Vehicle incapacitated, no enemy seen."

"I can see," said Al over the airwaves. "I have them on thermal."

"What they doing Al? Give us a clue," demanded George.

"Looks like they are regrouping, using the smoke screen as cover. I think these guys know their stuff."

"Stand by Don, stand by," said George waiting for them to show themselves. Donald fidgeted leaning on the bonnet, his heart pounding, adrenaline flowing through his body causing his aim to rise and fall with his chest as he breathed. "Here they come!"

Cam and Rory stopped running and tried to steady their breathing in an attempt to hear what was going on up ahead of them. Cam wiped away the sweat from his forehead and out of his eyes. Rory and Cam exchanged glances as the fire fight raged only just out of sight on the ridge.

"Come on, keep pushing up," wheezed Cam. Their thighs, filled with lactic acid, felt like lead and chests burned as they dragged oxygen into their lungs. They had to keep going, their friends needed them.

"Three round burst Don, conserve your ammo!" George was guiding Donald through his first contact. As they advanced up the hill to the contact they could hear the fire fight grow out of control.

"I'm out!" Screamed Donald.

"Quickly. Sort it, I'm running dry!" Rory and Cam listened; all they could do was move as fast as they could. The weight they carried and the incline of the hill was beating them but they could not slow down. They heard a 9mm open fire again indicating Donald had sorted out his stoppage.

"Magazine!" Now George was out of ammo. There was a lull as he must have been trying to reload. But George was a professional and it only took seconds for him to get back in the fight.

"Can you see them, can you see them?" Said Al.

"Nearly," gasped Rory. "There."

"Magazine!"

"I'm out!" The guys needed help, Rory and Cam somehow found the push to speed up. They were nearly there.

"Come on, come on." George was struggling to reload, bad timing as Donald was out too. "Shit! Here they come!"

"Ready!"

"Fuck! Grenade! Donald duck!" The explosion stopped the two men in their tracks. Cam looked horrified at Rory who could barely hide his amusement at the Donald duck remark. Within an instant they were up and running again.

"George, you OK?" Struggled Cam through his heavy breathing. "Don, you there? Shit Al, can you see anything?" With no answer Cam pushed on and up to the ridge.

* * * * * * *

Donald and George hid behind their vehicle. Donald tried desperately to reload his MP5 still dazed from the near miss from the enemy grenade. George jumped to his feet, ears ringing,

179

hooked the tripod of the Minimi on the side of the vehicle and reopened fire on the enemy. The second vehicle was now in sight; it had emerged through the smoke backing up the approaching enemy fighters. George could see the gun on the rear of the vehicle turn towards their position. The gunner hidden by metal shielding. George tried one last blast with his Minimi at the gunner. The rounds bounced off the armour plating only stopping the gunner for seconds. Soon he was back ready with the 7.62 machine gun and about to open fire on their cover.

George realised the damage the larger calibre gun would cause to their vehicle and dived behind the wheels of their truck. He hoped it would be enough. He gritted his teeth and waited for the impact of the enemy machine gun.

It never happened. The gunner was shot dead with one shot knocking him off the vehicle. One by one the enemy were shot down from their flank, they had not noticed Cam and Rory advance on them, weapons in the aim. Well-placed single fired shots cut down the enemy and silenced their guns. Cam and Rory split, Cam heading over to their own vehicle and Rory continued towards the enemy.

"Don, George. You OK?" Said Cam rounding the side of the truck.

"Yeah," said George rising to his feet and dusting himself off. "Christ that was close."

"Doesn't come much closer," said Cam helping Donald to his feet. The odd shot in the background rang out as Rory finished off the last of the enemy wounded. Cam turned his attention to the satellite dish that had been blown off the roof of the vehicle. "That's not good." He said picking up the dish. "Explains why we lost comms though."

"Yep, don't think we'll be hearing from Al again," said George taking the dish from Cam. He examined the dish assessing if it could still work. It was slightly bent and had a bullet hole in it. He tried to fold it shut but the buckling didn't allow it to pack away.

"Oh, whoops," said Rory returning to the group and spotting the satellite dish. "Is the truck still drivable?"

"Truck looks good," said Cam giving it a good look over. "It didn't take many hits."

"We need to get out of here, and quick." George didn't want to risk running into another convoy of hostage takers. "They might have been able to let someone know what was happening."

"Yeah," agreed Cam. "Lets get the hell out of dodge before any more show up." Cam opened the door and sat himself in the driving seat. The rest followed, George finally getting the front seat from Rory. As Rory climbed into the back he started giggling to himself.

"That was great," he said looking at George.

"What was?" Asked George looking confused at Rory's amusement.

"Donald duck!" He laughed. "Brilliant."

Chapter 23

The sun began to rise over the desert. Adrenaline that had been pumping through the veins of the four combatants started to ebb away. Fatigue settle in like a warm blanket as the sun's aura crested on the horizon.

"Christ! I'm so bloody tired," mumbled Donald. "Can hardly keep my eyes open."

"The excitement is wearing off mate, it's normal," replied Rory. "Get your head down, we're back in it again tonight." They had decided to stay up on the high ground, as it was daytime and get to a point where they could overlook Ataq. From a good vantage point on the high ground they would be able to conduct a good survey of the town before moving in.

"Funny isn't it," said Cam. "People watch movies on TV and think it's easy, don't they?"

"What do you mean?" Said George.

"Well, they see the shootouts and think that's all that's involved. They don't see the lack of sleep, food and how uncomfortable we are before and after. How exhausting it is."

"Yeah, I see what you mean. I guess he's finding out about that now," George said motioning towards Donald who was now sound asleep.

"I feel like we should do something to him." Said Rory desperately searching around for some inspiration of what to do. Behind him, shoved in amongst the other baggage, was an orders kit.

Rory pulled it free from the mess of equipment that had been hurriedly packed into the vehicle and opened it up.

"Yes!" He exclaimed finding a number of coloured marker pens used for drawing up quick battle orders. With these he gently started colouring some big rosy cheeks and a red clown nose on the unconscious Donald. Extra to this, as he wasn't going to wake for anything, he added some purple to his eyelids.

"Doesn't he look lovely?" Said Rory.

"You know what they say," said Cam quietly to George. "Little things please little minds."

* * * * * * *

Midday had come and gone by the time they found a spot to observe the town of Ataq. Donald was still fast asleep so the other three exited the vehicle quietly in a rare show of compassion to their inexperienced colleague.

"Wow!" Said George reaching the edge of the cliff face. "That's one big town."

"That's not how it looks on the maps we were given," said Cam pulling out a map of the area from his trouser's map pocket." "We sure it's the right one?"

"Unfortunately, the sat nav doesn't lie," he said holding up the sat nav. "That's the place."

"Yeah, look," said Rory. "I can see the old airfield on the outskirts of the town over there." He pointed to the northerly edge of the town.

"Well, that's the place then." George slid the sat nav back into its pouch on his tactical vest hidden by his outer overcoat. "Maps of this area are well out of date. We can't trust them."

"That's why we got the U.A.Vs" Said Cam. By this time Donald had realised the car had stopped and he was alone in the vehicle. He wearily got out and went over to where the guys were on ridgeline.

"Well, good morning precious!" Said Rory as he joined them.

"Is that Ataq?" He yawned closing his jacket around him.

"Yep, that's it," said Cam. All four men stood in a line staring at the town lost in their own thoughts. An early evening breeze blew through their hair and clothes refreshing them after the long night cooped up in the truck. Before them the town that they would soon be entering sprawled out in front of them.

The sun was still bright but low in the sky and if they had been there in any other circumstances it would have been a different moment altogether. Rory realising the irony in the situation jokingly reached his hand out towards Cam's. Cam quickly and instinctively pulled his hand away and threw Rory a look of confusion. Rory still looking at the scenery and with a slight smirk on his face continued the search for Cam's hand.

"What the hell you doing?" He shouted at Rory.

"What?" He said turning to face him. "It's a beautiful moment." Cam turned and walked off in the direction of the truck.

"Come on we got work to do before the light fades."

"Great," Rory said running after him. "I'm flying the U.A.V" George and Donald just looked at each other in despair and followed them to the vehicle where they were already unpacking the Unmanned Aerial Vehicle.

The kit consisted of the vehicle itself and two laptops. One of the laptops was for the pilot and had some extra controls attached via a USB port. The other was for controlling the camera that the vehicle carried. To this laptop a simple joystick was plugged in to move the camera and to zoom in on the terrain.

"Are you sure you can fly this thing?" Said George looking at Rory who was sat on top of the vehicle ready with the pilot controls.

"Yep."

"Cause you said you could put the sat phone together," said George in a condescending way.

"I can fly it."

"Because we only have this one and a back up."

"I can fly it," he repeated. The others looked at each other and as Donald shrugged his shoulders the others smiled in an unconvinced manner. Rory saw this and just shook his head and grinned in disbelief at the lack of trust.

Cam, knelt next to the packed U.A.V, started to construct the wings and snap them into position. Once unfolded the aircraft was less than one and a half feet long with a wingspan of two and a half feet. The Wasp Three, Unmanned Aerial Vehicle was as light as a feather; they were designed to be man portable. They could be carried into the battlefield and launched by hand and used to snoop on the enemy.

Cam held the U.A.V in one hand, horizontally to the ground and gave the signal for the engine to start. Rory started the engine remotely from his laptop; the small nose-mounted propeller hummed into action. Cam cocked his arm back ready to launch it.

Rory shouted for the U.A.V to be launched and Cam, with all his might slung it forward at a slight upward angle. The aircraft travelled unaided for a few metres steadily gaining height, until Rory took control. The aircraft went into a sharp climb for a brief second then nosedived to the ground smashing into the floor near to the ridgeline.

"Whoops!" Said Rory on seeing the U.A.V shatter into pieces and spread itself across the ground.

"What the fuck!" Shouted Cam.

"You said you knew what you were doing," screamed George, now showing a hint of anger.

"I do," he said back trying not to laugh; even Rory knew he had to show at least a little remorse for this one. "It's just," he struggled for an excuse. "I thought up was up, when it's not, it's down," even he looked confused at his own explanation. "Err, for up?"

"Well, we only have one more shot at this and you ain't getting another go," said Cam.

"I can do it," he said. "It was an honest mistake. Just stand near the edge next time and I'll have more room for error."

"No, Rory!" Said Cam. "Not room for error. No errors."

"Just throw the bloody thing, I know what went wrong that time." Cam looked at George and Donald who clearly didn't want the responsibility for the second and possibly last flight.

"Fine!" Cam said unloading the final U.A.V. "Just don't mess this one up," he muttered. Rory pretended not to hear him and unnecessarily practised with the controls. When it was ready to go, they repeated the launch process only closer to the edge. As soon as Cam threw it the U.A.V was in clear airspace and flew uneasily away from the group towards Ataq.

"Take us south west, I want to check out the old airfield first," said Cam. "Make sure there's nothing to worry about." Rory carefully steered the U.A.V left. With a bit of a wobble he found the right heading whilst Cam opened up the camera laptop. He turned it on and waited for the toughened screen to boot up.

Entering the frequency of the U.A.V unlocked the camera and gave Cam control of the bird's eye view from the aircraft. He angled the camera down from its default position ahead and twisted the control stick to zoom in. There, in the distance was the old airfield on the north-east side of Ataq.

"Should be abandoned, right?" Asked Donald looking over Cam's shoulder as the airstrip came closer into view.

"Should be," he said. "However, things change round here and we don't always get to hear about it."

"Anything could have shacked up it there in the last few years and we wouldn't know," said George joining Donald on Cam's shoulder.

"Take it further east and do a sweeping turn on the right of the bird." Rory followed Cam's instructions altering the course even more left to skirt round the side of the airfield.

"OK, lets have a good poke about," said Cam moving the camera right keeping the airstrip in sight. He zoomed in on the small radio tower on the north side, taking it as far as it would go. "Steady as you can mate," he said to Rory who tentatively took his hand off the controls allowing the aircraft to guide itself in a semi circular motion round the airstrip.

The radio tower was a one-storey building with nothing but a small antenna on the roof. There was no movement around the building and it looked relatively un-maintained.

"Nothing much to see there," Cam said.

"Could that be the antenna we're looking for?" Said George. "Could that be it?"

"Well that would make this a whole lot easier," said Cam. "I'd rather just get in there than a police station in the centre of town." Cam zoomed out away from the radio building. "But, all we got to go on is what Al's told us. Let's take a look at the tower." He found the aircraft control tower and focused the camera in as close as he could. The level of movement around the tower was much the same as the radio building, very little if anything. "No movement," Cam said if only for Rory's benefit, as he was busy piloting the plane he couldn't see what the others were seeing.

"Cam, do you want another pass?" Shouted Rory feeling confident about his new-found piloting skills.

"Looks dead mate," he said in response. "Leave it on this course, I'll have a quick look at the hanger. The last in the collection of run-down buildings was a corrugated iron hanger. Once Cam had it in view it was clear the airfield hadn't been in operation in quite some time.

"That's enough Rory," Cam said. "I'm happy with that. Move on to the main road into the town."

"Roger that," he said getting a bit too carried away with the controls and nearly causing the aircraft to flip onto it's back.

"Easy, wing commander!" Shouted Cam. "This is our last bird." Rory righted his mistake and flew at the main route into Ataq. The N19 was a decent metalled road taking the main flow of traffic through the centre of town. "Give it an easy left hand turn and take us round the west side of town.

Traffic that time of day was a little more than they would have liked. However, they would be entering the town after dark and the volume should have died down a little by then. Rory flew the bird across the road and Cam used the camera to survey as far north to south along it as he could.

"Normal road movement," he said. "Nothing out of the ordinary." The unmanned aircraft flew onwards over the town like a vulture hunting its prey. Cam focused on the sites that Al had identified as possible extraction points. The disbanded stadium and the open area park. Both sites had the space to get the extraction helicopter in and were also away from buildings, especially the intended target building.

"Both extraction sites look good," Cam said studying them with the bird's eye view camera. "I like the look of the secondary; the stadium looks more in use than we thought."

"What about the airfield?" Asked Donald. "It's deserted." He looked around in turn at the others. "And it has functioning heli pads." George and Cam both nodded to themselves impressed that Donald was thinking tactically.

"Good thinking, shame we can't tell Al," said George.

"We could still try, but we won't know if he gets the transmission or not," said Cam. "Hopefully he's watching via satellite."

"How about if all goes well and we get in and out no problem, we just head to the old airfield well out of the way and wait till they come for us," suggested George. "If he is watching they'll come right at us, if not we can send up a flare." He looked around at the others. "Agreed?" The others all agreed that this was a good plan, safe and simple.

Cam continued with the aerial surveillance of the target and zoomed in on the police building.

"OK, this is the police station," said Cam. "Rory, slow it down a bit."

"What do you mean, slow it down? There ain't no hand brakes up there mate."

"Just throttle back a bit, need time to look at this place. It's one big building." Cam was scanning round the police station, which appeared to be the tallest building in the town. At three storeys high it towered above the other lower flat-roofed buildings.

"I've got in it a good flight path now," said Rory. "How about I just let it circle here?"

"OK, that'll do." Cam zoomed in and out in an attempt to see as much as he could. "Three storeys; normal government-style building." Cam give a running commentary of his findings. "Main central entrance, building extends to either side of the entrance. Large windows, some metal stairs on the exterior. Flat roof with some antennas dotted around it."

"That's got to be it," said George.

"Yeah, must be," continued Cam. "And now we know what the directional antenna looks like it shouldn't be much of a problem to find."

"It's just a busy building," said Donald. "How are we going to get in without being seen?"

"Easy," said Cam.

"How is getting in there," said Donald pointing at the populated police station, "going to be easy!?"

"Chill out kitten," said Rory sensing that Donald was getting nervous at the thought of being caught. "This ain't our first rodeo."

"Cam's like a ghost, quiet as a mouse," added George. "And you got me and him if things go loud," he said pointing at Rory.

"It's when it goes loud that worries me."

"It won't come to that," said Cam, finishing checking out the building and now looking at the approach roads. "See, nothing's happening." The aircraft circled over the police building and the camera allowed them to see everything they needed. The town in general was virtually empty.

There was, however, some movement around the police building, probably this was what Donald was getting concerned about.

Cam trained the camera on the building one last time to have one last count of the guards. Three were counted, armed, but the lack of motivation was obvious. They stood around in one place, around the main entrance. Not a problem as it was the last means of gaining entry that they would use. The guards were more interested in chatting and smoking.

"Wait!" Said Cam. "Damn! Have we been spotted?" One of the guards, for some unknown reason, suddenly looked up. And continued to look up. "Has he seen us?"

"Can't have, how high are we?" George shouted over to Rory.

"We're a good few thousand feet," he replied. "We must be nothing more than a dot to them."

"Do you think he hears it?" Asked Donald.

"Nah, could he?" Cam thought for a second. "Nah, it hardly makes any noise." He zoomed out a little, the other guards seemed not to wonder what he was looking at and continued with their conversation. "We've seen all we need, bring it back." Rory allowed the bird to continue in its trajectory, when it was facing their direction he levelled the wings and started it back to their position.

"Right," said Cam turning off the laptop he had been using. "This is the plan as I see it. Wait till dark, move in, we'll go past the old airfield as we know it's quiet. Down main street to the vicinity of the police station. When nearby, figure out a way in, play it as it goes." He looked around for approval of his plan so far. "Find this antenna on the roof and get out and head to the extraction point. If all goes well it'll be the old airfield, if not the park. OK?" Everyone seemed to be in agreement.

"Full fighting order," said George. "Just in case." He added as they started to hear the whine of U.A.V engine approach from the south.

"What do you reckon?" George said nodding in the direction of the incoming aircraft. "Do you think he can land that thing?"

"We might be surprised," Cam said optimistically. "Then again he might land it like he did the last one."

"We're about to find out, here it comes." The U.A.V wobbled side to side as it grew larger the closer it came, dipping up and down under Rory's control. He now sat open mouthed in deep concentration.

It crossed the ridgeline with its engine speeding up and slowing down in quick succession as Rory tried to keep it under control and bring it down safely. From Cam's point of view it didn't look good from the start and the inevitable happened with the last of their U.A.Vs slamming into the ground and splintering into pieces.

"Yep, thought so," said Cam. Rory slowly closed the laptop he had been using to fly the aircraft and hopped down from the top of the vehicle.

"Sorry. My bad," he said.

"Hope we don't need to use that again." Everyone was looking at Rory as he smiled one of his huge smiles. "Pick that shit up," said Cam pointing to the wreckage. "Get your kit together. We're out of here. And as for your new job as pilot," Cam stared at the smiling Rory. "You're fuckin fired!"

Chapter 24

"I think we need to ditch this vehicle," said George. They had been on the road into Ataq for about twenty minutes and all they had seen pass them was beaten up old pick up trucks. Their new-looking four-by-four with all the mod hons looked well out of place. It had a few bullet holes in it but from a distance you couldn't tell.

They could see the attention their new, all be it, dirty vehicle was attracting. All were hiding beneath shemaghs, which they'd wrapped around their faces to hide their western looks. Outer coats had been draped over tactical vests and grab bags that were packed full of extra ammunition, frag and flash grenades. Split between the group were a few trip wires and claymores.

Cam drove with his head covered by an old beige hooded top with an outer dirty green jacket, his HK G36 rifle lay on his lap. Next to Cam sat George with his sat nav in hand, a long dark jacket hiding his equipment from view.

"That might be a good idea," said Donald sat in the back seat in faded desert camouflage and a green woolly hat. "We're getting a few stares from the locals." Another beat up old car passed with the occupants trying to see who they were.

Rory resisted the urge to hide from the prying eyes that drove past. He knew they looked the part. He had a brown woolly jumper on with some frayed holes in it, dirty khaki trousers and a Chitrali hat. A hat he had picked up in north-western Pakistan. It was a traditional dark flat top hat made of a fleece type material; he pulled it further down his head so only his eyes could be seen between the shemagh and the hat.

"I think he's right," he said gripping onto the pistol grip of his Minimi that he had exchanged back from George. "Where can we get another vehicle?"

"I see some buildings up ahead," said George with the sat nav up to his face. "Possibly a farm of some sort, it's off the beaten track." He looked up from the sat nav. "I think it's worth a try."

"OK, sounds good," said Cam agreeing.

"Next right, maybe hundred and fifty metres." Cam turned into the road and took them away from the main highway. What came into view was indeed a set of farm buildings set among some low stone walls. Cam entered carefully. He saw a vehicle that might blend in better than theirs, an old smashed up, stinking looking pick up.

"Really?" Said Rory.

"Well, maybe it has a radio to listen to." Cam pulled up near to the pick up as a local man and his small son came out of one of the whitewashed houses. George put away the sat nav and Cam turned off the engine and switched out the headlights.

"OK, nice and easy," said Cam, opening the door and stepping out. George and the others followed and the farmer froze when he saw the weaponry. He raised his hand and pushed his son behind him to protect him from the armed men that had just arrived on his property.

"It' OK," he said placing his rifle on the seat in the cab. He put his hands up and tried to look as none threatening as he could. "It's OK," he said again. "Donald, can you see what you can do?"

"See what I can do with what?" Asked Donald.

"Whatever happens, we're leaving with that vehicle," said Cam with no emotion in his voice so that the farmer would still be left not knowing their intentions. Donald walked over slowly to the farmer after he too placed his rifle on the back seat. He knew the farmer would die if he could not convince him to swap vehicles.

Donald began an exchange of words with the farmer who was shocked to hear a western accent talking his own language. The others watched as the two men from completely different backgrounds talked. Donald pointed back to their vehicle and then to the farmers. The farmer nodded and pointed at Donald who didn't seem to understand the comment.

The Yemeni farmer said a few more words that seemed a little more light-hearted. Donald looked over his shoulder at Rory then turned back and started to rub his face. He looked at his fingers and said a few words in Yemeni. The farmer roared with laughter as Donald rubbed furiously at his face.

Once the exchange was completed and the farmer was happy with his nearly new, top of the range vehicle the four men grouped together next to their new ride.

"Who did it?" Said Donald knowing the answer.

"What?" Giggled Rory. "I recon that's what got us the deal. He found it funny."

"It's permanent marker, I can't get it off!"

"It got us the deal, didn't it?" Laughed Rory.

"Enough," said Cam. "Come on, let's get going, time is not on our side with this one."

"What about the kit in our vehicle?" asked George. "Is any of it classified?"

"It's worth nothing to us, but probably a year's salary to him though," said Cam. "Take some fuel, water and rations. Enough to get us into Ataq." They quickly loaded up and got underway, leaving the farmer admiring his new four-by-four. Donald took a back seat next to Rory who still had a smile on his face, happy that his face painting joke had worked out so well.

* * * * * * *

The vehicle they had acquired was allowing them to slip into the town a little more discreetly. The looks had stopped and they started to feel confident about their ability to get to the target building. From then on was dependent on what they would find.

"Hey," said Rory loudly. "Check to see if this radio works." George tried the tuner and some Arab music bleared through the crackly speakers. He tried to tune into another station – more messy, loud music. George, out of curiosity pressed the CD button on the face of the radio. Some recognisable tunes filled the cab.

"Is that Phil Collins?" Asked Rory.

"Yeah," said George surprised. The vehicle fell silent except for the well-known singer and his nineties classic. "Maybe this is just getting into the charts round here," he listen to the song that was playing. "What is a Su Su Sudio anyway?" He said after a short pause.

"No idea," came the response as they moved deeper and deeper into the town. Closer and closer to the police station. The song finished and they started going through Phil Collins repertoire.

"Must be 'the best of' or something," said Rory when the next well-known hit began. "Turn it up, I love this one." Rory started to sing along with the track, out of pitch and adding harmonies that weren't in the song. Soon the others had joined in and the track finished only for them to continue on with the next one. Cam stopped singing when he realised it had gotten too loud in the cab.

"Guys, I'm not sure this is a good idea," he said over the singing. "I don't think many people in this part of the world can sing along to this type of music with perfect English accents."

"You might be right," said George turning down the music. He looked at the sat nav to confirm their location. "We can't be far now, keep going, about a mile or so." The pick up chugged on, blending in to the town's traffic deeper and deeper into the centre to where the police station was.

"I can see the stadium," said George. "Over there on our right." It was lit up; not the right choice for the extraction point. The park was a far better option, the reason they couldn't see the park was because it was blanketed in darkness making it a safer option if they needed to get out. That was if Al would send someone for them. They had tried to send a message with their plan, using the damaged sat phone dish but it was impossible to tell if he received it.

Up ahead, the police station came into view. The height of the building made it instantly recognisable. Also lit up, it looked like a dangerous place to be getting close to in the darkness of the night.

"Looks like more than a police station to me," said Rory looking between the seats at the target. "Shall we think about getting off the main road and making way on foot?" He was right; they were close enough to use side streets and alleyways now. Cam turned right, down the next street, it was less lit up than some of the others and he felt they could use that to their advantage.

"Shit!" Said Cam as soon as he got a look down the street. "Roadblock! God damn it, wasn't there before."

"No," said George. "But it's there now." Cam applied the brakes and slowed to a crawl. The makeshift roadblock was now only about thirty metres ahead, and the guards were starting to take notice of the car. "We look suspicious, we need to make a decision."

"What can you see?" Said Rory trying not to move, his instinct told him to look but he resisted so as not to draw attention.

"Nobody move," said Cam quietly. "Got a roadblock, six, no, seven guards. Long weapons." Two guards now started towards them and Cam stopped the pick up completely.

"They know something's wrong, we need to make a choice." Rory looked backwards through the rear windscreen. "Shall we reverse out of here?"

"No, I don't think this thing's got what it takes for a chase." Cam looked around, his eyes peering through his shemagh-wrapped face. "Shit. George, turn Phil Collins off."

"Do you think Donald can talk us out off this one?"

"Not from the back seat," said Cam. "He's gonna come to me." The guards came closer, growing increasingly more suspicious at the car full of men who were just sat staring out at them. "We're gonna have to do this, aren't we?"

"I'm afraid so," said George. "I don't see any alternative. But the question is do we run for it or go for the target?" Cam thought for a second but the answer was obvious.

"We go for the police station," he said.

"What!" Said Donald. "Are you crazy, lets get the hell out off here."

"Donald!" Said Cam loudly. "This is what we're here for. This is who we are." Cam sighed. "Stay calm and listen to what you're told, there's a lot of experience in this car."

"We're screwed if we don't get back to the stadium." Donald was starting to panic at the thought of another fire fight.

"We're screwed either way!" Cam turned to face Donald. "We need to stay together and work as a team. OK?"

"OK." Agreed Donald warily.

"I just hope Al's watching and will get someone to us in time."

"OK, say when," said George moving his rifle into a position, ready but still out of view.

"Don, follow my lead," said Rory. "Hand on the handle, when these two start we get out and provide cover."

"Get out, into the open?" Questioned Donald.

"Vehicles are bullet magnets; we don't want to be in here when the shooting starts. Be ready." Donald gripped both the door handle and his MP5. Slowly and without too much movement Cam reached down with his left hand and grabbed the door pistol that sits all the time in the side door compartment. The two guards moved into a position that Cam was happy with, they looked on edge now, peering at the people in the vehicle. They had no idea what was about to happen. The amount of firepower that was about to come out of the vehicle would be devastating to anyone unfortunate enough to be in the way.

"Rory, Don, when you exit take out the guys further back, we got these two assholes," said Cam. "And Don, go wide, I need to get out and I don't want shot in the back. Use the darkness and shadows and any other cover you see."

"Got a side street to our rear, it goes left towards the police station," said Rory. "I suggest we split left down there."

"OK, get ready gentlemen," said Cam. "This is it. On your shot George." George flipped the selector lever of his rifle to full automatic with a click.

"Best of luck guys. GO, GO, GO!"

Chapter 25

The windscreen shattered into a million pieces as George fired on full automatic fire through the glass. The noise inside the cab was deafening as the rifle fired over and over again sending round after round through the holes in the glass.

George had turned his rifle on its side and pulled the stock into his chest. The red hot empty cases ejected from the breach, instead of hitting Cam in the face, bounced of the roof and landed in his lap. A few of the spent, burning metal cartridges bounced free and lodged themselves between his neck and shemagh, melting to his skin.

Cam was too busy to feel the pain, blindly firing the door pistol alongside the repeating SL8 fire. The pressure built up in the cab like sound waves pounding out of a stereo speaker, relieved slightly by the rear doors being flung open by the two passengers.

"Push left. Push left!" Shouted Rory instructing Donald to move away from the vehicle. "Cover on!" Now Rory was firing on the roadblock. The Minimi made short work of the other guards. The ones that weren't hit straight out dived for cover from the terrible and accurate fire.

George and Cam soon exhausted the ammo in their weapons, for less than a second they had a view through the windshield at the roadblock. The two guards that had been approaching on their vehicle were nowhere to be seen, cut down by the bullets and glass sent at them.

Cam threw the spent pistol into the centre of the cab and struggled out of the driver's seat dragging the shattered glass that had settled on his lap with him. George moved too, pressing the magazine release catch he detached the empty mag as he went. With ringing in their ears and the smell of cordite in their noses they joined the others outside the vehicle.

Cam and George knelt next to the pick up. Now with loaded weapons prepared whilst moving. George flicked the selector switch back to single fire to provide more accurate fire and also to conserve precious ammunition.

"Cover on!" Shouted George firing into the enemy blockade. Cam too fired well-aimed single shots into the roadblock guards' cover.

"Donald, Rory! Move back. Go!" Shouted Cam struggling to be heard above the four weapons firing.

"Moving!" Came the response from either Donald or Rory he couldn't tell who. They both stood and swivelled on their toes as they ran for cover further down the street. Rory changed magazine as he ran so he would be ready when he stopped, he had spent a lot of ammo from his box mag in this initial exchange. Donald not as well-trained, and without the years it took to build up the muscle memory needed for slick drills, took longer. His hands shook with both fear and adrenaline.

Rory found a broken sidewalk with a concrete block jutting out. He slid into cover behind the low-sided stone block, rolled onto his front and extended the tripod on his Minimi. He saw in his peripheral vision Donald was taking cover behind some metal bins. Knowing this was not sufficient cover from fire he shouted for him to find better. He ducked into a doorway and leaned out from behind a tall brick wall.

"Cover on!" Yelled Rory projecting his voice as far as he could.

"Moving!" Screamed George once he felt the rounds from his cover fly past him into the enemy.

Cam and George now turned back down the street, making ground between them and the roadblock. Changing magazines on the move they tucked the nearly empty ones down their tactical vests, to refill later. They moved past Donald and George closer to the side street they wanted to get to.

"Cover on!"

"Moving!" The process repeated until they found themselves level with the entrance of the alley they had identified from the vehicle. Cam took a good look down the side street. It was narrow, had doors that looked like they entered private dwellings leading off it. Barely lit and with limited cover, it was the best they could find. It was all there was, they had no choice.

"Split left!" He screamed over the firing. "Rory, the alley, Go!" Rory was up and running, he had been waiting for the order. With the weapon skyward in a safe direction, he sprinted passed George who was shooting his rifle at the enemy at the roadblock. The guards kept presenting themselves by peeking up over their cover trying to see what was going on, only to dive back down when the fire team zeroed in on them.

"Last man!" He shouted as he passed George's position. George left it a few second to let Rory get closer to the alley then he too was up and running. Sprinting flat out for the alley that Rory had reached and was now readying himself to provide cover for the rest to get there.

"Last man!" George passed Cam's position. Cam followed George who disappeared into the shadows of the alley. Cam could see Rory lying prone, curled half moon shaped around the wall of the alley firing away with the Minimi.

"Donald, the alley! Move now!" Commanded Cam slapping him on the back to be sure he heard and would follow. All three seeped into the shadows of the alley under cover of the automatic fire of the Minimi under Rory's control.

"Don! Change mags!" Cam shouted. "Be ready they'll be coming for us. Rory! Cease fire!"

* * * * * * *

Somehow three roadblock guards had survived the vicious hail of fire that had come their way and had now plucked up the courage to investigate where the men that had attacked them went. They reached the side street that they had disappeared into, now deafeningly quiet. One brave guard sneaked a look down the alley to find it deserted.

One stepped round the corner entering the alley and another followed close behind. The last man stepped into the shadows AK47 in hand pointing down the alley, like the others that went before him. One whispered something in Yemini to the others that probably only Donald could understand. He didn't know that they would be his last words. The next sound was also the last sound they would hear. Clack, clack. BOOM! The claymore mine exploded scattering hundreds of metal ball bearings through the three guards. They were ripped to pieces by the shrapnel from the curved anti-personnel device.

The dust settled and four figures, guns in the shoulder, emerged from the doorways either side of the alley. The silence after the explosion added to their buzzing ears. Up on aim the figures scanned up and down the alley for movement. They saw nothing; they were at least for now, alone.

"On me!" Said Cam calmly shifting his aim up the alley towards the direction of the police station. "Don, rear cover. If you see anyone I want to know about it. George, Rory, watch these side doorways. Move." They advanced methodically up the alleyway, a pair of eyes and a weapon muzzle covering every direction. With the sounds of battle gone and the ringing of their ears dying down they started to hear the ambient noises of a Middle Eastern town.

Some music from one of the abodes polluted the air, shouts and the voices of panicked civilians, now well aware that something is occurring in their neighbourhood, echoed around the stone walls. A mobile phone rang the old Nokia ring tone as anxious friends and relatives tried to find out what was happening. The smell of fire and unfamiliar cooking wafted around the four men moving tactically towards their objective.

Cam moved smoothly and steadily covering slightly left and right as the alternating doors either side of the alley came into view. One of the wooden doors flew open only a few metres ahead of him. Cam stopped in his tracks, his rifle was already pointed in that direction, whoever was coming through it was about to have a bad day. Below his point of aim he saw movement, he lowered his rifle to see a small boy, he had ran out into the street. Cam hesitated; the boy stopped and stared wide-eyed back at him. He had frozen in terror. Cam lowered his aim, took his left hand off the front pistol grip and moved his extended finger to his lips.

"Ssshhhhhh," he whispered. He gestured with the back of his hand for the boy to go back in the house. The boy turned and ran, back the way he had come, slamming the wooden door nearly off it's hinges.

Cam carried on past the door, waving to the others and pointing at the door with his hand, indicating for them to pay close attention to the door, realising danger could come out of it any moment. He had to keep the team moving towards the target building. Then there it was.

The police station was ahead. Across a road and sat on an angle to where they were at the end of the now cleared alley. Alive with activity, now alerted to the presence of an enemy force in their area. Police, who were armed more like military personnel, spilled out of the station like ants out of an ant hill. Some took cover, some stood around unsure of what was happening.

Cam, who was on point, stopped short of the entrance to the alley. Still in the shadows he observed the police station illuminated by streetlights. The others huddled in the darkness taking cover from view but still keeping an arc of fire down the way they had come. There was confusion on the side of the police, they knew something was happening or had just happened, what and where was unknown to them.

"We can take em!" Said Rory. "We have to keep the momentum going."

"Wait!" Said Cam. "Lets see what they do." He lowered himself behind some boxes and watched the chaos unfold in front of them. Police ran in all directions, none of them seemed to know the direction of threat. For the moment Cam and the team were safe to collect their thoughts and wait for their opportunity.

Out of the building, barking orders, emerged someone of authority. Shouting commands and waving his men in the direction he wanted them to go. He was trying to organise a defence for the police station with what he had available. Nothing more than an ill disciplined but well armed militia. They had to take this guy out of the equation, then maybe they stood a chance of fighting their way through.

"That bastard has to go," whispered Cam. He could not be allowed to get these guys into some sort of order, if he did it would be a lot harder to assault this building. Cam could see George had been thinking the same thing and was taking aim through his magnified scope. Cam knew if he took the shot they would have to go for it then and there. He also knew George wouldn't take the shot without being told to.

"Do it," Cam said. George understood and fired one shot. The officer hit the deck, his organising a defence over. The police stopped and seemed even more confused than ever. Cam had to act. "Now! Go! Rory covering fire!"

Rory stood and leaned on the corner of the wall and opened fire on the mass of police in front of him. As they started to be cut down by the 5.56 automatic rifle the others streamed out of the ally to places of cover. Once in cover they too opened fire on the figures running wildly around in the open.

Rory moved out of the ally whilst the others covered him. Keeping low he threw himself down into some cover and continued the sustained fire on the enemy. Cam moved, changing mags as he went, screaming at Donald to follow him, then George and Rory. A makeshift section attack slowly started to take shape.

"Keep low, Don!" Shouted Cam on their next bound. Donald was presenting himself as too much of a target and Cam was concerned that they would soon be taking incoming fire. Sure enough some random bursts of AK47 fire zoomed over their heads. Then more and more erupted around them, some bursts more accurate than the others. They now had a fight on their hands.

"George, the windows!" Cam had spotted some police that had not left the building and were now returning fire from an elevated position from within. However they were leaning out the windows and not firing from inside the rooms and were an easy target. George lifted his aim and picked them off with his scoped rifle.

"Rory!" Screamed Cam trying to gain his attention. "Cover us, keep their heads down!" Rory intensified his fire, faster but shorter bursts firing on each target, forcing them to stay in cover.

"Don! You're with me!" Cam and Donald sneaked their way round to the right of the defending police cowering behind their cover. "Change mags, Donald!" He said reminding him to refresh his weapon. They kept below the height of the street furniture edging their way to flank the defenders.

"Wait here," Cam said softly motioning with his hand to tell Donald to get on the floor. Donald lowered himself to the deck and crawled forward to where Cam was, crouched behind a car. Donald crawled up to him and waited for the next command. Cam looked down at Donald and with his left hand pointed to his own eyes with his index and middle finger, then to the other side of the vehicle they were hiding behind. Donald looked the way Cam indicated and saw the police hiding from Rory's sustained fire. Pinned down they were now open from the position they had worked their way to.

"On my shots," Cam said softly nodding his head. Donald nodded back and crawled under the car, gaining an even better position to fire from. Cam peeked at the hiding defenders round the front of the car. They were not paying attention to this direction, only to where the shots were coming from. He moved, quickly and smoothly. He sped across the open ground and leapt a low wall that was designed to stop cars from ramming into the police station.

Now Cam was crawling closer to the enemy, covered from view and fire by the vehicle mitigation wall. He could hear the police shouting to one another frantically trying to figure out some way to save themselves. Cam was so close now he could see the front door to the station; it had been left wide-open as the troops piled out into the street. He readied a frag grenade.

He pulled the pin but held the spring lever in place, took a deep breath and released. The lever sprang from the grenade and spun off to the floor. Cam counted, one, two, then lobbed the frag through the open door and braced for the explosion.

Dust and debris bellowed out of the front entrance and shocked the terrified police even further. Cam popped up from behind the wall and opened up into the remainder of the armed police. As he fired, cutting them down he could hear the 9mm MP5 belonging to Donald firing behind him. Between the two of them the last of the police outside the station were cut down.

Cam ran over to the door and, still from the outside, looked into the corridor that led away to the left and right. He could smell the hand grenade; the dust was only just starting to settle after the explosion. He listened for movement. He heard nothing.

"On me!" He yelled. "On me!" Waving his hand and patting the top of his head, signing for his team to come to his position. The others ran for the front door. "Grab yourself an AK!" He shouted. "We might need 'em!" Whilst running, Rory and George swiped up an enemy rifle and slung it on their backs. "Don, find AK mags." Cam said pointing to the bodies of the dead police.

Donald routed around for spare 7.62 magazines stuffing them into his grab bags.

"Get yourself an AK." Said Cam. "And sling it." Donald pulled a rifle from underneath one of the bodies and slung it behind him.

"What's this?" Shouted Donald picking up an AK with an attachment.

"Mine!" Cam shouted back. "Throw it here." Donald threw the strange weapon to Cam who checked its state then slung it. "It's an under-slung grenade launcher. Does he have any grenades for it?" Donald searched the body further as George and Rory arrived at the door.

"What now?" Said George.

"The roof, find the antenna," said Cam. "We'll have to clear our way to the top."

"Then what?" Said Donald handing Cam a satchel full of grenades for the under-slung launcher.

"Don't know," he said looking inside, counting the grenades. "Hopefully we can be extracted from the roof."

"That's if he's watching," said Rory. "He might not even know we're here." Cam attached the satchel to his tac vest and acknowledged the fact that they might be on their own, with a nod.

"Yeah. That's a possibility," he sighed. "But we must get the bearing of this antenna to Al somehow." He looked a George. "How many mags mate?"

"Loads," he said. "One thing these lads weren't short of is ammo."

"Share it out."

"I don't need much I got hours left in this," Rory said, lifting his Minimi.

"OK. Don, you are rear guard. Watch our backs and if anyone appears let 'em have it. We aint got mates out here." Cam shortened the stock on his G36, ready for close quarter battle. "I'm on point, you two know what to do." Rory and George nodded. "Who's got the ball cam?" He asked.

"I have," said George taking the wrist device out of his tac vest and strapping the smartphone-like device to the inside of his left wrist. This way he would be able to look at the screen whilst still up on aim.

"Good, we may need it." Cam looked into the building. The corridor to the right looked more favourable. "We're going right," he said taking in the details of the corridor. "Long corridor, multiple doors either side, some open some closed. On me."

Cam stepped into the building weapon in the shoulder; they were now in the enemies' backyard. George followed then Rory and Donald entered last, watching the rear.

Chapter 26

Stacked up in the corridor, Cam, George, Rory and Donald moved clear of the entrance to the police station. Leaving behind them the bodies of the police under the glowing streetlights of Ataq. There was a ten metre stretch of corridor before the first of the doors leading off into un-cleared rooms. Cam placed the shortened stock of his G36 in the centre of his chest and peered through the red dot sight. This way he could move forward, front on, more accurately.

"Who's got a claymore?" Asked Cam.

"I have," said George.

"Place it; we need to know if anyone follows us," Cam said. "On a trip." The trap would be set off if anyone was following them into the building, killing them and anyone with them. George set the trap and let them know he was ready by tapping Cam on the shoulder. Cam moved on; they would have to clear the rooms as they moved.

"Closed door, right," he said calmly. "Make a split on the door." Cam advanced past the closed door; George and Rory stacked up one on each side and Donald stayed at the back of the team, covering the rear. George nodded at Rory, signalling him to open the door.

Rory tried the handle and pushed the door inward, it swung open easily. George rolled in a grenade after cooking it off so it would go soon after he threw it in. The grenade exploded causing a pressure wave to be pushed out of the doorway into the corridor. George and Rory were in, clearing the room immediately after, checking their corners and ensuring the room was clear.

"Contact front!" Shouted Cam as someone appeared through a door halfway down the corridor. Cam fired two shots hitting the individual and sending him crashing to the floor. "Xray down," said Cam as the two empty cartridges clinked onto the floor.

"Room clear!" Came the shout from within the room once they had it confirmed that the target in the corridor was down.

"Clear ahead," said Cam. When nothing came back from Donald he asked if it was clear behind.

"Yeah, clear behind," he said. The two in the room were waiting for the all clear before exiting the room. When it came they rejoined and stacked up in their original positions. They tapped each other on the shoulder from the rear position to the front to let Cam, who was permanently up on aim, know that they were ready to move.

"On me," said Cam on receiving the taps and he advanced down to the next door. Cam looked constantly through his red dot sight above his 4x telescopic sight. Where the red dot went the bullet would go.

"Closed door left," he said moving the team to the left hand side of he corridor. "Split, same as before."

Boom! In went the door and in went George and Rory.

"Room clear!"

"Clear ahead!"

"Clear behind!"

"On me!"

"Closed door right, split!" They methodically cleared down the corridor until they reached the body Cam had shot. "Stairs," said Cam. "He came down the stairs," he said stepping over the body.

Cam wanted to get to the roof as soon as he could, that meant going up. "Don, get his ammo." Donald checked the dead body and pulled some AK47 mags from his pouches putting them into his grab bag. "OK, all round defence." The four-man fire team took up a formation like a diamond, a gun facing every direction, like a spiky bubble moving up the staircase. Every area was covered as they climbed the stairs. As a new area of landing came into view someone claimed it. Their eyes were everywhere.

The staircase took them to the top floor. On the top landing Cam pointed at Donald and gestured for him to cover the left of what appeared to be a t-junction at the top of the stairs. Cam took the right.

"What do you see Don?"

"Corridor, extending to a dead end," said Donald. "Some doors open, some shut. I don't think this is the way to the roof."

"OK, we go right," said Cam. "We need to get up top. On me!"

"Cam," said Rory. "We are low on grenades. We need to conserve."

"Switch to flashbangs. On me!" Cam led them along the top floor corridor in search of a way to the roof. Arms began to ache from constantly having their weapons up on aim, beads of sweat formed on foreheads and soaked into clothing. "Closed door right, split." Now in a rhythm the team moved swiftly only using less lethal flashbangs to disorientate rather than to kill occupants of rooms.

"Got a body in here!" Shouted Rory from the room they had just entered. "Must be one of the shooters George took out."

"Take his ammo," shouted Cam. Rory searched the body taking his 7.62mm ammunition.

"Room clear!" Called George.

"Clear ahead!" Shouted Cam.

"Clear behind!" Yelled Donald.

"On me!" The men tagged on and tapped to confirm they were ready. Cam moved off to the next door. "Closed door left!" Cam began to transition to the left of the corridor when the door swung open and a police officer, terrified, stumbled out into the corridor. "Contact front!" Screamed Cam aiming his floating red dot sight on the man's chest and fired two well-aimed shots into the centre body mass. The two rounds thudded into the police officer and he was thrown to the floor, lifeless. "Xray down." Cam didn't stop the momentum and continued to the now open door.

"Open door left," Cam said correcting his earlier order. "On me." George closed in on Cam's shoulder and took over the front cover as Cam now concentrated on the open door in front of him. He kept as close to the wall as he could without scraping it and approached the door frame. He stopped before his muzzle crossed the threshold so not to alert any possible occupants that they were there.

"Stop me if you see anything," said Cam quietly as he slowly moved out into the corridor in a semicircular motion still facing into the room. More of the interior came into view as Cam came a full 180 degree on the door frame.

"Don," whispered Rory. "Watch the closed door on the right." Rory was worried about a closed door nearly opposite their position. As he was about to enter the room with Cam, he knew they had to have a gun covering it. Cam was now looking into the room facing back the way he came with George facing front. "On me," he said softly. Rory stepped up and tapped Cam on the shoulder signalling he was ready. And in they went.

"Room clear!" It was empty, the now dead police officer had been the only one in the room.

"Clear ahead!"

"Clear behind!"

"On me!" Called George now front cover. "Closed door opposite, split!" The team went straight to a split position on the door opposite. "Contact front!" George let off a series of shots. "Shit! Missed the little bastard!"

"What do you see?" Cam asked.

"Last door at the end of the corridor. Someone opened it, saw us and ducked back in."

"OK, keep eyes on. Rory, frag this room." Rory opened the door slightly and rolled in a grenade.

"That's our last frag." The explosion slammed the door shut again only to be kicked open by Rory who was in like lightning.

"Room clear!" He said.

"Clear ahead!"

"Clear behind!"

"On me!" Shouted George now leading the team to the last door. The door which had at least one enemy in. "Closed door left! Last door before the corridor bends to the left. Split!" Cam and Rory stacked up on the closed door. George took front cover and Donald the rear.

"George," whispered Cam. "Ball camera." George searched his pouches for the ball camera and handed it back to Cam. The small tennis ball-sized camera had ten or so lenses imbedded in it facing different ways giving it a complete 360 degree view. Linked to George's wrist device it would gave a 3D image of the room once rolled in.

Cam nodded to Rory who was nearest the door handle. He reached for it and turned the knob and opened the door enough for the ball camera to be rolled in. Cam rolled it in bouncing it of the wall allowing it to roll towards the middle of the room.

"Two guys," George said looking at his wrist. "Hiding behind a desk with a bank of computers." He swiped the screen moving the view around. "That's it, easy shots."

"Rory, easy with that thing," Cam said meaning the Minimi. "I want those computers intact." Rory nodded and mouthed one, two and three. He kicked in the door and two shots one from each weapon hit their targets. "Shit!" Screamed Cam upon seeing a grenade roll from under the desk. "Grenade!"

Cam dived for the rolling grenade, desperately trying to see if the pin was still in it. It wasn't. With an automatic response he flicked it with his outstretched hand sending it bouncing into the corridor.

"Grenade!" He shouted horrified at what he had done. "Corridor! Get down!" George ran for the bend in the corridor only a few metres ahead of him. He dived round the bend. Donald had nowhere to go; he made it a couple of steps but not far enough.

BOOM!

Cam rushed to the doorway. He saw only Donald laid on the floor.

"Don!" He screamed. "Don!" Cam got to him and rolled him over onto his back. Donald took a deep breath in. He was cut up badly but alive. He coughed and some blood frothed in the corners of his mouth. "Can you walk?" Asked Cam.

"Yeah," said a dazed Donald. "Yeah." Cam helped him to his feet and assisted him limp to the cleared room.

"Got stairs!" Shouted George from the corner at the end of the corridor. "I think it's the way to the roof." George knelt by the corner using it as cover as he looked back down the rest of the corridor. "Do what you need to, I got you covered."

Cam placed the shrapnel-damaged Donald down against the wall. Rory was already messing with the computers inserting USB sticks that would automatically download all information from them. Cam conducted a secondary survey of Donald's injuries; apart from some superficial wounds he appeared OK.

"I'll be OK, I'll be OK," he said blinking, attempting to clear his head.

"Damn right you will be," laughed Cam, picking up the nearby ball camera, relieved he hadn't killed anyone with his mistake.

"Contact rear!" George fired off a what sounded like a full magazine from his SL8. "Fuck me! Contact rear!" A further few shots rang out. "Magazine!" Rory calmly walked to the door of the computer room leaving the USB to complete it's download. He stuck his Minimi out of the door frame and blindly fired down the corridor.

"Have some of that!" He screamed as he struggled to hold the machine gun steady from such an unusual stance.

"Ready!" Yelled George once he had reloaded his weapon. "Xray down," he said once Rory ceased fire and withdrew his Minimi from the corridor. He walked back over to the computers to find the USB had finished downloading the information. "Contact rear!" George opened fire once more. "Xray down! Come on guys, the roof. The roof."

"Clear!" Shouted Rory. Cam helped Donald to his feet. He was still clearly dazed and confused.

"Coming out!" He said.

"Yeah, clear, come on!" Screamed George. Rory led the way followed by Cam assisting Donald. "Get yourselves up there, I'll stay here. I think there's more of them coming.

"OK, don't be a hero." Said Cam.

"No chance," replied George smirking. "Get up there and find that damn antenna!"

"OK, lets go." They climbed the set of concrete stairs tucked away down the recess they had just came around. At the top of the stairs was a painted wooden door. They could see the early morning light seeping through around the edge. Cam wanted it open but able to close again so Rory started to work on the lock.

"Can you hear that?" Said Rory.

"What?" Replied Cam holding up Donald.

"That, sounds like a chopper."

"Shit you're right, come on lets go!" Cam took a few more steps closer to the wooden door dragging Donald one step at a time.

"Contact Rear!"

Chapter 27

Rory smashed through the wooden door into the dim light of the morning. He advanced out onto the roof-top in the aim, scanning the flat top of the building.

"Clear!" He yelled to Cam who came out onto the roof with Donald. The sound of firing from down below them continued with George finishing off the last of a desperate attempt to stop the intruders. "There!" Pointed Rory. "Heli, coming in from the north."

"Yeah," cheered Cam. "You're gonna be alright Don!" He placed him down next to the low perimeter wall of the roof-top.

"Which one's the antenna?" Shouted Rory. Cam looked around trying to identify an antenna that was similar to the one he had found on the oil-rig.

"That could be it, there." Cam rushed over to a tall metal antenna tower. He jumped up to grab the last rung of the ladder and hauled himself up, fighting against the weight of his equipment. Once fully on the ladder he bounded up to the antenna. "This is definitely it!" He shouted down to Rory who was looking out towards the direction of the approaching helicopter.

"Just take the bloody bearing and get down!" He called back. "This don't look good." Cam was already on the case.

He had pulled out his electronic compass and was taking a bearing.

"Forty degrees!" He screamed, looking down at Rory. "Jesus!" Said Cam at a volume only he could hear. From his heightened position he saw past Rory and Donald. A mass of troops was being formed up and still more poured out of the town's stadium. Cam clambered down at such a speed that he bounced of every rung. He fell the last seven or eight feet to the floor. "Oooff, shit!" He moaned as he hobbled over on impact sore feet. "Have you seen that shit?" Rory had and was just staring lost in his own thoughts.

Out of the stadium flooded a small army. Men, vehicles and weapons. This was where the helicopter was heading to, one of their pre-arranged extraction points. The Chinook made it's distinctive sound as it thundered towards the stadium. Then it started to take incoming fire. It was hit straight away and smoke began spilling out of one of its engines. The large troop carrier turned and started back in the direction it came.

"No!" Screamed Cam. "No!" George appeared at the doorway to the roof and ran over. The others hadn't even noticed the firing stop in the building, they were too wrapped up in what was happening outside.

"What's going on?"

"Well," said Rory. "Our ride out of here has buggered off without us and we have a small army heading our way."

"Oh," he replied. "Is there any bad news?" He laughed nervously.

"We better start preparing a defence." Said Cam. "What's happening down stairs?"

"I think I've killed every police officer in the town," said George shrugging it off as if it was a normal statement. "I got their ammo as well." He opened his jacket and allowed a dozen or so AK mags fall to the floor.

"Good, share 'em out," Cam said. "Get Donald's stash too. Leave him with his 9mm, for personal defence." Cam looked out at the force heading their way in the bright morning sunshine. "We are gonna need all the ammo we can find." Rory went over to Donald's side and crouched down.

"Don mate," he said compassionately. "You still got the sat phone?" Donald nodded and retrieved the sat phone and damaged dish from his grab bags. Cam was walking in small circles taking in every part of the roof-space. On the other side of the roof-top from the doorway that led inside the building, was a space behind a separate low wall. This would give them protection from the direction the enemy would come from and room to fire down in all directions on the advancing troops.

"Behind that wall!" Ordered Cam. "Come on, Don," he said, lifting Donald to his feet. Donald groaned in pain as the adrenaline wore off and the injuries started to come to his attention.

"George, pick at them when you can," shouted Cam, placing Donald down in their safe zone. George joined him in the walled-off area on the west side of the building.

"Cam!" Rory, who had vaulted the wall, wanted Cam's attention. He was looking down the west wall of the building." "Look at this." Rory showed Cam the metal fire-escape stairs that they had seen from the U.A.V. There would be a drop of eight or so feet to the ground, obviously to stop anyone climbing to the roof, but still a route of escape.

"Should we make a run for it?" Suggested Rory. Cam thought for a minute. It was in the direction of the park that was their secondary extraction point. He leaned over to get a better look. To get to the park they would have to make their way through a residential area.

"And run where?" He said sullenly. "We don't know if anyone's coming for us."

"OK, I'm going to try the sat phone." He lifted the battered dish that he had taken from Donald. "Worth a try."

"Yeah," said Cam looking up, reminded that Al might be watching via satellite. "Don mate," he said still looking up. "Do you think you can watch these stairs?" He knew that a point of escape was also a point of entry. "A few shots at anyone thinking about it will give them second thoughts."

"OK," coughed Donald.

"Anyone still got claymores?" Cam shouted to his team as they prepared themselves for battle.

"Yes mate," answered Rory setting up the satellite dish on the wall.

"Lay it ten metres this side of the door. On command wire."

"Just a minute," said Rory struggling to unfold the dish.

"Leave that for now. We need to be sure we stop anyone coming through that door." Rory did as he was told, then he vaulted the wall for a second time heading back to the door through what was going to be their kill zone. He removed the claymore from it's satchel and unfolded its tripod, then placed it on the floor with the curved side towards the door. This would spread the metal ball bearings in a wide arc, wiping out anyone unfortunate to be in the way. He connected the command wire and reeled it out back to the safe zone over the wall. Once on the safe side he connected the other end of the wire to the clacker.

"Claymore ready," he said hanging the clacker from its wire over the wall. "Two clacks and it'll go." He turned his attention back to the satellite dish half unfolded on the wall. "Don't waste it."

Unexpectedly George fired a shot. He was knelt next to the wall with his SL8 steadily leant on the top. He had his telescopic sight to his eye and was preparing to fire again. They were now in range and he was picking his targets.

"We got another claymore downstairs right?" Shouted George remembering they had laid one.

"Yeah on trip," replied Cam watching the enemy advance.

"Should we retrieve it? We don't know what route they will take through the building." Cam watched the troops advance, studying their movements.

"It's good I think," he said thoughtfully. "Look." He motioned with his chin. "They always go round things on the right hand side." He looked at Rory working on the sat phone. "I bet they go right inside the building, straight into the trip."

"Good logic." Rory nodded, finishing the set up just as a burst of AK fire hit the building below the line of the wall. Cam ducked and saw George shift his aim and fire a well-aimed shot. There was no more incoming fire. Rory began sending a distress call which included their location, Donald's injury and also the direction of the antenna. He repeated the message over and over having no idea if Al would ever receive it.

More AK fire hit the building. George was now shooting almost constantly. Donald coughed again, doubling in pain. Blood was now frothing more and more in his mouth. Cam crawled over to him as more fire hit the building.

"Don, you OK?" He said lifting his chin. Donald took a breath in and the pain was evident in his face. Cam could hear a slight gurgling sound as he inhaled and exhaled.

"R.P.G!" Screamed George once again shifting his aim. The whoosh of the rocket propelled grenade flew over their heads disappearing into the distance, probably to explode in the residential area behind them. "He's down," said George taking out the grenadier.

The bursts of AK fire became more frequent some hitting the building some going wild over their heads. One burst came too close causing George to take cover, abandoning his sniping position. The same burst knocked the satellite dish off the wall, landing near Rory.

A second bullet hole had appeared near to the old one shot there in the attack by the Somalian pirates. Rory scooped up the dish and raised it to his face. He looked through the holes, they were an exact fit to his eyes. He looked over at Cam who was watching what was going on. He lowered the dish and Cam saw the grin on his face.

Cam shook his head in disbelief that he was finding the situation funny. Rory tossed the useless satellite dish to one side and crawled over to his side.

"Is he alright?" He asked.

"No," said Cam. "I think it's something like shock lung."

"What the hell's that?"

"It's like drowning in your own blood," Cam looked at Donald who was coughing up more frothy red fluid. "It's basically when a force ruptures lung tissue and blood vessels, blood slowly leaks into the lungs and you drown in your own blood."

"Will he live?"

"It takes a while to die from it. We need to get him to care and soon," Cam said. "What's the chances you got through to Al?"

"Honestly," he said. "I don't think I did." This was one of the rare moments that Rory was serious. It was times like this when Cam knew the shit had hit the fan and they might not get out of this. "What's the plan?" Cam sat side by side with Rory as the enemy fire intensified. He looked over at George who had now abandoned his fire position as it was too dangerous to be there, exposed on the perimeter wall.

Cam sat thinking as the AK fire cracked and thumped over their heads. He took out the ball camera and turned it in his fingers, deep in thought.

"I got an idea," he said. "Rory, George, over by the wall." Cam crawled with them over to the wall that was being hit by the enemy fire. It was far too dangerous to put their heads up over the wall and observe the army heading their way. They had to figure out another way of getting a look.

Cam threw the camera up into the air and watched it slowing down and falling back towards his hands. He caught it, pleased not to have lost it.

"Large column of enemy coming towards us," said George looking at his wrist device, swiping at it and zooming in pinching his fingers on the screen. "Rory take the mass of troops in the centre, left of the two-storey building. I've got the guys trying to sneak round the back of us and Cam send some grenades at those sods advancing on the front door." Everyone studied the screen of the device, identifying their particular targets.

Cam switched to his AK47 with the under-slung launcher and loaded a grenade into the barrel. Once ready he nodded.

"OK, ready. Go!" All three stood up simultaneously and began firing. Rory dumped a massive amount of lead down on the larger group as George picked of the one or two sneaky soldiers who thought they would try for the fire-escape. Cam fired two grenades down on the assault team rushing for the door to the police station, followed by a third. Despite his best efforts they kept coming, numbers outdid fire power.

"They're in guys," he said. "They're in the building." He let rip with his AK; 7.62mm rained down on the stragglers running to the door. BOOM!

"Nice one," said Rory. "Didn't think that hippy shit would work." The enemy soldiers had entered the building and gone right setting off the claymore. Cam and the others fired more rounds down on the soldiers and Cam let off one more grenade round. Then it was their turn. The enemy seemed to fire all at once; AK mixed with R.P.Gs slammed into the side of the building causing the three men to dive for cover.

It was now a waiting game as the soldiers streamed into the building. How long it would take them to ascend the two floors and arrive at the entrance to the roof-space was anyone's guess. They might run the whole way up and be there in seconds or they may be more cautious now they had stumbled into a trip. Cam removed his outer jacket and shemagh. The sun was heating up and he was also anticipating a major fire fight.

Everyone reloaded their weapons. George was still popping up and taking pot shots at the enemy, trying to slow their progress into the building. Cam and Rory peered over the low wall at the door on the other side of the roof. Donald remained where he was; between coughs he checked the fire-escape for movement.

The firing outside the building faded to the odd burst of AK fire, ineffective and didn't concern the guys on the roof. Soon the enemy would be on them. The air was quiet, much quieter now the gunfire had ceased. They listened for movement on the stairs, the other side of the door.

Rory thought he could hear some shuffling. He looked over at Cam who was straining his ears, open-mouthed and eyes squinted. He nodded back and aimed his G36 at the door, mindful of the AK next to him with a grenade up the spout.

"George," he whispered. "The door." George turned his attention from the troops outside and he too took aim on the door.

Chapter 28

The sound of movement echoed in the passageway that led to the door at the top of the stairs. They were there, moving around, shuffling hesitantly up the stone stairway. The three men, only just visible over the wall behind their weapons, could only wait for them to present themselves. Cam grew impatient.

"Fuck this!" He said picking up the AK leaning on the wall next to him. He looked through the launcher sights and pulled the trigger on the bottom of the tube. The grenade round thumped out of the hollow tube and was sent flying in a curved trajectory to the open doorway.

The grenade disappeared into the stairwell and exploded hitting the far wall inside the passage. What was left of the wooden door splintered off onto the roof followed by dust and smoke. Cam loaded the last of his grenades into the tube, sliding it shut as the others laughed.

"That'll slow 'em down," giggled Rory. George had a smile on his face as he shook his head at the unexpected shot. Out of the smoke appeared an enemy soldier AK in hand, followed by another then another. They darted out onto the roof in a suicidal rush for cover. "Or maybe not!" Shouted Rory as he pulled the trigger of his Minimi.

Two soldiers fell to the floor knocked down by the burst of 5.56. One made it to some cover behind one of the concrete air vent covers that dotted the roof-space. The soldier took a look round his cover. George took his shot hitting his target squarely in the face.

The first three were not alone; they were closely followed by many more that seemed to materialise one after the other. The three men desperately defended their roof-space, magazine after magazine fell to the floor. They switched between their original weapons and the captured AK47s, the odd shout of 'Magazine,' to indicate they were reloading and needed time to replenish.

The enemy soldiers climbed over their comrades and slowly gained ground inch by inch, hiding behind the air vents and the bodies of their fallen. One got close enough to throw a hand grenade. He lobbed it over his air vent cover and it dropped amongst the defenders.

"Grenade!" Screamed Cam who was closest. He scooped it up with his fingers and in one smooth motion sent it back to where it came from. It rolled across the roof exploding behind the attackers. It knocked some down only to be replaced by more soldiers.

A second then a third grenade landed in their safe zone. Cam dived left and right like a goalkeeper, flinging them back at their throwers.

"Magazine!" Shouted George and Rory simultaneously. They looked at each other in horror, with Cam diving around the floor there was no one left returning fire. George grabbed the claymore clacker and snapped it twice. The claymore blew spreading an arc of shrapnel that sliced through the enemy. Rory looked up over the wall at the carnage before them. The bodies practically blocked the doorway. Some of the soldiers were only injured or incapacitated and rolled around on the ground crying out in pain.

"How many more of them can there be?" He said. "Cam, George bomb up; I got the doorway," he said attaching another box of ammo to his Minimi. Cam and George sat back against their defensive wall loading individual magazines with spare rounds from bandoliers that were slung around their bodies under their tactical vests. Cam who had fired fewer rounds than George finished first. He slid some mags into his ammo pouches and the rest went back into his grab bags. He spun round and rested his rifle on the top of the wall and waited for it to start again.

"Ready!" He screamed breathlessly. Everyone on their side of the wall was struggling to keep their breath, they heaved up and down as they sucked in the dry dusty air. The smell of battle, all too familiar, filled their nostrils. It was quiet again, the only sound was the moaning of the injured enemy and Donald coughing up blood. The only other sound was George clicking rounds into his magazines, putting the springs under tension, and the distant sound of rotor blades.

"Do you hear that?" Asked Rory. "Rotors."

"Yeah, more than one," Cam said. George stopped and listened.

"Chinook?" He asked.

"More than one engine, so could be," said Cam but thinking that it didn't have the distinctive Chinook sound. Cam had a bad feeling that it was enemy reinforcements or worse, a support helicopter. He didn't verbalise his thoughts. Donald, slumped behind them, was now breathing more rapidly. His lungs gurgled with his own blood, which he was spitting out in disturbing quantities. Cam and the others could do nothing for him; they had to stay on aim.

"Ready!" George joined them, now reloaded. Just as he settled his aim the soldiers began their second wave. Like before, they pushed forward at great sacrifice to their own numbers, but there were many of them and they could afford the losses. With more places to hide, they crawled under cover behind the bodies of the first wave and gained vital ground across the roof.

Their weapons smoked as they overheated. Cam could feel the burning heat of the barrel through the hand guard. He didn't notice the rotor sounds approach from behind until he felt the down-wash of the blades. The next thing he felt was something raining down on him from above. He ducked behind his cover and curled up in a ball.

What Cam thought was enemy fire from above were hot empty cases from a 7.62 machine gun mounted in the doorway of a SH60 Seahawk helicopter. The rounds were not aimed at them, instead they were firing into the enemy who were now dangerously close.

Cam looked over at Rory and George who were also in the foetal position as the cases landed on and around them. George was squirming, picking hot cases out from his collar. Rory knelt up and peeked over the wall, the enemy were either falling or diving back inside the building.

Rory looked around and saw a Viper attack helicopter hovering in the distance, the AH-1Z attack helicopter was waiting for something.

"We need to get off this roof!" He screamed. "He can't get that Seahawk down on here!"

"Secondary extraction!" Shouted Cam over the noise of the blades and firing. "Get to the park!"

"Get Donald down!" Yelled Rory pointing at the fire-escape. "The stairs. Go!" Cam stood up and screamed for everyone to tap on their earpieces, he punctuated this by pointing to his ear. He heard a series of beeps as the earpieces were activated. They would need comms now they were to be separated. Rory turned back to the doorway as the Seahawk veered off left, the fire from above temporarily gone. Cam grabbed Donald to his feet.

"Come on mate!" He said as the limp Donald was hoisted up onto his shoulder. He stepped over the wall onto the metal gangway and started down the steps. The Seahawk lapped the police station with the door gun pointing at the building. Cam glanced at the helicopter as it passed him starting its second lap. He made eye contact with the door gunner, a stocky man in mixed civilian and military clothing, his scraggy beard hiding the features of his face.

"Always nice to see a friendly face," he said between the heavy breathing caused by carrying Donald and his equipment. His thighs were burning when he reached the last stair. "Sorry, Don mate," he said dropping him the last eight feet. Donald crumpled in a heap. Cam jumped down and dragged him by the back of his tac vest to some cover across the road from the police station.

George was already on his way down the fire-escape taking three or four steps at a time. Above, the firing had started again. The distinctive sound of a Minimi being fired in short bursts bounced off the walls of the street, as George took cover behind some street furniture. The Seahawk was getting into position for more support fire when George saw the gunner in the doorway.

"Is that Bull?" He said. Cam heard through his earpiece as George was out of earshot, twenty metres away.

"Yeah," he replied. "Rory, get your ass down here!" There was no reply. Bull opened fire on the roof-top once again. "Rory, can you hear me?" Still no reply. The Seahawk continued to fire and a figure slid low over the wall and landed on the metal staircase. Rory was off the roof and bounding down the stairs, rattling them as he went. The fixings of the fire-escape were not used to having people with this much equipment on bouncing down its stairs.

"Contact!" Shouted George through his mic. "Enemy, left corner of building." George opened fire on the soldiers as they came round the corner of the police building. Cam moved to a position where he to could get some rounds down on the new enemy location. A burst of fire slammed into the bricks above his head.

"Contact right!" Cam announced returning fire on the second of the new threats.

"R.P.G!" George spotted a rocket-propelled grenade being prepared to fire. Before George could react it was away, flying towards the Seahawk. "R.P.G!" Another was launched in the same direction. George was annoyed at himself for letting them get past him.

The first narrowly missed its target, going between the tail rotor and the main rotor blades. The second missed by a long way slamming into the building above Rory's head. The resulting explosion tore the fire-escape from its bolt holds and it started to fall in a concertinaed fashion.

The metal staircase fell down around Rory and collapsed to the ground in a pile of twisted metal. Cam and George could only watch as Rory fell twenty or thirty metres and out of sight behind some vehicles abandoned by the police station.

The soldiers moved in on the area into which Rory had fallen, intensifying their fire at the two others.

"Shit! Man down!" Called George going to stand and, on instinct alone, move towards his fallen colleague. The accurate incoming fire forced him to stop; he took cover and looked for Donald and Cam.

"Cam!" Said George into his mic. "Can you get to him?" Cam fired at the enemy and tried to formulate a plan. He could see Donald gurgling for breath, the enemy moving in all around them and the Seahawk circling overhead.

"Rory!" Screamed Cam hoping the comms might work now he was closer. "Rory, can you hear me?" He looked again at Donald then to the helicopter moving into position over the park. He had to make one of the toughest decisions of his life.

"No. We got to go." He had to clear his head; they were still a very long way from being safe. He grabbed the casualty handle on Donald's tac vest and dragged him to an alleyway that led the way towards the park. George covered them as they moved.

"George! Come to me!" George moved as Cam kept the enemies' heads down.

"Rory, can you hear me?" George had one last try before they would be out of range. But to no avail. Rory was lost. The Viper slewed closer and opened up with its nose-mounted chain gun raking the street with 20 mil rounds. Next it fired off a volley of its Hellfire missiles and rocked the police station, causing half of it to collapse. Cam and George moved down the alleyway, Cam weighted down by Donald.

"We're going in the wrong direction," said Cam breathless. "We need to head more west." The alley was bending the wrong way taking them away from the park.

"Here!" Shouted George from behind. "Through here!" George kicked in the door to a private dwelling and moved inside. Cam turned and doubled back hampered by the weight of Donald on his shoulders. He saw some movement at the entrance to the alley they had just come down. He grabbed for the handle of the AK slung on his back. He slid it forward with his one free hand made harder with Donald in the way. He let rip with the last 7.62 mag he had. His one-handed firing wasn't accurate but it smashed all over the area he intended. He might not have hit anyone but he wanted to ditch the weight of the AK and just needed to use it up. For good measure he fired the last grenade before casting it aside and entering the home of a civilian.

George had passed through the house and was out the back as Cam carried Donald through the living area and food preparation area. The family huddled in the corner of one of the cramped rooms terrified, the children protected by the parents, using themselves as shields.

Out into the open and into the next house, whatever way they needed to go they went, no matter if it meant smashing their way through walls and fences, they would get to the park as the crow flies. Sweat poured down Cam's face and Donald's blood soaked into his clothes, his chest burned from over excursion and his legs wanted to give up.

George led the way and Cam followed, they kicked down doors, ran through ordinary civilians homes and broke through fences. Anything it took to get to the park. Whenever they were outside the Seahawk was overhead seemingly leading the way to safety. Gunfire behind them continued to ring out as the enemies' confusion caused them to fire on each other.

Cam entered another house through a side door that George had opened for him. He was nearly out the other side when Cam was confronted by a group of young adult males. They had hatred in their eyes and makeshift weapons in their hands. They fancied themselves as heroes, imagining the rewards and praise they would get for catching the infidels.

Cam didn't want to kill them; they were only in their teens, but they came at him swinging their clubs. With Donald on his back he wasn't fast enough to bring a weapon up to bear. He went down under a series of blows to the stomach, knocking the wind out of him. A swipe by one of the older ones took his legs out from underneath him and he landed heavily on Donald.

Cam looked up to see one of his assailants raise his club above his head ready to inflict a lethal blow. Cam lifted his right leg and stamped it into the young man's belly. Cam grabbed his Glock pistol that was still in his thigh holster and squeezed the trigger. A 9mm round grazed his knee as it flew along the length of his leg hitting the Yemini civilian in the stomach. He fell backwards no longer a threat.

The three others stopped and stared at their friend, flat on his back holding his stomach and howling in pain. They didn't expect anything to go wrong; they were going to be heroes. Instead they turned and ran. Cam, angry at the attack, fired his Glock from the floor, hitting two in the back, missing the last.

Cam hauled himself to his feet, groaning. He still had a long way to go. He steadied himself by reaching out and leaning on the wall. A man appeared in a traditional thawb and shemagh rapped round his head. He pushed past him and collapsed to his knees next to the young man with the serious stomach wound. He howled in anguish, turned to face Cam and began a torrent of verbal abuse.

Cam presumed the man was the boy's father; his son had a wound he would not survive. The hatred in his eyes burned into Cam. He raised his pistol and took aim at the man who stopped shouting and was now returning the stare. Their eyes locked in a gaze. Cam lowered the pistol. He left the man to watch his son slowly die, the stomach wound would be a painful death.

Donald was lifted once again onto Cam's shoulder, he was now unconscious and Cam should have checked to see if he was even still alive. He was not going to leave him behind for the enemy, so it didn't matter. He left the grieving man and continued after George, pistol still in hand. He came to the rear door of the home; it was closed even though George must have passed through that way.

Cam went to the unhinged side and eased it open slightly with his fingertips. He put his head close to the wall and tried to see down the street. Echoes of gunfire bounced off the walls of the alley making it difficult to know which way it came from. He opened the door further and slid out into the alley. A muzzle of a gun appeared in his face.

Cam raised his pistol but didn't pull the trigger, something was wrong with the picture he saw. The weapon pointing at him was a 5.56 Minimi. Had the enemy taken Rory's rifle? The answer was no. Behind the weapon stood an exhausted-looking Rory. He lowered the barrel of his weapon.

"How the hell did you do that?" Gasped Cam.

"Do what?" Replied Rory. "You OK? You look like shit." Rory started to help Cam with Donald. "Give him to me, we're nearly there. Come on." Rory took Donald and ran off down the alley. The park was in sight and the Seahawk was hovering in a clearing.

"What?" Said George seeing Rory appear with Donald on his shoulder. "How? I thought you were a gonner!"

"Nah," said Rory. "The idiots thought that too and turned their backs on me. Big mistake." Cam emerged from the alley limping on a battered leg. He looked ahead and saw the Seahawk coming down in the clearing. Bull was in the doorway of the helicopter still manning the machine gun. He beckoned furiously.

"Come on!" Shouted Cam running forward. They had only fifty or sixty metres to go. "Come on!" Everyone went for it in one last dash. They were in the clearing, near to the chopper when a single shot rang out, loud and clear. Rory dropped to his knees then fell face first on the park's grass. George turned to see what had happened.

"Man down!" He screamed. "Rory's down!" He ran back to where he and Donald were clumped on the ground. "Cam, help me!" Cam, double backed to assist. George pulled Donald off Rory and looked for signs of life. He was out, shot in the back. The gun in the Seahawk fired on a building in the distance, peppering it with 7.62.

Cam grabbed Donald's tac vest and pulled him across the grass to the waiting helicopter, George carried Rory and threw him into the chopper. Between Cam and George they lifted Donald in along side Rory. Bull was still firing, switching directions with every burst.

Cam and George climbed aboard and the chopper lifted off and its nose dived down giving it forward momentum slewing it over the tree tops. Cam and George lay on the metal floor of the helicopter at Bull's feet that were stepping from one side to another as he sprayed Ataq with lead.

Once free of the city limits and the incoming fire, Bull stopped and knelt down next to Cam and George. The crew chief set to work on the two injured men, patching them with field dressings and putting up fluids.

"Typical bloody Yanks," said Cam to Bull. "Always turning up late like the bloody cavalry." Bull patted him on the shoulder and laughed.

"U.S saving the day again," he bellowed. Cam crawled over to his injured colleagues through the empty cases that littered the floor of the chopper.

"Are they going to be OK?" He pointed at his two friends unconscious on their backs. The medics had placed an airway into Rory's mouth and were busy inserting an endotracheal tube down Donald's throat. Both had cannulas in their arms with bags of fluid dripping saline into their veins.

"They're alive now!" Shouted back the U.S Air Force crew chief. "That's what matters. That was a hell of a job you guys did down there."

Cam sat back against the airframe of the helicopter, tilted his head back and sighed a huge sigh of relief. He then placed his head in his hands.

Chapter 29

Cam and George followed Bull through the narrow corridors of the U.S.S Carl Vinson, one of the U.S Navy's Nimitz class Aircraft carriers. Less than three minutes ago, they had watched their two friends being dragged off the SH60 Seahawk by the ship's medics and rushed to the medical bay. Now they were on their way to be debriefed.

The Carl Vinson had been in the Gulf of Aden in support of the mission to find the missing C.I.A agent. When the Americans' N.S.A satellites had located the group that had taken the agent, Cam and his team had been the only ones able to respond in the time frame available. Al had been more than happy to volunteer his Assets to help; he wanted international recognition to build the program. Now with the attempted rescue of the agent and Bull's involvement, Al's Assets were now stepping more into the international spotlight.

Cam and George walked like zombies, dragging their feet with exhausted leg muscles, their tired eyes only able to focus on Bull's back. They turned corners multiple times into corridors that looked exactly the same as the last ones. The ship's crew got out of the way when they saw them coming, standing with their backs pressed against the grey-painted metal walls.

"Do you know where you're going?" Asked George with what seemed to be the last of his energy.

"Yeah," replied Bull. "I spent some time on the Chuck Wagon, in fact I dropped a very important passenger off the ship not long back." George and Cam did not respond, too tired to realise what Bull had meant.

After the twists and the turns, Bull entered a large control room that looked like it should normally be bustling with activity but now strangely quiet. The control room was dark; there were glass partitions throughout the room with crayon writing scribbled all over them. The yellow and white writing revealed ship and aircraft locations but Cam was too tired to take any notice.

Bull motioned towards some seats by desks covered in paperwork and coffee cups, the two men slumped down into them. Their equipment, still on, dangled off them uncomfortably but they didn't care anymore. George had a look around at the surroundings but Cam stared at the floor. Bull took up a position in the corner of the room; he leaned his shoulder on the wall and crossed his legs.

"Cam, George." A voice, eventually, appeared out of nowhere. They immediately recognised the owner of the voice. "It's Al," said the voice. Cam nodded slightly but still only looked at the floor. "I'm glad you guys are OK, I thought I was going to loose you." Cam and George were too tired to speak back; they just stared at the floor and walls of the control room.

"What you have done is quite incredible," said Al. "Because of your actions we now know the location of the General. And," he continued, "with a little luck we might be able to get some intel from the information that Rory downloaded from the computers in the police station." The mention of Rory's names caused the two men to shuffle on their seats.

"Look, I'm sure they're going to be OK. And that is down to you two; I was watching the whole thing. I saw what you did to get both of them out. If I could put you in for a medal I would." Cam and George stirred at the mention of medals. They hadn't done it for that. They were their colleagues and were not going to be left behind.

"OK guys," said Al on sensing their reaction. "Get some rest, I'll brief Bull. He's with us from here on. He'll give you all you need to know after you sort yourselves out. All we know is we have to react fast, the General will know what happened in Yemen and might be spooked into something stupid. You'll be going in tonight."

"Tonight!" Exclaimed Cam. "That doesn't give us long, Al." Cam and George looked at each other. "If you know where he is now why don't you just send in an airstrike."

"He's still in Iran and you know fine well we can't bomb Iran."

"Why the hell not? You just bombed the shit out of a town in Yemen."

"There's a huge difference in bombing Iran and bombing Yemen," said Al. "Nobody cares what happens in Yemen, whereas Iran will retaliate. We must make this look right or the world will suffer as a result."

Bull left his spot against the wall and walked over to where the two men were sat. He patted them on the shoulders and they stood up wearily. Once on their feet Bull walked them towards the entrance of the control room. Bull could feel the tension in the room. Cam and George were visibly upset, exhaustion interfering with thoughts and emotions.

"I've got a couple of cabins where you can clean up and get your heads down," said Bull leading them out of the control room. "Leave things to me; I'll get everything set. We're off the carrier in six hours, make the most of it." He stopped and looked at the two exhausted men. "This is what we do. Suck it up and get on with it." He turned and led them down more grey corridors to their individual cabins.

* * * * * * *

Bull returned to the control room. He had left Cam and George to get prepared for the next phase. He was concerned; they were close to breaking point. Bull had tried to kick them back into reality, to get them in the right frame of mind but they didn't seem to react.

"Al," said Bull entering the control room. "You still there?"

"I am, Bull. How are they?"

"I'm worried, they are physically exhausted. Have they ever been tested like this before?"

"Yes," said Al. "They are the best I have. I know their capabilities and they can cope. Having said that we have no choice."

"Meaning what?" Bull sat himself down on a swivelling chair and put his feet up on a desk.

"Info coming back from the USB stick that Rory got for us." Al was clearly analysing information in real time as he was speaking. "It could be worse than we thought."

"Give it to me," said Bull opening up a can of soft drink and taking a gulp.

"We have a location, an island off the southern coast of Iran. I've tasked a satellite to get us some pictures but it'll take a little time; I'll have them for you before you deploy." Bull listened, drinking his drink and stroking his beard.

"Still chemical weapons?" Asked Bull. "Not nuclear?"

"Still only chemical, that we're sure of. We have a weapon, a delivery system and a launch platform." Al paused and made some sounds like he was reading and thinking. "Right," he said. "This is what we know: he's been blackmailing surrounding countries for either money or alliance. He sent out people he trusts and got them into positions where they can get to people of power."

"And those are the guys you sent your men to?" Said Bull. "To gain intel and find the directional antennas?"

"Yes, that gave us his location, simple triangulation," said Al. "It appears he is asking for funding from some and military help from others. If he doesn't get what he wants he will attack them with the weaponry he has acquired."

"Military help!" Said Bull. "Help against who?"

"That we're not sure of. Israel maybe or Saudi, they're not best of mates. Whatever his exact goal is, isn't entirely known, but it's hard to work out what this madman wants."

"War, power, the usual," said Bull crushing the can and tossing it into a bin across the room.

"Yeah," sighed Al. "So, the aircraft he supposedly crashed in was a Russian SU 34, loaned from the Russians for a test flight, the same as the ones they are reported to be looking into buying. It went down but there was no wreckage, search or a rescue. The SU 34 is now on the island with the X-55 missiles that were smuggled into Iran. The General was tasked, a few years ago, with adapting chemical weapons for aircraft launch. All about the same time that Saddam Hussein's blister agent went missing and reportedly crossed the border into Iran."

"That's a lot of putting two and two together," said Bull lighting a cigarette.

"Well, it's becoming more factual by the minute," continued Al. "The only thing we're not sure of is what he's going to do with all this stuff."

"Does it matter?" Said Bull blowing smoke rings. "We gonna put a stop to him, right?"

"The U.S.S Ohio is in the Persian Gulf. You have S.E.A.L equipment on that submarine don't you?"

"Oh, yeah," said Bull smiling. "Everything we'll need is on that boat."

"Good, I'll transmit everything I get to the Ohio. Wake up Cam and George in a few hours, get to the Sub and kit yourself up."

"OK," Bull said standing up and stubbing out his cigarette. "I'll be in touch."

* * * * * * *

Cam stood in the cleanest cabin he had ever been in. He was standing looking at himself in the mirror. He now knew why everyone had got out of their way as they had walked past. He was covered in blood, Donald's blood. It had soaked into his clothes and now, mixed with the dirt and sweat; he was black from head to toe.

He couldn't tell if the reason why he was swaying from side to side was because of the motion of the ship or from sheer exhaustion. He unclipped his equipment and tactical vest and let them fall to the floor. He was now starting to feel the cuts and bruises that he had collected from the contact. Not only from the attack by the teenagers but from diving around the roof-top deflecting hand grenades. From sliding into cover on hard ground and bumping into things and not noticing in the heat of battle.

He sunk to the floor and sat hunched up leaning his back on the lower bunk bed. He reached into one of his pockets and pulled out a bundle of documents. He fanned them out in his hand. There were four passports, an American, British, Australian and a Czech Republic. Each had the same photo in it, the dead

C.I.A agent. Was the U.S passport under his real name? 'Caleb Goodman.' He might never know.

Along side each passport was a credit card, one under each name. He knew he was thinking something that he shouldn't. He could use these cards. He could put the money to good use. The families of his fallen colleagues would benefit from the huge funding the C.I.A has. It would mean committing fraud, but the C.I.A's budget was so massive they surely wouldn't notice.

He placed his head in his hands and closed his eyes. Tiredness wrapped around him like a warm blanket. His body was trying to trick him with warmth into falling asleep. He didn't feel like he had full control of his limbs, they kept dropping away from him as parts of him went to sleep. He needed to stay awake, he needed to shower, to eat, drink then he could sleep.

Instead his eyes remained closed, he saw Rory fall from the sniper shot to his back, he saw Donald coughing up blood, he saw the rounds and rockets fly overhead and bounce off walls. He watched it all back in his near-sleeping head and he knew he was pushing his luck. How many more times could he put himself in situations like this and keep getting away with it? These new memories would join the old ones stuck in his head to be replayed over and over.

Finally he succumbed and fell asleep, adrenaline totally faded, he could no longer hold on to the waking world and gave up. He had not had such a sleep for a very long time.

Chapter 30

Cave Complex Xray
Shawal Valley, June 2008

In the darkness of the caves Cam could barely open his eyes. When he tried, the blood stung at his eyeballs. He could not believe he was still breathing, but that was all he could hear at the moment. The world outside his head was nothing more than a blur of hissing and buzzing.

There was movement; the pounding of feet running past where he was laid was all he could feel until the hands started grabbing at his tattered and ripped clothing. They were pulling at him trying to drag him out from under the limp, lifeless bodies that had protected him from the explosion.

There were voices too. What they were saying was impossible for him to say. Were they friendly or not, he couldn't tell. Even the language they were speaking was a mystery to him. Cam let out a scream as he was pulled free, the pain was excruciating. Locating the source of the pain was also difficult; everywhere hurt.

There were more shots fired, he wanted one to hit him, to end it before they got him. Cam's worst nightmare was to be taken alive by these people; he never thought it would be worth it. What he would go through would be hell and with little chance of ever getting away. He had visions of him kneeling in front of a webcam waiting to have his head sawn off live over the internet. He made a choice then to fight to the death or antagonise them so much they would kill him quickly out of anger.

There was another explosion of light; glowing red through Cam's closed, blood-covered eyelids. The hands released their grip and he fell helplessly to the ground. Something landed on his chest knocking the wind out of him. Cam struggled to suck in air when more hands grabbed at him.

"No, no!" Cam managed to get out through desperate attempts to breathe. "No!" He screamed again and again. Cam heard another voice, closer this time, near his face. He felt a hand slap his cheek then grab his shoulder and shake it. The muffled voice continued to shout but Cam couldn't make out any of it. A gloved hand wiped away the blood that was keeping his eyes from opening and allowed him to see.

From down on the ground Cam saw the inverted head of a U.S Ranger shouting at him. More shots filled the room as the Ranger pulled Cam along the ground by the shoulder straps of his equipment. He felt every inch with sharp stabbing pains shooting up his legs and into his back.

Cam tried to reach down his right hand side for his pistol. It should still be there, attached by its lanyard to his leg holster but he had no idea if his arm was even moving. He felt paralysed. Without any warning he was pulled from the cave complex and out into the sunshine. The rays on his face felt good, he knew he was safe.

"Hey man, you are one lucky son of a bitch." Never before had Cam felt so happy to hear an American voice. The voice was only just audible; his hearing was slowly returning.

"Where's everyone else?" Said Cam, barely able to get anything out.

"Where's who man?" Said the strong southern American voice.

"Swanny, the Boss. Where are they?"

"You're the only one, man."

"We have to go back; there are five others in my team. We have to get them out," pleaded Cam.

"Sorry man, you don't understand. They're all gone, you're the only one left." A feeling of dread, of failure washed over Cam. The thought of it was too much; his brain could not process the information given to him by the Ranger. He tried to speak but couldn't. Instead, he passed out.

Cam woke. His eyes were still shut. He didn't want to know where he was. He heard a loud rumbling noise and could feel vibrations underneath his body. He went over everything he knew in his head. They been caught up in an ambush, he had lost everyone in his entire team. He was the sole survivor of Charlie Troop.

He had been rescued by the Ranger support that had followed them into the caves. He had been dragged from the caves and he had been badly messed up. How bad am I? Cam thought. He opened his eyes and tried to lift his head. He strained his stomach muscles and looked down the length of his body. He needed to know if it was all still there.

He was covered in blankets, but as far as he could tell he was in one piece. Exhausted he dropped his head back into the lying position he had started in. He looked up to see two drip-stands, one either side of him slowly dripping fluid into his arms. His eyes were dry and he blinked in an attempt to lubricate them. He could still taste a mixture of blood and cordite in his mouth.

After taking in his surroundings he realised he was in a Hercules transport aircraft, a British one. He was near the front of the aircraft. He arched his back as best he could and took in the rest of the aircraft. There were a few more wounded personnel on board and a medic moving between them checking their condition.

"Well, good afternoon," said the British airman. "It's good to see you're awake."

"What's going on? Where are we going?" Croaked Cam through his dry throat.

"We're on our way back to the UK; we'll be landing in a few hours." Cam looked at the medic. He could see the emblem on his t-shirt visible through the v-neck of his shirt. He was an R.A.F Aeromedic.

"How bad am I?" Cam asked, not sure if he wanted the answer.

"You're bashed up big-style, but after what happened you're lucky to even be here at all. You're going be fine; there shouldn't be any permanent damage."

"What happened to my team?" Again Cam did not want an answer but he had to know.

"They didn't make it. You guys were walking straight into an ambush." Cam didn't say anything; he couldn't. He just stared at the Aeromed.

"Look, you did all you could," the medic put his hand on Cam's shoulder. "There were too many of them. Get some rest, we'll be landing soon."

The hours passed slowly as he waited for the aircraft to land. Cam's mind wandered to the friends he had lost in the caves. Swanny had a young family. They had always struggled to get by on his small Army wage, now it would be even tougher for them. Cam thought about Denise and the two little ones. He vowed that they would not want for anything, even if it meant that he would have to go without.

Chapter 31

"Welcome to the Persian Gulf, gentlemen," said the submarine's second-in-command holding on to his hat under the down-wash of the helicopter. "I'm the XO of the boat and I'll be looking after you whilst you're on board." It wasn't every day that he had been ordered to surface to have three unknown visitors fast rope on to his vessel. He was visibly excited to receive, who he assumed were three special warfare operators on board his boat. This was to be the first live test of the new special warfare delivery systems that had been installed a few years ago, and with the Captain away, he was in command.

His three visitors looked unimpressed by their location since they had been operating in and around the area most of their careers. The XO realised what he had said and quickly ushered them inside the submarine. The interior was clean and bright, a stark contrast from the outside elements and the roar of the helicopter.

"The U.S.S Ohio," said the XO, once everyone was inside the submarine, "is one of eighteen ballistic, nuclear submarines in the U.S fleet. Only four of the eighteen have been converted to allow you guys to be inserted into the battle, underwater." The

XO motioned them to follow him. "If you'd like to follow me I'll explain."

Cam, George and Bull walked behind the officer as he led them towards the rear of the boat. Cam and George, still weary from lack of sleep, had been woken by Bull and boarded a helicopter that had taken them here. After a long flight they had fast-roped down onto the deck and now they were following an overexcited navy officer. Bull, who was a veteran of operations like this kept quiet; he let the officer have his moment.

"We have twenty-four vertical, nuclear missile tubes," he said pointing down the length of the ship. "Two of them have been converted into lockout chambers." He stopped in the corridor and turned to face the three visitors. "A relatively new concept for us, but one we look forward to trying out for real." He pointed to either side of the corridor. Two of the three mysterious visitors nodded and looked in interest at the chamber, not fully understanding what the Naval officer was talking about. Bull who had been involved in the sea trials stood cross-armed hiding his grin under his thick, bushy beard.

"Right," he continued. "Follow me, I'll take you to the briefing room. I believe there's an update for you." He paused before moving off, he appeared to be intrigued by their mission. It was rare for an operation like this to come in and for the boats command structure to be kept in the dark. The briefing room was similar to the control room aboard the Carl Vinson – dark, cluttered and with glass partitions covered in writing. This time though, Cam could make out the boat's location and course: the Persian Gulf, south coast area of Iran. The officer took them over to a map desk in a quieter part of the briefing room.

"This was transmitted to us via secure link half an hour ago." The XO handed Cam a sealed envelope that he had been carrying in an inside pocket of his tunic.

"Thank you mate," said Cam to the naval officer who seemed taken aback to hear a British voice.

"Thank you Sir," said Bull, in his booming New York accent. His respectful interruption drew attention away from Cam, while at the same time hinting that they were to be left alone to open the envelope.

"I'll be right over there," said the XO clearing his throat, "if you need anything at all." He nodded, not needing to finish his sentence. However desperate he was to be involved, he gave them the space they needed and only when he was far enough away did Cam rip open the envelope. He glanced over the documents, handed them to Bull and folded his arms. Bull speed-read the text chewing on his lip.

"OK," he said. "Not much has changed." Bull arranged the map that was on the table by spinning it around to their viewpoint. The map was a naval map of the Iranian coastline, the Persian Gulf and the Gulf of Oman. "Faror island," he said pointing with a pen at a small egg-shaped island off the southern coast.

"That's where he is?" Asked George.

"Yeah," answered Bull. "It's a protected nature reserve; only a handful of inhabitants, mostly government officials."

"And looking at the names," interrupted Cam, "most are sympathetic to our General Pourali and are the ones he has been sending out to do his bribing and whatnot."

"And he's made the island his hideout," said Bull. "Nobody gets to set foot on it for the," Bull made air quotes, "conservation work!"

"What's all this on the satellite photos?" Asked George circling a collection of buildings on the east side of the island.

"That's where he is," confirmed Bull. "Thermal imaging and past photo comparison show construction work over a period of time. Here, look." Bull moved the point of the pen to an area inland of the buildings. "This is a makeshift airfield, cut into the rock and covered over with the most up-to-date camouflage. Virtually impossible to find if you're not really looking for it."

"Impressive," said George leaning in for a closer inspection. "You would never know it's there."

"Exactly," said Bull. "The rest of his compound is hidden with netting. Anti-thermal infrared coating, it's the top of the range stuff. We didn't know they had it. He's getting help from somewhere."

"Are we sure that's where the missiles are?" Asked Cam.

"We can't be sure, but it's a good bet."

"The General, the missiles, the chemical weapons and the missing aircraft all under one camouflage net!" Stated Cam unbelievably. Bull looked back at him and shrugged.

"He was put in charge of converting KH-55 missiles for Iranian SU 24s," said Bull.

"KH-55?" Said George. "I've heard of X-55s."

"Same thing," answered Bull. "We know Iran had a number of these smuggled in, and then they went missing. Along with Saddam's blister agent. Now, we think the General failed to convert the SU 24s and asked Russia for a loan of their new SU 34s for a test flight."

"Pretending to be thinking about buying some off them?" Said Cam.

"Yeah," continued Bull. "It disappeared, supposedly crashed. We know this to be fabricated. SU 34s can launch X-55s, and that gives the missile even greater range."

"So we do have it all in one place?" Said Cam.

"Damn right we do," said Bull. "All the locations you have just been to, to find those directional antennas. They were all his people sent out either to bribe or gain loyalty under duress." Bull moved some paperwork to expose more of the map. "Dubai: rich pickings. Those oil fields we went to: rich pickings." Bull waved his hands at most of Iran's neighbours. "Yemen, probably for manpower for whatever he is planning."

"That Saudi diplomat I was watching in Malta," added Cam.

"And all the antennas point to here?" Said George pointing at the island.

"It all comes together. They used highly directional, encrypted antennas so we couldn't intercept them," said Bull. "Look, the powers that be are concerned that he is either wanting to start a war or take over Iran with some kind of coup. Whatever he's doing he must be stopped. Especially when it comes to weapons of mass destruction."

"What's the plan?" Asked Cam. Bull grinned through his thick beard.

"Your gonna love it," he said smiling. "This sub, like the XO said, has two lockout chambers. They are converted missile tubes. We get into them, flood them and swim out." Cam and George looked at each other and, watched by Bull, gave each other a look of disbelief. Cam had done this once before, but was by no means an expert in this sort of operation. George on the other hand, was trained in underwater insertion but had no experience.

"Don't worry guys," said Bull. "This is what I do. I got all the gear for us. My buddies on board have sorted everything we need."

"OK," said George with a sigh. "We are out of the boat, how do we get to the island?"

"Like I said, this is what I do. Let me get us there. I'll land us here." Bull moved the pen so it rested pointing at the east coast of the island, there was a beach near the collection of buildings. "A small pier where we can pop up unnoticed." He then slid the pen to the hidden airfield. "George, you plant a charge on the missile store, I'll search the buildings for the General and Cam you plant a GPS bomb on the aircraft."

"A GPS bomb?" Asked Cam.

"Yeah, it's set to go off when the aircraft leaves the end of the runway here." Bull thumbed the area where the runway ended. "Just in case the aircraft is set ready to go with some warheads. Just make sure the missile stash doesn't go up before you get the GPS bomb planted. We don't want to give them a warning."

"What if the plane never takes off?" Said George.

"It can be triggered remotely; it'll go when we're making our escape and give us some cover as we get back to the pier and get submerged."

"You're loving this, aren't you?" Said Cam.

"I've wanted to do this for real for a long time," said Bull. "Sir!" He shouted to the XO. "Can we have a minute?" The XO hurried over to the crowded map table, hungry to be part of what was happening. "Sir," said Bull greeting the officer. "Can you let us out here?" The XO studied the map. Bull was indicating an area off the coast of Faror island, a position south-east of the pier.

"No problem," agreed the XO. Bull nodded back and when the XO turned to issue the order to his crew for a course change, he leaned forward on the table with both hands taking his weight. He lifted his right hand and tapped loudly with his index finger three times on the beach near the buildings.

* * * * * * *

The General's evening walk around his island compound was far more hurried than usual. He passed by people he would normally stop and talk to, his odd behaviour attracting attention of his loyal co-conspirators. They all sensed that something had changed, that the moment was close at hand.

They were right, only not by the General's choice. During the day, he had been informed of some developments in Yemen, the place he was recruiting more troops into his private military force. He had been demanding from the Yemeni government manpower, or else face the consequences of his chemical weapons.

The Yemeni government had given into his demands and was gathering soldiers to be transported to Iran for his Quds Force. These soldiers belonged to the Revolutionary Guards but were tasked with exporting Iran's Islamic revolution. It was made up of Iranians but also foreign troops recruited abroad and trained in Iran.

What was worrying the General was that a group of western fighters had attacked and infiltrated the very building his envoy was using to recruit these soldiers. They had then decimated these soldiers. And there had only been four of them. Who were they? And what was their reason for being there?

He paced through his compound past the stockpile of chemical weapons and the SU 34 he had acquired. He ignored everyone as thoughts raced around his mind. Would he have to put his plan into action now before some foreign intelligence service puts a stop to him?

He had an army of ninety Quds Force, a dedicated and well-trained group. Also, he had twenty Takavar Special Forces – commandos trained in every method of combat. He had enough helicopters to get them to their destination; the Chinook helicopters would have to carry a smaller load of thirty troops each to have the capacity for extra fuel to get them to the city of Esfahan.

Esfahan was the choice for the new capital of Iran. Tehran was slowly being downscaled and its infrastructure and defences moved, due to security reasons and the fear of potential damage from earthquakes.

His plan was simple: destroy the government buildings in Tehran with precision bombing, using the SU 34's KAB 500 laser guided bombs. His troops secure Esfahan, the Special Forces taking the new and still unused government buildings and allowing him to seize control of Iran. Once the existing government was out of the way, and he was in power, he would unleash his chemical weapons on selected members of the Arab League that he despised for their comments on Iran. Whether they had paid their ransom or not, he would strike. Iran must control the Arab world.

Now, after the events in Yemen, he was concerned he had come to the attention of the western world that couldn't help but stick their noses into everyone's business. His hand had been forced. Tonight would be the night; the night Iran showed the Arab world that it was their natural leader.

He left the compound and headed across the beach to the small wooden pier that jutted out a few metres into the Persian Gulf. He stood on the wooden planks and listened to the tranquil sound of the waves washing through the stanches. He became aware of footsteps behind him. They came closer, near to the pier. He heard the footsteps stop when the boots touched the wood. He turned to face the person who had disturbed him.

The pilot of the SU 34 stood waiting for his orders. He needn't say anything, the General was aware of what he wanted. All he needed was the nod, the approval to go. The General took in a deep breath, looked up towards the sky then returned his gaze to the pilot. He nodded then returned to the view of the sea.

The footsteps faded as the pilot walked away. The General stood mesmerised by the moonlight shimmering on the waves. The sea was calm.

Chapter 32

The LAR V, the Navy S.E.A.L's closed circuit oxygen re-breather had been used on so many special operations it was second nature for Bull. Cam and George however, had never used one before. The three operators were checking their equipment after entering the lockout chamber and being sealed inside.

"They won't hear or see us coming with these babies," said Bull securing the diving set to his chest. The re-breather would allow no bubbles to float to the surface as opposed to other traditional scuba equipment.

"I'm afraid Rory was our frogman," said Cam checking his equipment. "We're more like enthusiastic amateurs."

"I bloody hate wearing these things!" Complained George pulling at his black wetsuit. For Bull these 5mm wetsuits and rubber diving boots were like a second skin; he had spent so much time in them he hardly noticed they were on.

Cam stood above his full set of equipment and counted off each individual piece in his head, making sure he had everything. Bull's mates had supplied them with a full complement of kit: silenced P226 pistols, diving gear and better satellite communication equipment, small headsets and microphones that would allow them to be in full contact with Al once out of the water and HK

MP7s. This short, 4.6mm rifle carried a 40-round magazine and was capable of penetrating some body armour at two hundred metres.

They each had tactical vests full of extra ammo and had waterproof dry bags attached to their backs that kept their rucksacks dry. Each man had their own vital equipment in these rucksacks. Cam carried the GPS bomb for the aircraft and George had demolition equipment for the X-55 missiles.

They all struggled into their diving gear in the cramped space of the lockout chamber. Cam finished getting ready and sat down on a ledge to take a rest from the weight of the equipment strapped to him. He looked around the inside of the chamber. A metal ladder led towards a circular hatch that was opened by a metal wheel; this hatch would lead out of the submarine.

"Are we ready?" Asked Bull. Cam and George nodded and slid their diving masks over their heads and left them round their necks. "OK!" Shouted Bull giving a thumbs up to a man outside the chamber looking in through a toughened glass window.

A loud clunk rattled around the chamber and water began to pool around their feet and slowly crept up, covering their ankles then their calf muscles. The water was cool and Cam felt it soak into his wetsuit, his body heat would eventually warm up this captured water providing a layer of warm water trapped in the suit.

"OK," said Bull. "It takes about thirteen minutes to fill the chamber and equalise the pressure inside to the pressure outside. These re-breathers are best at depths no deeper than ten metres, so that's what we'll stick to. Once we're out I'll lead the way." He lifted the navigation board to show them. The board was handheld and had a compass, depth gauge and an area for writing notes and bearings. Bull had already scribbled his notes on it using a waterproof pencil that was also attached to the board by a lanyard.

"What do we do when we arrive at the jetty?" Asked George shivering as the water reached his armpits.

"Follow my lead, we'll de-kit under water and emerge weapons ready," said Bull. "Attach the kit to the pier using your karabiners." Those were the last instructions Bull could give as the water reached his shoulders. He spat into his mask and washed it out in the water before putting it in place. Next he inserted the LAR V's mouthpiece into his mouth and began breathing from the re-breather. Cam and George did the same and the water level rose above their heads.

Cam concentrated on breathing slow and steady, conserving his air. He adjusted his mask that wasn't sitting comfortably on his face; water seeped in and sat in the nose of the mask. Cam looked up, pressed the top of the mask against his forehead and blew out hard, through his nose, expelling the water.

The level of the water was now well above head height and about to reach the top of the lockout chamber. The area around them lit up suddenly as a number of bright LED lights turned on. Bull sprung into action. He gestured with both hands for his two diving buddies to stand. He turned, grabbed the metal ladder and, with his feet in his swimming fins, pulled himself up towards the top of the chamber. Cam and George followed, hand over hand until all three were at the wheeled, diving door lock.

They waited, suspended in the clear lit water, holding on to the ladder with one hand they bobbed up and down slightly as they breathed. Bull was holding onto the wheel lock with his left hand and with his right he gave an 'OK' sign to Cam and then to George. They both returned the sign, letting Bull know they were OK and ready. Seconds later the lights went out.

Cam could now see nothing in the new darkness that surrounded him. Until Bull snapped a cylume glow stick that he had attached to the back of his climbing harness. They could now see Bull in the glow of the chemical light as he began to turn the wheel.

Cam could hear the wheel turning, grinding metal on metal, the sound magnified under water. The hatch made a thudding sound as it opened. Bull pushed the circular hatch out into the sea on its hinge and swam out of the submarine and into the open water. Cam followed his fins out of the hatch only to be grabbed by Bull who was holding onto the outer hull. Bull guided Cam's hand down onto the same railing that he was holding and signed for him to hold on. He then did the same to George as he emerged from the chamber.

With the team out of the sub, Bull closed the hatch and locked it by screwing it down. With one more 'OK' sign given and returned, Bull let go of the railing and drifted backwards away from the sub. Once free from the hull he beckoned for the two to follow him. Cam and George released their grip and finned after Bull, who had now turned and was swimming away.

Bull held out in front of him the navigation board. He adjusted their course slightly and continued away from the submarine. He turned to make sure his two colleagues were following him; he passed a signal to tell them to stay close together. They acknowledged with one more 'OK' sign each.

Bull continuously checked their course with the navigation board. As the destination, the jetty, was so small he decided to use intentional error with his navigating. He aimed off slightly more south than he was heading, this way he would know which way to go when he hit the beach and there was no jetty. They would find it if they headed north-east and paralleled the beach.

They stayed less than ten metres from the surface during the dive, Bull leading the way. The water above, shimmered in the moonlight, silver ripples on the calm surface glinted down on the divers as they approached the shoreline. Lines in the sand created by the small waves showed the direction of the beach. Bull turned, putting the shore on his left shoulder, taking a north-easterly heading.

After a short while the jetty's supporting legs came into view, slowly fading in through the moonlit water. Bull tried to keep two or three metres of water above him during the approach but this was not easy as it was very shallow. He reached the legs of the jetty and held on whilst the others did the same.

Bull looked up at the wooden platform above, it looked clear. He started to unclip the re-breather, first the waist strap then the neck strap. Once it was free he attached it to one of the supports. All the time he kept the mouthpiece in place and breathed the recycled air.

He watched the others follow his example, when they were ready he unclipped his MP7 from the side of his body and beckoned his buddies forward. He took one last deep breath in and removed the mouthpiece. The three crawled up the rocks towards the shoreline, holding their breaths, still beneath the waves. Bull took aim up the beach and pointed left and right. Cam took the left arc and George took right. At the same time, all three emerged into the night air, weapons in the aim, covering the entire beach. Once sure they were alone they pulled their diving masks down and left them around their necks.

Alert to any movement on the beach and the tree line ahead, they extracted themselves from the water, slowly and carefully as not to create too much splashing. Bull noticed ahead on the beach, about four metres from the shore, a set of rocks that could provide excellent cover. He moved the three of them over to the rocks and set them down behind the cover.

"Sort yourselves out," he whispered. Bull stayed on aim and covered Cam and George as they set about opening their dry bags and readying their kit. Cam pulled out the radio and asked George to slot it into the pouch on the back of his left shoulder. He then did the same for George, who put on the headphone and mic set.

"Al, Cam. Radio check," Cam whispered.

"You're OK," replied Al. "I have you on the beach, no movement as of yet." Al was watching via satellite and would be able to direct them onto their targets. Cam slung the day sack that contained the GPS bomb on his back and, now ready, took over from Bull on front cover.

George completed his prep soon after and joined Cam leaning over the rocks, covering Bull as he prepared his kit for the assault. When Cam sensed George join him he shifted his aim slightly left, George took over the right hand side of the beach. Widening their arc of cover.

Bull took no time at all to get himself ready. He grabbed the three, now empty, dry bags and put them together, weighing them down with a few rocks.

"What can you see, Al?" Asked Bull ready for action.

"No movement," said Al. ""All that's between you and the compound is a small guard hut. No movement for a while, four or five guards at last count. All still inside." Everyone looked across the beach and identified the guard hut; it was just off the beach in the tree line – a small building with one door and one window on the aspect they could see.

"Got the hut," said Cam, "also two large hangar-type structures, amongst the trees."

"Past the hangars you'll find the buildings, not sure if you can see them from your position."

"No," said Bull.

"OK," continued Al. "They're there. That's where you'll probably find the General."

"He's mine," said Bull. "Let's move." Bull broke cover and moved on the wooden hut bathed in the shadows of the palm trees. Cam and George followed covering left and right, Cam pushed out his MP7 strapped around his body by climbing webbing. He focused through the red dot sight around the left of the hut, Bull and George covered the other areas. Bull pushed forward across the sand.

They reached the tree line and each of them took cover behind a palm tree, the guard hut was ahead. Light spilled out through the open window hatch, lighting up the sand in a semicircle. Bull paused and observed the guard hut. He could see movement inside – figures moving around the interior, casting shadows that flickered across the walls and out onto the forest floor.

Bull broke cover and advanced on the hut; the island's small guard force was inside. Bull wanted to be sure the guards would not cause any problems when they separated on their own individual tasks. They moved forward, crouched, weapons up on aim.

Bull slipped into the shadows of a waving palm tree when he heard voices emanating from the hut. The others followed suit.

"Movement," whispered Bull into his microphone. The door to the hut opened and silhouetted a figure that had his head turned back into the hut, talking to the occupants. The figure left the doorway and pushed the wooden door shut sealing in the flickering light. He walked away from the hut and slung his weapon behind his back.

"I think he's taking a piss," said Bull quietly. Without looking around, the figure moved in close to a tree and started to relieve himself. Bull silently broke cover and moved in on the man. One foot after the other, using his toes to clear the ground ahead of him of twigs that would give away his position.

He was close on the man who, having finished his business, turned unexpectedly. Bull reacted quickly reaching up and grabbing the man by the throat and pushing the barrel of his MP7 into his chest. Three muffled shots later, silenced by the sound suppressor, the man slumped onto Bull. He gripped the dead weight of the man and dragged him out of view and dumped the body into some undergrowth. Bull turned his attention to the hut.

Bull motioned to the hut's entrance on the right, indicating Cam and George to take the door. He moved to the window, which was nothing more than a hole in the wooden structure. Bull crouched under the window and looked over at his two colleagues stacked up on the door. He was about to signal them to enter and take out the occupants when he heard someone approach the open window.

Above him, Bull could see a man lean out of the window. He was looking around, maybe for the other guard who had not come back, or perhaps he had heard something. Bull reached down to his ankle and pulled his diving knife from its sheath. He plunged the knife up into the soft fleshy area under the man's jaw, forcing the blade up through the man's brain. With all the strength he could muster he pulled the man though the window out onto the forest floor.

Bull stood and raised his MP7; the shocked guards hardly had time to react before Bull started shooting. Mechanically and methodically he took out the greatest threats first. Four further guards lay dead in the hut.

"Tango's down," said Bull changing magazines. Bull still used American code words but Cam and George had worked so much with other nations they knew what he meant. George entered the hut to see the carnage that Bull had brought to the island's guard force. He made his way to the window hatch and closed it, bolting it from the inside. He next extinguished the lights and took the key from the inside of the door and locked it from the outside.

Bull pulled the knife from the dean man and after wiping it clean on the body, he replaced it in its holder. Cam and George picked up the body and hid it in the same fashion as the first guard.

"OK, well done," said Al. "I take it that the area is clear?"

"Unless you can see anyone else," said George throwing the key to the hut into the grassy undergrowth.

"No movement anywhere near you," confirmed Al. "All the action must be taking place inside the structures."

"These guys have got some serious kit Al, they don't look like they're messing about. They look like regular troops," said Cam.

"It's possible, Pourali had connections everywhere. Iran can't keep track of all its troops, they don't even know their full numbers for God's sake," said Al. "We need to get a look inside those hangers; they are your next objectives. Move out, I'll update you if I see anything."

"Roger that," said Cam. "Bull you look for the General in the buildings, I'll go with George and check out the hangers."

"OK," he said. "Moving now."

Chapter 33

Moonlight slinked through the waving leaves of the palm trees, shining shards of silvery light onto the forest floor. There was an orange light on the corner of one of the hangers that created some dark shadows along the side of the structure. Even though it seemed the wrong place to be, the shadow would provide some excellent cover as they moved along the building.

The two hangers were built at right angles to one another, the corners of each nearly touched but not quite, allowing a small gap that one person could fit through. Cam approached this gap first. Still hidden in the artificial shadows from the security spotlight above him, he peered around the corners along the front aspect of both hangers.

The one on his left had one half of its sliding doors closed, the door nearest to him, obstructing his view into the hanger. The other had its door wide open, displaying the interior. The runway that had been dug out of the rocks started almost directly outside this particular hanger. Cam could now see the whole tarmac runway leading off into the distance, hidden from view by what looked like amazing camouflage paintwork.

"I've found the aircraft," whispered Cam. "It's in the hanger closest to the original buildings, looks fully functional, armed and ready to go." Cam couldn't see any movement in the aircraft's hanger from his kneeling position in the shadows. The hanger's interior was well lit and as far as he could see, empty of anything but the SU 34.

"What's in the other hanger?" Asked Al.

"Can't see," said Cam. "No movement so far, but I can hear something from inside."

"Cam," said George. "If I was to take a look could you get to a position where you can cover me?"

"Yeah," he replied. "What do you think, Al?" Al pondered for a second as he scanned his bird's eye view.

"Go for it," he said after confirming to himself that there was no movement on either satellite view or thermal view. They had to locate the weapons and they were most probably in this other hanger close to the SU 34 and the runway.

"Moving," said Cam as he broke cover and slipped into the open hanger, disappearing even from the watchful eye of Al. Cam entered the brightly lit hanger, standing out in his black wetsuit against the light walls. He headed, after confirming the hanger was empty, for the tail of the aircraft. The shadow cast by the tail might provide at least some cover from view.

"OK, I'm in. Go." George moved straight away, darting out of the darkness and along the closed portion of the hanger door. Under the cover provided by Cam, he took up a position at the edge of the door. He could now hear the movement that Cam had detected.

"There's definitely at least two people in there," he whispered. "Moving in." He then slipped around the door and entered the second hanger. This one was more crowded with objects and was not so well lit.

Plenty of hiding places presented themselves to him and he used what he could find.

"What have you got George?" Asked Al. He could not reply. He was so close to the enemy that, if he spoke, he would be discovered. George had found the missiles, stacked in the hanger, under a large tarpaulin. Some looked like they had been prepared for fitting to the aircraft. One technician was working within the hanger under the watch of two armed guards. George had snuck in to a distance where if he breathed wrong he would be detected. "Let me know you're OK George," said Al. THUD, THUD. George tapped his microphone twice indicating he was OK.

Cam was the only other person who heard the clicking of the silenced MP7 as George took out the technician and guards; there was nobody else around to hear.

"Three Xrays down," said George. "I have the missiles."

"How many?" Asked Al.

"Not sure, maybe ten or so."

"That sounds about right," said Al.

"Al," interrupted Cam. "What's on this aircraft aren't your X-55s. These look like standard munitions. Maybe guided bombs, they look similar to Paveway."

"So, he's not about to use his chemicals?" Said Al almost asking a question.

"No," said Cam inspecting the aircrafts hard points. "Not from the looks of it."

"Whatever's going on we need to put a stop to it," said Al. "Continue with the plan. Plant your devices and get back to the beach. Bull where are you? I can't see you."

"I'm by the north-west corner of the main building," he said. "Al, there's a lot of movement west of the compound. Can you make out what it is?"

"Negative, the IR shields they seem to have are incredibly effective. What is it you see?"

"Not sure Al," said Bull straining to make out the mix of shadows reflecting through the trees between him and the collection of unknown objects. "Permission to take a closer look?"

"Granted," said Al. "Careful Bull, lets keep this one quiet."

"No problem," said Bull. "Quiet's my middle name." Bull moved off towards the movement, snaking through the trees until he could see what was going on.

"OK Bull, I've got you on screen. What can you see?"

"Damn Al," said Bull taking in the scene ahead of him. "This is bigger than we thought." Bull slinked in behind a palm tree and took a knee. He could see troops up ahead, hurrying around loading equipment into helicopters. All this hidden beneath a large camouflage net suspended three stories high. Three guard towers set in a triangle shape held up the netting, a guard in each tower kept a close eye on what was happening around the area.

"What do you see Bull?" Asked Al anxious for information.

"I got troops," said Bull. "Well-armed troops, at least one hundred. Four Chinook helicopters being readied for something, all guarded by towers under a fuck off huge net. And you can't see any of this?"

"No," said Al sighing. "God damn it, what the hell is going on? I can't see anything under that netting, otherwise we would have spotted this well before now."

"Do you want me in there?"

"Cam, George. How long are you going to need?"

"Done in five," said Cam setting up the GPS bomb on the tail of the aircraft. George was rushing around the missile store setting charges. He was silent, working to the same time frame as Cam.

"Yes, Bull," said Al after mentally analysing the information he had just received. "Move in slow and quiet. Get to a vantage point and wait for the guys to finish in the hangers. Once they are done guide them in where you want them. This must end tonight."

"Copy that," said Bull. He eyed each guard tower, looking for the weak link. One was not paying attention; he was looking down on the action in the helicopter staging area and not looking out. That would be his best vantage point. He moved in, weaving his way to the bottom of the ladder that would take him to the guard platform thirty metres up.

"I've lost you, Bull," said Al as Bull entered the area under the netting. "Keep me updated verbally." Bull spoke softly into his microphone explaining his movements and observations beneath the netting.

"Heading up," he whispered gripping the lower rungs and ascending the ladder. He kept a fixed eye on the top of the ladder as he climbed, ready to swing his MP7 up if needed.

He stopped short of the platform and lifted his weapon, now one-handed he climbed the last few rungs. Peeking over the top of the ladder he saw his target with his back to him leaning right over the railings looking down at the preparations going on below. Bull climbed onto the platform in silence.

He pulled his diving knife from its sheath, the blade stained with dry blood glinted in the silver moonlight as Bull crept up to his prey. When within reach he gripped the man's hair and yanked his head back. He kneed the back of his legs putting him off balance and plunged the knife into the man's throat. He forced the knife out of the front of his throat, slicing clean through the windpipe, then stabbed him in the groin severing the femoral artery. Bull slowed the unfortunate mans fall to the floor of the guard tower, where he squirmed, holding his slashed neck as it gurgled dark red blood.

Bull held the man's head to the floor with the sole of his boot and raised his eyes above the level of the railing. It didn't take long for the squirming to stop, if the ripped out throat hadn't done the job the severed femoral artery would have caused him to bleed out in minutes. Bull looked down on the scene the dead man had been looking at only seconds before. He saw what appeared to be the final stages of some kind of preparation for a possible ground assault. The soldiers looked well-equipped and well-trained. A smaller group of soldiers, who were keeping themselves to themselves, caught his eye. He cursed silently to himself and slid down behind the tower railing. He was going to need help.

"How long you guys gonna be?" He said into his mic looking around the floor space of the tower.

"One minute," came the response.

"Good," Bull said relieved. He spotted in the opposite corner of the tower, near the body of the guard, an R.P.G and a bag of spare grenades for it. "Al, they are prepping for a ground assault of some kind, we ain't got much time."

"OK, Bull," said Al. "Cam, George. I'm going to lead you to where I lost sight of Bull, from there Bull will take over. Listen to his quick battle orders."

"Roger that," said Cam. "George are you done?"

"Yes mate," he said.

"Good, on me." George left the safety of the missile store and headed for the hanger that housed the SU 34. He entered the lit up space and saw Cam who had moved to the other side of the building, ready to leave and be directed to Bull's position.

"Al," said Bull. "I have seen some Iranian Special forces down there."

"What!" Exclaimed Al. "How the hell did he get these kind of resources?"

"There is a group of Takavar Commandos boarding a CH 47." He paused, allowing Al to absorb the information. "They're bad news, Al."

"Are you sure?" He said eventually.

"Oh yeah, I've had run-ins with those bastards before," he said recalling back to when he had last come up against them. His team hadn't come off too well.

"Damn it," said Al. "Cam move out now, head north out of the hanger." Cam tapped George on the shoulder indicating him to move out. He stood and took one step forward and stopped. He stood still and listened.

"Al," he said. "I got voices out there. You see anything?"

"No," said Al. "No, nothing." Cam and George stayed in place like two stone statues, listening. "Yes, two Xrays moving in on you, hide yourselves! Quick!" The two figures had emerged from the netting hiding the edge of the runway and were crossing the open ground closing in on the SU 34 hanger.

Cam and George looked desperately for cover from view but the hanger was sparse and there was nowhere to go. They turned and faced the direction of the incoming voices and brought their weapons up on aim. It was not long before two enemy turned the corner into the hanger. Cam and George opened fire hitting the two with multiple shots. One went straight down but the other pulled a pistol and fired four loud shots as he fell dead to the floor.

Cam and George didn't move. The shots had been loud and bounced around the hanger making the four shots sound like many more. Cam had the awful realisation that things were about to go horribly wrong.

"Were they who I think they were?" Said George.

"Yeah," said Cam. "Al, we have a problem."

"What's going on guys?"

"Um, we just killed the aircrew."

"That ain't your only problem," said Bull. "I think the entire world heard the shots and they are coming to check it out."

"Jesus!" Said Cam. "Al, what do we do?"

"Abandon, get the hell out of there. You too Bull. Back to the beach."

"And how do you want me to do that," said Bull. "I'm surrounded by the little bastards."

"Damn it!" Cursed Al.

"Right!" Said Bull. He grabbed the loaded R.P.G and lifted it above the rail of the tower and let it rip. The rocket propelled grenade whooshed towards one of the Chinooks and slammed into its main rotor engine. He threw the spent R.P.G launcher to one side and swung up his MP7. He fired some silenced 4.6mm rounds at the other guards in the two towers hitting one; the other dived for cover.

"We're going in Al!" Shouted Cam as they rushed passed the two dead pilots and out into the forest.

"No!" Ordered Al. "Get back to the beach!" Cam and George ignored the order and ran off in the direction of the firing. Bull had slung his own MP7 and had grabbed the dead guard's AKM and was now raining 7.62mm down on the Iranians. When the magazine ran dry he ducked down into cover and reloaded it. He also reloaded the R.P.G from the bag of spare rockets.

Incoming fire from the ground was now smashing into the guard tower causing wooden splinters to shower down onto Bull as he prepared himself for the next round. With extreme courage he took up the same firing position as before and let off another rocket taking out another Chinook.

Cam and George moved in with intent of offering some support to Bull so he could make an escape. They could hear AK fire as Bull emptied another magazine into the Iranians. Bull could feel the guard tower losing its structural stability as he reloaded for the third round. He aimed the last R.P.G at another Chinook only to see a trail of white smoke heading for his position. The surviving tower guard had plucked up enough courage to fire one of his own R.P.Gs; this one hit Bull's tower destroying the tower's legs.

"Christ!" Shouted Bull as the tower toppled like a tall tree being felled. "Whoooh!" Cam and George saw the tower come crashing down and from the comms from Bull it was all too obvious what had happened.

"Bull, You OK?" Said Cam stopping in his tracks. "Bull, say something!" The gunfire continued. "Bull!"

"Get back to the beach!" Ordered Al. "Now!" Cam looked at George, gritted his teeth, shook his head and begrudgingly turned and headed back towards the beach. Soon they started taking incoming fire from the Iranians as they fanned out and located their attackers.

Cam and George pepper potted back past the hangers and the small guard hut and dashed across the beach. Under fire they threw themselves behind the row of rocks where they had prepared their kit on the way in. They took up fire positions and returned fire on the advancing enemy soldiers.

Through their earpieces they could now hear Iranian voices. Had Bull been captured? Surely he would have found some way of letting them know. All the signs pointed to the worst possible outcome.

"Do you hear that, Al?" Said Cam between bursts of fire.

"Yes, I'm afraid so," he replied. "Get the hell off that island, we've done enough!"

"George! Get in the water. Kit up!" Shouted Cam changing magazines. George crawled into the water and felt for his re-breather under the surface. He unclipped his fins and started putting them on under covering fire from Cam. As he fitted his re-breather to his front the firing started to die down. Cam had taken out most of the Iranians who were advancing on them. The rest retreated back into the trees.

"Cam," said George now kitted up. "Your turn."

"Wait," he said in response. "Do you hear that?" George listened but all he could hear was gunfire in the background. He shook his head. "That's 4.6mm not 7.62."

"So!"

"That's Bull. It must be. He's removed his silencer to let us know he's still fighting." George joined Cam back on the firing point. Both men listened to the fire fight that they couldn't see.

"Get in the water, get the hell out of there!" Commanded Al.

"He's still out there Al," said Cam.

"You need to get back to the sub, now!" He got no reply; he could still see Cam and George lying prone on the shoreline. They were ignoring him and there was nothing more he could do but watch.

"I know he's there," said Cam. "I can hear him." George agreed silently, there still was hope. There was a lot of fire in the compound for no reason unless he was still alive.

"There!" Cam pointed at a black-clad figure sprinting through the trees making a dash for the beach. It was Bull firing behind him as he ran. "Yeah!" Screamed Cam firing past him into the trees, providing what cover he could. "Al! Blow the missiles, give them bastards something else to think about."

Behind the enemy soldiers erupted a huge explosion, engulfing the hanger that contained the missiles and flattening the surrounding trees. The pressure wave knocked down the enemy combatants providing Bull time to make his escape. Bull raced across the sand arriving at the rocks and dived behind. Cam looked over at Bull who looked as calm as ever. He could see he had no earpiece and microphone, he had lost it in the crash.

"Get in!" Shouted Cam at Bull. "Kit up." Bull rolled into the water and began to don his diving equipment. Cam fired burst after burst, three rounds at a time. With all the noise of battle he didn't hear the whine of the jet engine start up.

"Bloody hell!" Shouted Al. "The SU 34, it's taxiing." The aircraft was pulling out of the hangar and rolling out onto the runway. The aircraft spun on the pan and the engines roared, accelerating it down the runway until it emerged out from under the covering net and lifted off the ground. Its undercarriage raised up into its belly and it banked to the right.

The explosion shook the island as the jet turned into a fireball and crashed down into the Persian Gulf.

"Fuck Yeah!" Shouted Bull struggling into his re-breather. Cam turned his attention back to the enemy soldiers in the tree line; more had come now, they had chased Bull to the beach. The incoming fire started to intensify once again.

"Get in the fucking water!" Shouted Bull. "Both of you!" Bull had his full kit in place and was ordering them off the beach. He reached up and grabbed the edge of the jetty's floorboards and with one arm, hauled himself out of the water. His MP7 in his free hand, he laid down covering fire as Cam and George slid into the sea.

Once he had run dry he dropped his MP7 into the water and let himself fall with a splash back into the sea. Cam had only managed to unhook his equipment but not put it on when he was grabbed by Bull and pulled beneath the waves. He held his breath and fumbled for the re-breather's mouthpiece. He located it, put it in place and blew out hard to clear it of the salty water.

Cam held onto his re-breather for dear life, as he was pulled deeper under the waves away from the incoming rounds. He could see nothing through his clenched eyes; he had to trust Bull to drag him back to the sub.

Chapter 34

Cam drove his rental car north on the M11 towards the A1 that would take him all the way home to Edinburgh. It was going to be a long drive, especially after everything he had been through in the last few weeks. Only two days ago he had been airlifted off a U.S submarine in the Persian Gulf and flown out of the area along with George and Bull.

Now he was on home soil once again, the sky was grey and the air had a crisp bite to it. He drove slightly over the speed limit in a hope of making good time back up north. He weaved in and out of traffic as he overtook the commuters.

He and George had left Bull in the airport; he was flying home back to the States. They had said goodbye at the car hire desk, then, he and George left through the glass doors and they too went their separate ways. He didn't know where George was going home to, it wasn't something they had ever discussed. George was one of Al's Assets but for what part of the country would remain a mystery. As Cam's mind wandered away from the thought of the long drive ahead of him, he pondered if he would ever work with them again. He had worked alone for so long, he had forgotten how it was to be part of a team, to exchange banter. He realised he missed it.

Al had contacted them shortly before they went their separate ways. He wanted to fill them in on what had happened on the island after they had extracted. MI6 sources in Iran had reported that the government had taken control of the island. Pourali had been in the aircraft when it was destroyed by the GPS bomb as it took off. Tons of blister agent had apparently been found in underground bunkers beneath the other buildings. However, that had since disappeared. Pourali was dead and his private army destroyed or in Iranian hands. Mission accomplished, Al was happy. Cam had wanted to ask about Rory and Donald but was afraid of what he would hear. He decided to wait for Al to get back in touch with him. He had things he needed to do. The passports and credit cards that he had taken from the C.I.A agent in Yemen were about to be put into use. He had to get home to where his work had allowed him to make contacts in the underworld. These acquaintances could alter the passports and hack into the accounts the credit cards belonged to. The C.I.A had a huge budget, surely they wouldn't notice some of their wealth disappear.

He thought about his two companions; Bull had earned his respect; the man never looked stressed or put out, it was as if the man was completely oblivious of the danger. He didn't seem to posses that part of the brain that processed fear. And George, he always got away injury-free. He was the sort of guy that would be put through the worst situations imaginable and would always walk away without a scratch. Cam was not that guy, he was used to being knocked about, if something was going to happen it would happen to him.

He stretched his legs as far as they would go under the dashboard of the car. He still ached from the action over the last few days. He was bruised and cut all over his body. Muscles were starting to cramp up and would spasm if he moved or sat the wrong way. The smell of scuba gear and salty sea was still in his nose and he was still digging grains of sand out of his ears.

This was meant to be an easy assignment, a holiday almost. Instead it had turned out to be one of the biggest operations he had ever been involved in, rivalling the caves back in 2008. At least he made it out in one piece this time, unlike the other guys from Charlie Troop. He was about to make it better in the only way he could, but first he needed to defraud the C.I.A.

* * * * * * *

It didn't take long for George to get home, although getting through the centre of London was never easy, he made good time. George jogged across the road outside Big Ben to the Tesco on Bridge Street. His apartment was above on one of the upper floors. Having left his car in the secure parking under Big Ben, reserved for politicians and government workers, he bought a sandwich and a can of coke before heading up to his apartment.

He locked his door behind him and slid the chain into it's housing. His place looked the same as it always had; he recalled the time when he got it. It was one of the first assignments that Al had detailed to him. He walked over to the window that overlooked the tower and in the distance to the right, St Margaret's Church. Between his flat and the church was Parliament Square, where the target of that assignment was protesting against the war in Iraq and Afghanistan.

He had spent quite some time sat at this window with that guy under surveillance, watching and reporting his every move, every visitor. He wondered how many innocent people had been checked out by the security services just for stopping and chatting about what he was protesting about.

"Bloody tree-hugging hippies." He laughed at the dwindling collection of protesters lounging around. Walking into the kitchen area he could hardly believe that he had been able to convince Al to keep the place on after the assignment finished. He had now lived there for years and had been the main Asset for London. A role that had kept him very busy.

George dropped the sandwich and can on the kitchen counter and opened the cupboard next to the cooker extractor fan. Inside were the apartment's heating controls. He flicked the central heating and hot water tank on and closed the cupboard.

The apartment had been empty for a good few weeks now and a layer of dust had settled. The radiators started to heat up and burned the dust, giving off that empty flat smell. He walked into the bedroom and sat down on the end of the bed. His double-glazed U.P.V.C windows kept out the noise of tourists and red double-decker buses in the street. The only sound was a ticking clock that he had on his bedside cabinet; it helped him sleep.

Al had told him to go home and rest up, to take a few days for himself. George didn't like having nothing to do; he had been constantly on the go for years and that was how he liked it. He didn't want time to think, he needed his mind to be kept active, a distraction from the mess his life had been before Al found him.

The clock ticked as the silent seconds past, he sighed and stood up. He opened the top drawer of his chest of drawers and moved the folded t-shirts to one side. Under the clothes was an upturned photo frame, he picked it up after a short pause. The hesitation was to be sure he wanted to put himself through the train of memories that would follow.

He spun the frame round and stared at the photo. It was the only one he had, the only picture of his wife and son. He would be much older now, five years old in the picture, now he would be a teenager. Probably raising hell if he was anything like his father.

After another sigh he replaced the photo frame back as he found it and covered it up with the t-shirts. There it would remain until the next time. He looked up from the chest of drawers and saw himself in the mirror. He looked tired, he wondered if she would even recognise him now.

He turned his face slightly to each side and sighed for a third time. He looked much older now, she was probably still as young and as beautiful as ever. After she had been forced to leave, she would have had a stress-free life, as a witness she had been given everything she would have needed. With a new identity, money and, above all, a safe life, she had to leave. All he could offer was danger. She had nearly been killed when she got mixed up in an attempt on his life. That was no way for her and his boy to live. They had to go.

George opened the drawer in his bedside cabinet and picked up one of his many mobile phones. He turned it on and waited for the messages to pile up. The phone buzzed and bleeped as the messages and missed calls registered. He began to read the messages and a smile appeared on his face. Jokes about news stories and drunken text messages left by his friends made him laugh out loud.

He phoned one of the drunken idiots.

"Dean mate," said George smiling. "Where are you? Yeah I'm back. Where are you?" George listened nodding, they were where they always were: The Westminster Arms, on the other side of Parliament Square. "Sweet, I'll be there in a minute."

George put the phone in his pocket alongside his Asset phone and grabbed a jacket and swung it on. He picked up his sandwich and left his flat heading for the pub. After wolfing down the sandwich he pushed open the doors and entered the pub. As soon as he was inside his three mates cheered announcing their location in the pub.

"George!" Shouted Matt. "Where the hell have you been?" As far as they were concerned he was a mobile phone engineer and was constantly sent all over the world repairing systems.

"Hey guys," said George. These people were his escape, the hours he spent drinking and chatting with them allowed him to forget and live a normal life. If only for a few hours at a time.

"So?" Asked Pete. "Where they send you this time?"

"Some shit hole in the desert."

"How was it?" Asked Dean.

"Hot and dusty," said George scanning the round table his three friends were sat around. "You guys look a little dry there," he pointed at the nearly empty glasses. "Same again?"

"Good to have you back George." Smiled his mates.

* * * * * * *

Sunderland, Swanny's home town. Cam had been home, seen his contacts in Edinburgh's more dodgy areas and had managed to get the passports and cards adapted. He now had passports with his picture in under the name of Caleb Goodman; he was now a Czech, Australian and U.S citizen. With the documents altered he was now a very wealthy man and about to make someone else wealthy too.

He stood nervously at the front door. He had rung the bell with his trembling finger and was waiting for the door to open. Eventually it did. Denise looked truly shocked to see who the visitor was and Cam waited for her reaction.

"Oh my God, Cam!" She gasped smiling through the look of surprise. "What! I... Sorry!" She said placing her hand on her forehead. "I mean how have you been?"

"Oh, you know. Not too bad," he replied.

"Wow," she said regaining her composure. "How long has it been?"

"A few years," he said. "Six, seven maybe." He knew fine well how long it had been. Before the 2008 deployment to the caves was the last time they had seen each other. He didn't want to mention it as he had no idea what her reaction would be.

"Christ," she said. "We're getting old aren't we? You look tired, are you alright?"

"I'm not sleeping too well these days."

"Oh," she said with a sadder tone. "Yeah, I think I understand. Do you want to come in?" She stepped to one side and gestured him into her house. Inside he could hear the noise of kids arguing. He tried to calculate the age of her kids now, her oldest must be twelve or thirteen.

"Um, no, I'm OK out here," he said. "I've actually just stopped by to give you something." He held out an envelope.

"Oh, what is it?" She asked taking the sealed white envelope.

"Nothing much, just open when I'm gone. OK."

"Yeah, sure." She took some time to look at him then smiled a thin smile. "Cam, it's been you hasn't it?" Cam didn't react to the question. "The money I mean. Just appearing in my bank every so often, that was you right?"

"Just look after yourself, Denise," Cam said softly taking a step back from the door, "and wait a bit before you open that." Cam turned and walked a few paces down the garden path.

"Cam wait!" She shouted after him. Cam turned to face her. "How did he die?" Caught completely off guard he looked at the ground, taken aback by the question.

"I honestly," he sighed. "I honestly don't know." He flicked his eyes up to her face only for a second then turned and walked away. He heard the door close and without looking back he rushed across the road and tucked himself round the corner of the last house on the street.

He waited, checking the door to Denise's house. Only seconds after slipping round the corner, her front door flew open and Denise stepped out, open envelope in hand. She frantically looked around but he was nowhere to be seen. Cam smiled, something he hadn't done for a while.

He leaned with his back against the wall out of sight of Denise's house. He snorted a silent laugh through his nose and thought about what she would be able to do with all that money. She wouldn't have to worry about anything ever again. Now he had to think what he would do with his share. He had a few ideas.

He felt his phone ring in his trouser pocket. His heart began beating faster as he pulled it out and looked at the screen. It was Al. His thumb hovered over the answer button.

"Cam, it's Al."

"I know," he said. "For the last time Al, your name appears on the screen. For God's sake!"

"OK, OK." He said. "Cam, huge developments over here. The Yanks want in on the Asset program. So do most other countries, funding has gone through the roof." Al continued to explain all the changes that were about to take place, and it was big. "But," he said. "There's some bad news Cam."

"What is it?" Said Cam not sure if he wanted to know. He had been dreading this phone call. He really didn't want to hear what Al was about to say.

"I'm so sorry, Cam." Said Al.

"Just tell me," he said. Al explained and Cam held the phone so close to his ear it started to hurt. What he heard was so unexpected he lowered the phone in his hand to the side of his leg. His other hand ran it's finger through his hair. "Shit!"

Bull stood outside his house in Virginia Beach, after all he wasn't allowed to smoke inside. He looked at his home, almost picture perfect in the afternoon sun. He dragged on his cigarette knowing that they were not expecting him home this soon. The deployment had meant to last at least another month but due to getting mixed up with Al and the Assets it had been cut short.

The front door opened and his wife cautiously stepped out staring in disbelief at what she was seeing. They had known each other since school back in Queens and had married within a few years of leaving high school. She was his partner and had supported him through everything he had done, even though it must have been hard for her at times.

"Dwayne," she said softly. "Is that you?"

"Yeah baby it's me," he said flicking the cigarette out and crossing the road.

"Dwayne, oh my God. What are you doing here? Are you back early?" She said throwing her arms around him.

"Yeah Trace, it's over for now," he said returning the hug. "How my girls been?

"We've been OK, just waiting for you," said Tracy stepping back to the threshold of the door. "Molly," she shouted into the house. "Look who's home." After a few seconds a little girl appeared in the doorway then ran at her dad.

"Hey baby girl," said Bull catching his daughter. "Look at you Molly, you're getting so big. He had been away for so much of her growing up it seemed like a new child every time he came home. She was nearly five now and he hoped he might get to spend the first birthday with her since she was born.

"Daddy," she said. "Will you take me to the aquarium tomorrow?"

"Umm," he mumbled taken aback at the random request. He looked at Tracy who just shot back a confused look and shrugged smiling. "Yeah sure baby girl." He stood up lifting Molly up off her feet and the three of them went into the house.

Molly ran around the living room finding all her latest toys, handing them one at a time to Bull. She explained who each of her soft toys were and gave their names.

"Wow, Trace," said Bull. "We gotta take her back to Queens more often, she's picking up a right little Virginia accent." Tracy giggled still in shock at having her husband back so soon. So happy, she forgot that she was about to go do the weekly shopping.

"How was it Dwayne?" She asked coyly knowing full well he would hold back most of the details.

"Not too bad," he said playing with a stuffed white rabbit. "Worked mostly with new guys, so…" He shrugged.

"So you haven't heard about Davey?" She said.

"Davey? No, what's happened?"

"He was killed," she said. "About two weeks ago."

"Drunk Davey or sober Davey?" He asked.

"Drunk Davey," she replied.

"Damn," he said passing the rabbit back to Molly and being handed a pink piglet. "What happened?"

"Same as ever," she said making air quotes with her fingers. "Training accident." Things like this were now a regular occurrence. All the families left behind lived in fear of the knock on the door. When it happened, the other families in the street noticed and were ready to offer support, as they knew it could easily be them.

"Where are his family now?" He asked.

"The Navy flew them home," she said. "We did a collection, but, you know…" She tailed off. "Anyway, that beard of yours needs to come off. Every time I see you it's longer and longer."

Bull laughed. She knew it would have to stay, most members of S.E.A.L Team Six had long facial hair. It was needed in the places they were deployed. But, she would at least try to get him to trim it down and tidy it up.

After a couple of hours catching up Tracy remembered the shopping trip she had planned and Bull accompanied her and Molly to the Walmart Supercenter. Molly had insisted on riding in the shopping trolley and Bull agreed after asking permission from his wife.

"So," said Tracy. "How long have I got you for then?" She had to ask, even though she didn't want an answer.

"Well, I need to talk to you about that," said Bull pushing Molly in the shopping cart. "I've been offered a transfer."

"What, away from the S.E.A.Ls?" She said surprised as the S.E.A.Ls had been her husband's life. All he had ever wanted to be was a S.E.A.L and she had been through the entire journey with him.

"Yeah," he said sensing her surprise. "How would you feel about living in Oxford?"

"What, Oxford Mississippi?"

"No," he laughed. "Oxford, England."

"Really! England. We're going to live in England?" She smiled at the prospect of the change and the opportunity to live in Europe. She had seen the other S.E.A.Ls wives go off to the likes of Milan and Germany and she had always wanted to go but it had never happened.

"And I'll probably be home more often than I am these days."

"And I get to have you with me?" She was trembling with excitement, Molly could feel the happiness from her mother and started to jump up and down in the trolley.

"Yeah," he smiled at the reaction from his family. "I'll be around more, these guys only deploy for short periods of time.

So no more long tours." Tracy had tears of joy in her eyes, welling up from happiness. Bull and his two girls hugged in the biscuit isle of the Walmart.

"This is a cause for celebration," she said. "Lets have wine tonight. And I'm not talking the five dollar rubbish I'm talking the ten or fifteen dollar stuff."

"Easy big spender," said Bull in a jokey way. "I'm not made of money."

Chapter 35

Cam's mind was not on the road, it was still thinking about the phone call he had received after visiting Denise. He had been prepared for bad news but this was unexpected. He drove on autopilot; his eyes were on the road but his thoughts elsewhere.

He heard a vibration, plastic on plastic. It was his mobile phone that he had placed on the dashboard. He could see it sliding in front of the speed dial. He reached through the steering wheel and picked it up and looked at the screen. He sighed pressing the receive key and put it to his ear.

"Cam, it's Al." He didn't answer, he just sighed again. "We got you heading in the wrong direction," Al continued. "Where are you going?"

"I want to go see the grave," he said.

"Cam, I'm sorry about what happened. Believe me I am, but we have work to do. I need you down here."

"I didn't get to go to the funeral," Cam said in a monotone voice. "I at least want to pay my respects."

"Look, Cam, you wouldn't have been able to go to the funeral. Remember who you are, you are Cameron Sterling now. You are no longer Robert Cameron. He does not exist, he can't just turn up at a funeral where he would be recognised."

"I'm well aware of who I am, Al!" He said raising his voice. "I am Sterling. A mercenary. A bloody ghost."

"We have a new start down here," Al said trying to calm him down. "Things are changing and I need your input on how best to organise it."

"Not this time Al, I'll be down when I'm ready. I've got my own shit going on, leave me alone. I need time." Al paused not sure of what to say.

"You have to come back Cam, you know that," he said eventually.

"I know what I have to do!" Cam shouted. He wanted to end this call before he said something he would regret. "I'm driving," he said in a more civilised tone. "I'll call you soon." He hung up and threw the phone onto the passenger seat. He gripped the steering wheel tight with both hands and pushed himself back into the springs of the seat. He would be there soon, just enough time to calm down.

＊ ＊ ＊ ＊ ＊ ＊ ＊

He parked near the graveyard and stopped the engine. He sat for a short while just to see if there was anybody else about. The small church was deserted and there was no movement in the area. It was safe to take a look around.

He entered the graveyard through the creaking metal gate. The black paint flaked off in his hand as he closed it behind himself. His feet crunched the gravel as he methodically walked up and down the rows of graves, picking out the newer ones. Then he saw it. Two headstones next to one another, one much older than the other.

He stood silently in front of the two graves. The flowers that had been placed between the two had started to wilt. The hand-written notes curled at the corners, the ink blotted by the rain.

"Beatrice Crossley," he read aloud sighing. "Beloved wife of Maximilian Crossley. Together again." He read the dates and realised they had been apart for fourteen years. This lady had given him a home when he needed it. He had used it to start his personal war on terrorism; it had been his base of operations. All that was over now since Al had got hold of him. He was still fighting terrorism but not the way he wanted to. He was controlled now but that would soon change.

He thought about when he had lived in the small cottage on her land. He started to remember all the times she had wanted to have a chat, probably lonely after losing her husband. However, he had never found the time for her.

He didn't even realise that she had lost her husband; she always talked about him as if he was still there. He wished he could have found some time for her but social interactions weren't his strong point.

As he stood contemplating his past and future he felt his phone buzzing in his pocket. He rolled his eyes up and looked at the clouds in the sky and let out an audible moan. He left it ringing; hoping whoever it was would give up. However, there was only one person it would have been.

"Al," he said after quickly, grabbing his phone and jabbing the accept button.

"Cam," said Al. "I've got some news for you."

"Really," he said unenthusiastically. "What's that then?"

"It's to do with Mrs Crossley." Al hesitated as if unsure as if the next thing he was about to say was a good idea. "But I need you to promise you'll make your way down here once you've taken care of business up there."

"You bribing me, Al?"

"Look Cam, there are huge changes going on and I need you. George is here and I've managed to secure a placement for Bull. He'll be a member of your team." Cam listened, surprised at what he was hearing.

"How did you get Bull?" He asked.

"I know people at DEVGRU, plus he wanted to work with you guys again. When Rory recovers he'll make up the fourth member of your team. We got four-man teams being put together as we speak, made up from all different countries S.F communities."

"How are they doing?" Asked Cam. "Rory and Don, I mean."

"Rory should make a full recovery, he'll be back before you know it. I sent him that Phil Collins CD like you asked." Cam snorted a laugh. "Donald's not so good. He's going to have problems with his lungs. He won't be back on active duties, but I'll find him a role here. We will always need a good linguist."

"We'll make a good team," said Cam exhaling.

"I know, that's why I want you down here as soon as you can get here. Your team will get anything you ask for, I promise."

"OK, fine. What's the news?" Said Cam.

"Mrs Crossley's lawyer has been trying to get in contact with you."

"With me?"

"Well, the old you, Robert Cameron I mean. If you want to check it out I'll send you an email with the details."

"Yeah, I do." He said. "I need one more thing, Al."

"What's that?"

"Just a few days. Five tops. Then I'll be with you."

"Deal!" Al snapped. "I'll see you then." Al ended the call and Cam placed the phone back in his pocket. He nodded, agreeing with his own thoughts. It was time to start again, to finish what he had started.

Later that afternoon Cam arrived at the lawyer's office in Carlisle. The office wasn't far from the town centre; he had passed the castle as he entered the city from the west and driven under the bridge shaped like a bow and arrow. He knew the town well and found a place to park easily.

He entered the building with the name of the lawyer's practice displayed on a brass sign next to the outer door. He introduced himself to the receptionist and she motioned him towards the seating area opposite the desk.

"Mr Bailey will be with you in a few minutes." It felt strange to call himself by his old name. Robert Cameron basically didn't exist anymore. He had been replaced with Cameron Sterling.

He looked around the waiting room and took in the features of the room. He paid particular attention to the door locks, cameras and their security system. It was something that he did automatically, he couldn't help it. Whilst waiting he would analyse how he could get into the place; it wouldn't pose much of a problem.

"Mr Cameron," said the man Cam assumed to be the lawyer. Cam stood up, acknowledging the man. "You are a hard man to track down. Where have you been hiding?"

"You'd be surprised," shrugged Cam rising to his feet.

"Follow me then," said the lawyer, "through here." Cam didn't like the look of the lawyer; he had a smug look about him and he took an instant dislike to him. "Have a seat, over there." He said pointing Cam to a specific seat in his office. Cam sat in the wooden armless chair and wondered why he wasn't good enough to have the more comfortable looking one.

"Crossley," said Bailey flicking through the files on the shelf on the opposite side of the office. "Crossley, Crossley, Crossley."

He pulled a file from the shelf and flung it onto the large wooden desk. "There she is, Crossley," he said as the file slid across the polished desk.

Cam said nothing, he just watched the lawyer, amazed at how insensitive he was acting around someone who was possibly grieving over a loved one. Bailey sat in his padded swivel chair and spun the file to face him with his fingertips.

"OK, Crossley left you almost everything she owned," he said thumbing through the papers in the file.

"Me!" Exclaimed Cam. "Everything?"

"Yes you," said Bailey in a condescending way. He looked around the room. "There's nobody else here." He smiled.

"No, there's not is there," said Cam sitting forward retaining constant eye contact with Bailey. Bailey cleared his throat and the smile faded from his face.

"Um, there's the house, of course, the land and a sizable sum of money." He handed Cam the papers. He read over the list of Mrs Crossley's estate; it stated that she had left Robert Cameron nearly three quarters of a million pounds. He nearly didn't recognise his name.

"I had no idea she had that much," he said eventually.

"Most of these elderly folks have more than you think. Half of them don't use banks." Cam mentally added this sum of money to the small fortune he had scammed from the C.I.A. Just more funds for his plans. "And it's all yours, all I need is for you to sign here and here." He pointed to a couple of dotted lines on the papers Cam was reading. "And here."

Cam signed the document resisting the urge to write Cameron Sterling, his new name, instead he signed it Robert Cameron.

"So what you going to do with your new-found wealth?" Joked the lawyer. Cam wanted to say 'Kill terrorists,' but instead he shrugged. "If you want any advice on how best to look after the money I have close connections with a financial adviser who…"

"No!" Cam said standing up pushing the chair away behind him. "I'll be OK." Cam turned his back to the lawyer and stepped towards the door of the office.

"Wait a minute, there's just one more thing." Bailey stopped Cam after he had opened the door a few inches. "I just need to see some form of identification that you are Robert Cameron. I mean, I can't just let anyone take this old lady's entire life savings."

Cam remained with his back to the lawyer, his face would give away that he was thinking how to get around this problem.

"Have you got a driver's licence or passport I can have a look at. I'll need a copy for my files."

Cam's eyes flicked side to side as he tried in vain to figure out how to get past this problem. He only had documents in his new name, his old identification having been erased by Al.

"Damn it," he said quietly closing the door. He turned to face Bailey. "OK, you're never going to believe this."

The Beginning of the end

This man deserved to die. The moment he found out what was happening on that yacht. What that man was doing was disgusting, ruining so many young lives. He was surprised to find out that his boat was still anchored up in the Blue Grotto in Malta, exactly where he had seen it last. However, it had only been ten or eleven days ago. It felt much longer.

After getting Mrs Crossley's estate signed over to him, with help from Al to prove his identity, he had visited the house he rented off her. His now. When he stood in the little cottage, which hadn't been used since he left, he was reminded of what his true purpose was. What he had wanted to achieve before Al had got hold of him.

Now he had the funding to put his plan into action, he had the weapons, the altered passports and the means to hunt out more of these creatures. Like the one he was watching now from up on the cliff top. It was too late to help the young girl that had just been brought to his yacht, not this time. But he could stop it happening again.

The warm evening air surrounded him and he could smell the sand and bushes cooling down from the hot Mediterranean day. The water around the yacht sparkled in the moonlight. It was about to start again; it had to be done. He reached down to his ankle and pulled out his diving knife. He studied the silver blade, it too reflected the moonlight. The blood channels would soon be full of Saudi blood.

He shifted his gaze back over to the yacht. This was the beginning of the end, he knew that. This was his second chance; unlike last time there was no going back.

ND - #0082 - 270225 - C0 - 234/156/16 - PB - 9781908487506 - Matt Lamination